Unlevel crossings

Unlevel Crossings

Michael O'Leary

Published in 2002 by Huia Publishers,
39 Pipitea Street, PO Box 17-335,
Wellington, Aotearoa New Zealand.
www.huia.co.nz

ISBN 1-877266-84-1

Illustrations by Gregory O'Brien

National Library of New Zealand Cataloguing-in-Publication Data

O'Leary, Michael, 1950–
Unlevel crossings / Michael O'Leary.
ISBN: 1-877266-84-1
1. New Zealand fiction—21st century. I. Title.
NZ823.2—dc 21

‘Even damnation is poisoned with rainbows’

– *Leonard Cohen*

Ki a Winsome Aroha.
He koha ngā kupu nei.
He whakaaro ki a koe.
Nō reira, nā ēnei,
ka puta tōku tino aroha ki a koe.

Ki ngā kaitiaki o *Unlevel Crossings*

Ray Bailey

Russel Buchanan

Moana Cleverley

Creative New Zealand
(for a grant to write 'Yellban Apocryphal')

Bill Dacker

Rowan Gibbs

Clive Hallows

Bob Harold

Bryan Harold

Linda Lees

Toby McAuslan

Clare O'Leary

Ben Partick

Don Polly

John Quilter

Patrick Rainsford

Helen Ryan

Patrick Ryan

Martin Schänzel

Iain Sharp

John Tamahori

Aroha and Te Amoraki

Niel Wright

Nelson Wattie

Nigel Yates

UNLEVEL CROSSINGS

The northern lights turned green where the Southerners cross at Goodwood. As the north-bound train pulled out he saw her from his south-bound carriage. He tried to catch her eye, and it was just as the moving window began to blur that she waved. He realised that she had seen him too. As both trains gathered momentum in opposite directions he felt an ever-rising sense of melancholy and loss, matched in intensity only by a great feeling of joy and happiness.

As he sat by the fire, smoking his pipe and musing upon this incident which had occurred in the future all those years ago, and had served in his mind ever since as a metaphor for their relationship – no, their aroha – he felt the anger of his passion for her once again ready to ignite in his heart, whence it would fan out through his whole body and then permeate his wairua. The flames in the fireplace lapped and licked softly at the edge of his consciousness as he sat alone in the lowly lit living room, and once again he found himself wrestling with the ever-changing, elusive puzzle of his life – her.

Her, and her magical web that held him. He shook his head in disbelief. The night was closing in and he walked outside to watch the last of the twilight as it darkened, bringing the sky and the ocean into ever-closing indefinite lines where they met at the horizon. And even the elements spoke her name, the wind carried it, and he could hear it coming from the far-off sound of the sea. Her form was in the ancient land. Her head, her breasts, her pregnant belly full of the promise of life, lay in his sight as he looked towards the south.

The wind grew cold as the last light of the evening was lost and he went inside for the physical warmth of the fire. Yet he did not feel warm ... he felt chilly and alone, cut off from his source – his mauri – which she somehow shared. The mystery of her was that when she was not there he felt only half. And it'd always been like that.

The circumstances of their lives kept them separate – not geographically any more, but otherwise. She was always inside him since the first day they'd met – even before that, perhaps. He thought about their first meeting and how he'd tried to replace her almost immediately. It was an act of desperation with a substitute her. Things went badly, as they had with every subsequent attempt at escape or denial. And now he was back – after all the years and diversions, all the drugs and alcohol, all the wanderings in the darkness of the spirit – here he was, back with the fact of her.

Building up the fire, the flames flickering and leaping, almost laughing, he thought of her as the only thing in the world he wanted, the thing he couldn't have. Not that he thought of her as a thing: that was just a linguistic nicety. But understanding the difficulty in this way, it paralleled the greatest things which are humbled – the mighty despair. His passion to be joined with her could bring down the heavens, he sometimes felt, and the heavens answered – oh yeah!

The outside wind gusted as if to agree, and 'like your master's kingdom, our love cannot be of this world', the long-ago line of a poem he had writ her blew through his soul as it sought to be united with her in the way of the religions. The faith he had in her was deep and disturbing. She attracted him in so many ways, and after so many years of being apart or partially together these strong feelings were more alive than ever. Yet, as he remembered further lines from his verse – 'and your husband and children/ stand between us like trees against the horizon/ at the point of sundown and the rising darkness/ I see you' – as the darkness renewed itself again for another day, there was the question of her ever-present absence in his life.

The fire burned on, the evening goods train going through the village below blew its whistle in a train's lonesome blues fashion, and all the night closed around him.

te pō
te pō
te pō aroha
the moonlight world
of our understanding
the Polynesian darkness
of light ...

The moon rose slowly, silently over the sea; above the cliffs the wind also rose and was wild. To the inland west the deep crimson sky merged into the darkness of the landscape as the last of the sunset displayed itself before the east-rising moon. Later, the wind dropped and the sky was alive with the light of stars, the shining of a million small moons, but the brightest was beside the one moon like a sentinel. With eyes that remembered a sort-of anniversary he looked towards the full moon and inwards at the full moon of exactly a year before – the last time he had been with her, in the twilight city.

One year: fifty-two weeks; twelve months: three hundred and sixty-five days. He could picture her leaving that last time, the confusion in which he had walked, the tears he had cried – he was still crying them inside ... and he looked up at the present moon, the same one which had burnt an impression of her leaving:

te marama who, when she shines
touches the silent, sleeping
soul of the earth
beyond those tall trees

that rising darkness
and sensuous sundown
of strange stark colours

and the moon flooded the sky with its light: diffuse, organic, milky-white light.

He awoke from the first dream fitful and disorientated. Where had he been? He tried to remember – he knew it had something and nothing to do with her, just like everything else in his life. The sky was beginning to lighten. He had heard a storm in the middle of the night; the heavy rain and high winds had pounded into the walls of the house and into his sleeping consciousness and his dream. But now everything was calm and, as he went outside for a mimi, the first golden-red rays of the sunrise broke along the horizon and through the trees. The sea and sky and the land separated into their own distinct forms after the cloak of darkness, te pō, had made them one.

The heavy chugging echo of a diesel engine reverberated around the early morning hills as a train made its way through the steep, winding cliffs, following the route of an old coastal Māori path. The deep, steady, shaking sounds sent him sleeping into memory.

He knew he had fallen in love with her the moment they first met. She was standing over the range in a dark flat making porridge, stirring with one hand while her newly born first child was sleeping on her shoulder, held closely by her other arm.

'Darling, this is –'

Her husband's introduction had been interrupted by the baby suddenly beginning to cry loudly, and she excused herself and went off into the bedroom to feed the child. But at that brief encounter he felt they had recognised each other, and the rest of his life would be spent in search of what that recognition was.

The whistle of the train woke him again and he heard the clickety-clack of each carriage over the track and, as each echo went up the railway line, he was transported into a deep, dark sleep.

The Southerners crossed and he was fully awake. Another day without her was about to begin. He began making coffee and thought of the piece of pounamu he had got for her from the city. He tried giving it to her as a koha, but she refused it, taking only the piece of his hair he had cut off to put inside the silver locket in which the small, round greenstone was set like a bright-green eye held in a teardrop. The song he had written her came up like a karanga through the bubbles of water ...

When we are together
Holding hands and talking so sweet
The flow of life runs through me
And I feel I am complete

Then I forget about walls and buildings
In your eyes are the sky and the ocean
My spirit's alive with the secrets of life
From your touch and your emotion

Then it's our time to part
I feel the searing of my heart
As it tears asunder with the pain
My tears fall down like rain
My tears fall down like rain

... and it did begin to rain. The city re-entered his mind. When he had first gone back there he had wished she had been with him. As he walked down the streets his eye would catch something that would make him think that she would like to see this, or hear that, or go to that place. But she was a thousand miles away with her husband and their growing family, and his spirit fell at this realisation.

The rain fell heavily now and as he went to light the fire he remembered the rain dances of the road gang he worked on in the city UA! UA! UA! as he lifted shovel-load after shovel-load of gravel –

> I have carried you all day with me
> Through the hard-nosed life of a labouring man
> Your beauty is so strong that I weep inwardly

– he marvelled at how many points of connection in his life she made, and his shovelling became a meditation.

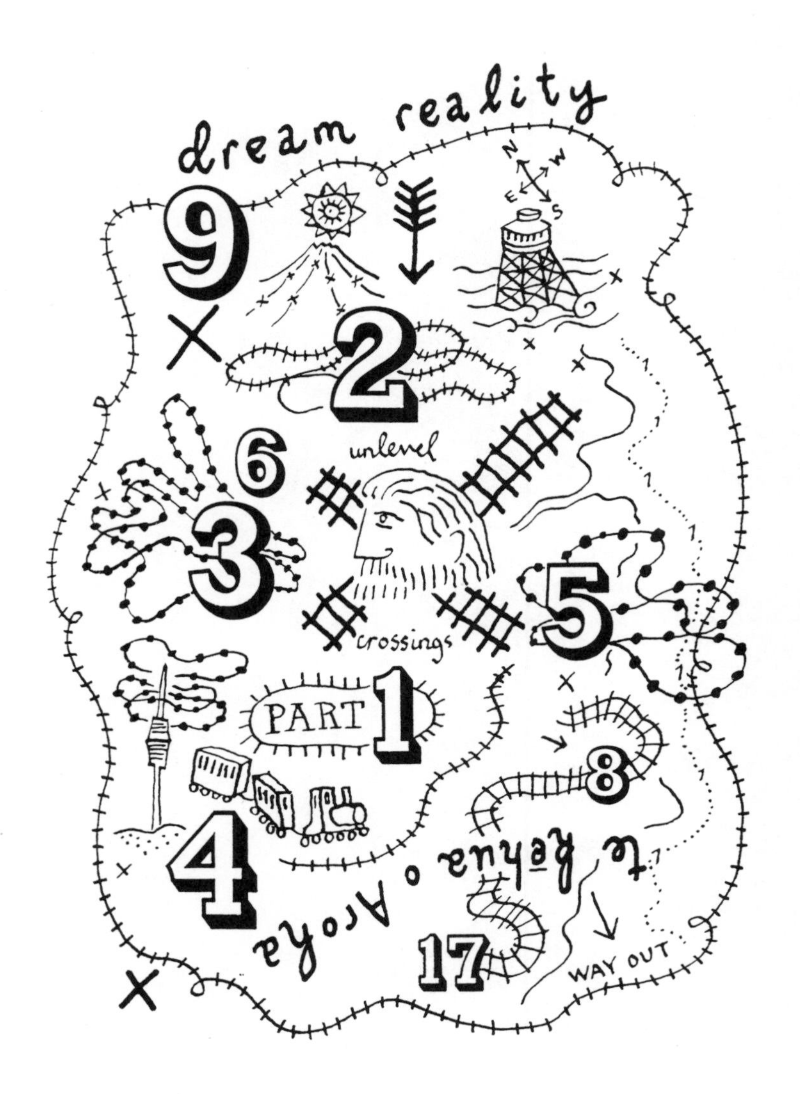

dream reality
N
W
E
S
9
2
unlevel
6
3
crossings
5
PART 1
8
4
te kehua o Aroha
17
WAY OUT

1

A sliver of dawn light appeared above the suburban rooftops. Patrick Mika Fitzgerald shivered with the early morning cold as he walked through the state-housing area where he had lived all his life. When he came to the small Māori cemetery he stopped for a moment as a mark of respect, as he always did, for his mother was part-Māori. While he never treated this as any big deal or got involved in any of the hōhā, he always had that recognition – much the same as passing a church.

He knew as he talked to the graves that if he ever met her she too would be Māori. As he walked on down Ngapipi Road the spirits of the night chased him and laughed at him and were all around, but finally they left as the daytime became more palpable. He looked to see if his train was coming, for he often lost track of time when he was talking to ngā tīpuna, but he hadn't missed it. He walked down the ramp from the road to Orakei Station and saw the usual group of his fellow commuters waiting.

The light from the train shone down the track. It came along the straight stretch from Meadowbank, highlighting the silhouettes of two fishermen, their lines cast from the road bridge into the inlet that takes the water out from the Orakei Basin. The train rattled along the raised causeway where it travels across the middle of Hobson Bay, and the first rays of sunlight set the waters of the Waitemata Harbour sparkling into life.

Passing the Parnell Baths he thought of his childhood and how much time he'd spent in the water, both there and at Okahu Bay. While the dreams of the previous night mingled with the thoughts of his past, the train pulled into Auckland Station.

After five minutes the train was clanking across the Parnell Road Overbridge, past Carlaw Park where he used to go with Uncle Alf to watch league long before it was in vogue, and then past the Ho Chi Minh Trail and the back of the Domain.

As the early morning train heads towards
Newmarket Station
Towards another day –
The bells ring
And the warning lights flash
At the Young's Lane crossing –
I look out the window
Expecting to see nothing
Other than dark-grey skies ...

The train crossed a maze of lines and points before entering the station where he had to change trains for the Waitakere Line.

A little shed and a gravel platform, collectively called Kingsland Station, soon appeared. When he stepped down from his carriage he could see the latest graffiti which had sprung up overnight:

their blue shimmer heightens
the fine-edged colours
graffiti gangs battle on walls
with slogans that defy each other
the power of television images
proven by these
New York subway copy-cats
and I mean cats!

Another rod came off the roller. Fitz took it in his big heat-proof gloves and laid it down on to the trolley ready to be bent into the curled shape of a stove element before being pressed and chromated.

'The boss wants to see you Fitz,' the foreman yelled above the factory noise.

'What?' Fitz replied. He had been doing his mechanical job mechanically, placing each rod neatly and efficiently, an expertise arrived at over many years of repetition. But while his hands were steady and functioned methodically, his mind and emotions were all over the place. Even the deafening sound of the vast array of machinery around him barely entered his consciousness.

He had been thinking of the turbulent night, of the dreams and images that had poured through his being, pounding like waves against his spiritual shores, scraping and shaping the sure rocks of his workaday life into confusion and excitement. Now the memory of images and nearly heard echoes of unheard sounds flooded his day with strange, unknown places – cliffs and the sea, huge hills and vast winds tearing at weatherboards and disturbing the very soundness of his mind. Te hau, te hau, te hau nui! The ancient karanga had called to him through his sleep, and she was there as a vision between the blasts, calling softly, calling his name, calling the name of his spirit.

'Fitz!' the foreman yelled again. 'The fucking boss wants to see you, ya deaf cunt!' Someone else came over to take his place at the end of the rod-rolling machine and Fitz made his way towards the landing, up the stairs to where the boss oversaw proceedings.

'Come in Fitz, me boy', said the boss with the familiarity that existed from a peasant–master relationship of many years. 'Come in and sit down.'

Slamming the door behind him Fitz beheld the factory floor that he had worked on for more than two decades. The word 'redundant' reverberated around inside his head, but he could not get it into a fixed position of meaning. Now he stood transfixed, looking, just looking. He watched the mechanical movements of his fellow workers, and things which only a few minutes before had had meaning and value now took on an unreal, arbitrary quality. It was as though scales had fallen from his eyes and he could now see clearly what had once been a blur.

All his anger left him and he could only feel pity and compassion for those who were left to carry on this industrious charade. As he stood there, machines hammering and chomping, rolling and gesticulating in what now seemed a meaningless jumble of noise and motion, he realised he was free!

Fitz said goodbye to his friends and picked up his final pay packet which included his redundancy money. He intended to go straight home and tell his mother what had happened and what he was going to do.

On the bus into town, a long trip at that time of the afternoon as the city readied itself for the evening rush hour, Fitz was set adrift, as though his quest for the grail of her was about to begin. The dreams of the night permeated and were made palpable through the faces and places of the bus journey ...

dreaming of a woman unseen,	tokotahi
	tokotahi wahine
travelling to town by bus,	he pahi
	he pahi kōwhai
beginning to find an unknown place,	he wāhi
	he wāhi ngaro

but the tears of Rangi fall
and the fire is extinguished

– a sadness comes from the only belonging
kei te kata nei ano
kua mamae te ngakau
a,
i te mutunga o taua
koa he pōuri
... so it is written ...

... and as the bus came down past Albert Park, turning into Victoria Street, Fitz found himself looking into all the faces of Māori and Polynesian women as they walked past the window, but he knew he would have to go a lot further in days and miles before finding her.

A thousand miles
is not a long distance
for dreams to travel
dreams have been known
to circumnavigate the earth
and even blast off into outer space
so it did not surprise me
when you arrived
in te waka moehewa ... off the bus he gets
rā huritau
ki a Aroha tāu
takoto iho ki taku moenga
me he ika ora au ki a koe, auē
ki a Wini nei
i muri ahiahi
ka hara mai te aroha
ka ngau i ahau
he waiata o rā huritau nei
i tupu mai, te mauri
te mauri nui, te mauri roa

te mauri whakaea
ka whakaputa ki te whaiao
ki te ao mārama
tēnā te whakaputa
nā ngā pū, nā ngā take
ka puta ki te whaiao
ki te ao mārama
mō tēnei karanga nōnamata
puakina taku aroha nei, awatu ...

Fitz sat in the public bar listening without knowing what was being said but understanding every detail, every word. Whilst not comprehending the meaning in the sense that he could retell what had been said, he knew instinctively that this karanga had come from his mother's people telling him of a clue in search for te wāhi moemoea, te wahine o te moemoea nō reira ...

His bus trip home was a blur of sleep – the last bus which he only just caught by yelling and staggering in front of its path, so the driver had to stop or he would have had a dead passenger ... a carnival of mind images, intermingled with the faces and voices of the various bars he had been to, and the black lights of the night city, boats bobbing in the harbour spotlit by lamplight and colour undercover of the rain-washed clouds which raced across the sky like the foggy few thoughts of his skull, rattling and sabreing their way through ... sleep, dream, then jerk awake, the bus turned a sudden movement, the horsemen of the alcoholic apocalypse dancing and prancing through the heathen's heavens ... noses, eyes held on plates, Santa Lucia pray for us, the bus lurched then settled into diesel dyke prosperity of the suburban dream, Spinoutza ya fishy swam through a sea of thought unbeknownst to modern mind

... re-dundant, with reference to the dundant, getting close, left hand down a bit, along Tamaki Drive, a long drive, a longing to dive into the safe umbilical water which sparkles all around him, to never re-emerge from immersion, into the drink ... fishy thoughts leading to the eternal ethereal, all those years a mechanical man, melancholy of moon dancing veil, half hidden like a mystery which reveals nothing unless it is peeled back and back and back ... sleep, then wake of a boat shining white water auē, auē, it's so sad moving through its own temporal forces, holding itself back, eternal fluid of gravity ... Fitz feels the bus climbing the hill, mouths are yelling, frothing, spitting at him, staggering and lurching away from and towards him, one mouth comes right up to his mouth – out comes a tongue ... he is awake as the bus turns at the shops, he pulls the chord and he's off, but not in tune ... the cool near-midnight air quickens his senses, standing for a moment and watching the bus disappear down the road, he slowly collects himself. Patrick Fitzgerald it is I am, made redundant this day of our Lord, so that I may follow the dream I was made for.

Fitz walked slowly down the path to the state house, surrounded by many other state houses, where he had lived all his life and from whose verandah, if you stood on tiptoes, you could see Rangitoto. He opened the front door and very quietly walked down the hallway, trying not to wake his mum. Her door was ajar, so he looked in the room towards her bed. She would have gone to bed hours ago, and he saw her asleep with her face looking at peace and restful in the light coming from the street lamp. She appeared to be sleeping at an odd angle and his instinct was to go over and lift her into a more comfortable position. However, he thought better of it, afraid of waking her up. Plenty of time tomorrow to tell her of the redundancy and beside it's probably just my haurangi perception of things, he thought. So he had a mimi and crashed on his bed exhausted and fell into a dark, dreamful sleep ...

Yet again my dreams are filled with you
Awaking from your visit of last night
Where we walked a disenchanted valley
Into the grounds of a small church
Whose green spire reached humbly skyward
All other loves have only reached roof height
Your love conspires to keep me downward bent
While I wrestle with
my unquitted passion for you
Which inspires in me such feelings
And thoughts, and indeed deeds
That to contemplate for too long
Would send me reeling; mad incarnate
Of some ancient unknown ...
We are together only when the waking world fades
And reason has lost its light of day
but while I sleep in your arms
I do not wake in them auē! auē! auē!

... and the dream travels on and on and on as though into eternity and his tears of grief and sorrow for the dark soul of the woman he hasn't met flow and drown the tree of love as though he is watering a barren vision which can never bear fruit, no matter how much he tends it. Walking into the street of a southern dream-like nightmarish city his spirit seems somehow lightened even though it is the end, and walking through these bleak thoroughfares he is consumed by the absolute ugliness of everyone's faces, the dreary desolation he feels now that she is no longer a possibility, the unrepentant nihilism in his soul now that the dream is over, as though decay and despair were the true liberating elements underpinning the nature of existence ... dark clouds sweep dramatically across the Orakei morning sky, as Patrick Fitzgerald comes to a slow comprehending consciousness. His head hurts and a drowsy dumbness pervades his mind. Waking and sleeping are still the one thing. 'Auē!' is the only word he can think and say. His drunkenness and dreams are still one!

The undrawn curtains let the sun, which intermittently breaks through the stormy sky, straight through his window and into his eyes. The words of reality and dreams roll his mind in irregular regularity. Redundant ... nihilism ... dark soul ... bus ... tongue ... rattling skull ... mechanical melancholy ... quickens ... ugly ... dumb ... boat ... mother ... Mother! He thinks of his last image of her, sleeping in a peculiar position. Just my haurangi mind, he thinks, uneasily reassuring himself ...

I'll make Mum a cup of tea, he thought, through the pain of his spirit. With great effort he dragged his old bones up, the physical hurt being less than the effort required to stay lying there with all these pōrangi ideas cascading tipi haere round his head.

As soon as he walked into the room he knew she was dead. He dropped the cup and saucer, sending hot tea and fragments of crockery flying. He ran to the bed and could see that this was the reason for her funny position. When he went to lift her from the bed her body was hard and intractable, like a lump of wood or stone. She must have been dead for many hours. Her colour was yellow, with red blotches on her arms which stuck out still and lifeless from the blueness of her nightdress. As though he were a child looking around for non-existent brothers or sisters, he uttered the useless, helpless phrase, 'I think she's dead.'

2

The tangi was a small affair: a few neighbours, some women from the local church group, and a handful of relatives claiming whānau rights whom he had never seen before and probably never would see again. One of these aunties rummaged through his mother's pots and pans saying things like, 'So that's where that got to!' and by the end of the day she left with many 'reclaimed' items which had apparently been borrowed from her many years before. The fate of many family photographs, icons and mementos was the same, as each unrecognisable family member recognised long-lost taonga. By the evening of the funeral's day, the house was depleted of its physical manifestations of spiritual nutrients and Fitz sat alone, exhausted and drained.

It took only a few weeks for Fitz to sort out his mother's affairs. She had been a simple-living, humble woman who never had much money to buy or accumulate things. He would have to find other accommodation as the house he had called home all his life was now deemed by the authorities to be too large for a single occupant. Housing New Zealand had offered him a one bedroom, semi-detached unit in Tamaki, and when he turned down that plus a similar dwelling in Otara, they said they could no longer help him.

So, after several weeks of being shunted from one government department to another, now that his mother's will and other outstanding issues had been resolved, Fitz decided that he would take an option previously uncontemplated in his life. He would leave Auckland in pursuit of the woman who had haunted his subconscious life. Without knowing whether she even existed, he felt he would know her as soon as he saw her. He felt that she too had been waiting for him.

The one thing which disturbed Fitz's dreamful future visions was the fact that the woman he always saw in his ethereal visitations was already married with children to another man. How could this be? Why – after all these years of searching or, in reality, not searching, for his partner in life – was she already spoken for? Why was she Māori? And why did her presence in his consciousness evoke such ancient and unexplained longing?

He did not doubt that she existed – she was as alive as the very air he breathed! Now that his mother was dead he wished that he had talked to her about the woman. She would have understood, he was sure of that. But when she was alive he had not brought it up with her, not least because he didn't really want to believe it himself.

Yet believe it he must. He spent the next few months in a state of constant denial, concentrically circulating the central problem of having to leave the city of sales, the down underworld merchant marine Gehenna of the south seas sailing. This time of indecision saw him leaping from tree to tree (the mighty lurch), moving from job to job, wheeling from deal to deal, travelling from place to place by car, train, boat –

in Auckland when the silver train is acoming you've got to move on now, roll on stoned immaculate into the next whiskey bar, spend your dough from station to station as it begins ... way to work way to go whoosh of smoke from the car in front's exhaust ... covers our windscreen as we drive blind instrument flying past Penrose Railway Station (as foreseen in Dockett and Becketty) ... seems funny to pickup and paymoney for sand-in-bags ... from a Mountywellington factoryfloor, wait for a factory whore-fact tory ... with the fleshfresh smell of the killing Westfields filling the moaning air ... and hitting the M'way northword two wards the siittee – a cross the Newmarket violation duct, eurythmic music pounding of flesh aloud as we are held fast, crazy! – drive o' the dead through

Grafton Graveyard – it's traffic to the right of, too right, it's traffic to the left, it's underneath and it's over the top! ... then down to the oily installations, the noise and the smell and the nose – who knows sea and sky knows life, and the sand which we bought now blasting through a nozzle knocking last generation's paint off petrol pipelines as the sun beats down hardy, tossing off the decibels ... as the nearly mourning train pulls out of Newmarket stationary engine driver standing at the kirk, it dives down towards Aucklana' Livinia Pluralla (the city of two tails, the terrible taniwha or T.T.2. foreshorette-fishnet stalkings and all), towards another day ... the bells are ringin', the warning lights are flashin' for me and my grill ... at Young's Lane lookin' indifferently out ta window lad, expecting (sex months, if it's a day) to see nothing other ... dark grey skysuits to the right, and right a golden shaft of light ... transforms the otherwise sullen l'scape ... beyond the marshes (spare the rod, matey) and swampthings of Orakei, guided straight as the gait slowly towards the gulflirth is Waiheke ... you two move too – the other daze ... Waiheke is the place where the light is heaviest – a conundrum as the humdrum enters the Parnell Tunnel plunged into devil's darkness ... Thursday night at the Naval and Family, Watson quickly evolving labrats fed on nought but grass – listening, looking, thinking and remembering the skill, the skill, the skill it takes to get to Connemara, through Cunard and other well-drawn blind lines ... first listening to the is-land band, janitors famed by day and inflamed by night, same old song week after week the rhythm moves my feet and the drink and the smiles make him feel that he's sorta at hommes, the voices and the words familiar and foreign ... lookin' outa the window at the O'Malley man's corner at Gayrodeo and ridehim cowboy following with eyes past other Karangahape neons up the lines of oldaucklana rooftops and Sunsetski ... then inside seeing all the pretty girls dancing, talking and singing and smoking cigarettes ... then thinking, why keep coming to this place wheresome knights round the table it's so cold in this age of shivverelry and here is aclue forfuture in threesome, not quite wholesome but as innocent as any pashion … no one else seems to no entice and the lifelong stranger he's been doesn't exist here … merembering the Pacific Island music his mother used to play on the gramophone, and the Pacific Island woman who shared his life and dreams fora flauna shorty wiles … the music wafts over him like waves as he stares into his ayeglass in anger at separation … crack! kai! whiskey! in mormarian of the easteregg uprising of the skirts of urale's daughter – sitting by the fire what's happening and where? … it's the place and it's the drinking, went to the garden of Eden Terrace factory twenty years ago today, industrial park in the dark – fitting place for the fall, kissed his love by the wall … but it's only a northern song!, and then … willego ta midnightmass or no? … in the pub talkin' and drinkin' – Finnucanes Walk one-legged, one-eyed drivin' through the night … the risin' of the mooo on, clouds are drifting … and everywhere the city grows and moves … so it's off with the top of the Tullamore Dew and down it goes (so it goes says Billy the Kidney, grimly) – firing up the organs like a mainline steam engine … is it yourself? … who knows, as all the con-straight constraints of reasonable morality leave and like a Cork only the eyerish see he gets tossed, lossed in the crack, the kai and the whiskey … it's a wild unremembered drive through the Balimoral night awakening in the morning to a legendary vision of O'Donnell driving straight towards a concrete wall … and for a thirty scent innercity fear hop onski the big yellow banana bus … from station to stoptostop initial surge of power throws you back, back, back all the dancing give me time to breathe as banana on wheels pushes past phoenix psalms oh, holly night … then flows around what once was a beach, now a road, into but past also anzac biscuit beach-head and the dairy of young turks … then, the battle having been fought, it's into the mainstream maelstrom to follow local custom, left … through the turquoise northern-great! The pacific south is lost now in large seas and the queen lies spreadeagled, eager to engulf all comers – up you go! And she is before you and following – the wise man walks behind ... as you move in fits and starts, a sexual epileptic-fishtank vision of the people and the crane-like cranes hang their elongated necks over building tops to cheque your progress as you check their progress at a red light ... a swarm of people descends and moves as you move ... bathed in golden yeahs wah, wah, aglow, hints of the wide open cuntryside, the banana moves up and up but never away ... auē! Now the fantastic voyage-movie is all but finished, the real illusion continues – they are building more of them and more of them ... just when you think you might get lost forever in the orgasmick firmament, going up further and faster than you can ever remember, the banana bends to the right, missing the sky by inches ... and slows, slows to reveal real human faces laughing and sad, moving and still in K'Rd ... time to hopoff the big yellow banana bus ... himself walks through streets of strangers expressing everything he doesn't feel and saying the things he doesn't think ... and Fitz is disoriented and uncertain but also excited by his surreal transformation of the pedestrian city and his own mind into a new synthesis of perception, whose doors seemed to have begun to swing slowly open for him assisted by the twin opiotic visions of love and death.

3

Unlike befive, the victorgy Fitz now talks to people he donteven know like a rhymestoned choirboy ... the camp bell rings down in the glen and the choir sings Ave! Ave! Ave! Mariavaderchi, but not yet goodbye, señor, on the Santa Lucia streetcar which held the machete to the throaty and the throatie went dry, and good old Pavlova Rotten sings this'll be the day, buddy ... in the house of publification he was told to go west yobro by black, powdered ganggreen, gombeen men – so, with next mon he sat at Morningside Station black and blue, the deep, dark black of the inner mother night and the bright blue sky in mid-winter warmth … sun beats down and heats the station seat … looking with redeyes at a red light in the distance … waiting to be seen the green-eyed colleen of Knock-na-Knee of the light too turns, the train ain't far away … its whistle blowing down the line (a straight line at last from the original) as it approaches … just outa sight of the bridge over the river, Newnorthroad, why? … gum trees glisten amongst single-storey factories … their blue shimmer heightens the fine-edged colours … graffiti gangs battle on walls with slogans that defy each other … the power of television images proven by these New York subway copy-cats, and I mean cats! nearly, yes T.S., practically instead of a dame, hello bosoms! – these pederants make feel si C.K.! … nearly, all Toosoon it is over stepping downon to the flat porm (annalmostbaptiste perfect concrete curve of olde world sensual technology) watt I ching (nott) the wagging train moving asa narrative towards the westwardho!-lick a mammory of love … a railway is the most melancholy mechanical and holy of transport modes, once aboard the motion is one of subtle love-making (sub-titled, sublove bellows the belt dive!dive!dive!) … as the train pulls out [sic] *from the station you stepped down at it is your lover leaving, rolling laughing stock down the track … all this 'ona, 'offa two minute, but not so small, trip to Avondale … deafend the Suburban services you hors de babbleon – romance (no pants) is not confined to the Orient Expression, and Mounty Albert is just as important as Montmartre if you live there! … once knew and unbeknownst, love is like a cryptic clipt railway ticket, clit und teke – stazalone in the male's fete, and like Rush to die, Fitz too felt that he was losing his city … in his following of dreams after death he was becoming a metaphorical migrant crossing the plains of past and future, moving out, out, out, but not down from the vortex of emptiness of Aucklandia Urbania, backyard birds chirping of things to come … driving out to Pihahaha, hightide of greengrass gathering mostmoss, rollintoned, immaculate mother fuha around to rock und cave music – get out of Muriwai, Mycarno packed, go cuz, go … M'Carno set to go, soup Togo … give the boys back their toys … not quite gone west or rather, overshot the runaway of Waitakere, ending up in cave not grave … at Whatipu the caves are hollow and hidden … no light or life can be seen in these solitary places … the heads of the western Manukau jut out to muri wai, buffeted by winds and undermined by rain and salt water … stand on the beach, feeling the force of the elements … look up to the safety and darkness of the caves … decide on te wāhi moemoea, shadows and the half-life or stand strong, kia kaha, be shaped and eroded down to the last pebble of existence … having been west and lived to tell the tail, fishy as it may seem, the compost turned now to the effluent sub orbs of the north … fatrickpitzgerald roamed in circumferential, evidently looking for demoncrats in the all together now, where devils may care more than the gods going the rounds round the bays, and berks in headgear onewahwahdomaighn to mak sense of horth nabour cough, cough, bogyrpardon hello litre of whiskers wrough, wrough, … the japs on knees, shaught peep holes, lookout – torbay!torbay!torbay! slipping through Waitemata waters, Rangitoto grandma blacksout during war as to be seen as the nirthborth beginneth to spread towards the platypus of Long Islandbay trolleybyse – 'I haaave a viiision!' – fast to the butcher … realing around the reality, it's aroundand aroundand aroundand goes the bus out of the site of the sea-saw, this suburb seems to go on and on, as we walktog ether alonga white con Crete path (not far from Rakikoti, where Monty Whikiriwhi's flying squad encircles the sky towering over Casino – always medalsome on a visit, ka pai e koro, tino pai tō mahi nei) the dark woman he is width, another creature from another in the middle of an island, in the middle of the O'Sean, or another time … Fitz thought of the love for Lidi, ah! He (master) Bates, writeswrongs the Polynesian woman who shared*

... afterwords she tells him what she knows ... so near to the sea, the sound is almost there ... inside a shell – over the bridge inside a bus back to the city carelessly they go to a movie or dinner ... next time Fitz goes to Torbay he is alone – same bus, same streets, same sane suburban sounds near the sea, he is in another island time, alone like the sound inside a shell ... but the freeze-frame shape has shifted, the janitor, the vagrant – anyone but Ler saw it ... Takapuna, buy the sea ... the hole country acts again like the auld Angstine Mug ... the peas ants, a gain no pain, duped – all that glitters in the gutters is not golden calf, silence, peat bog fool mounty gormlessly phrasing the life sentences of the middle of the road classes ... television pye rates, protectors of the pub, lick minds, and pilfer the public purses ... ka pai ngā kākahu hou o te rangatira o te Tīwī o Aotearoa, arā, kei te haere ia ki te toa hoko kākahu, kei te kiri kau ia, nō reira ... tell the yutha bout the prelatemorgan, nightly filled headonistic heds with age-old (soon to be old age) delusions, boats are looking for realestate, kick butt the leaders got the edge – same inane from the common torybox ... coming up – if you owned an under wateracre at Whangaparoa or Milford or Takapuna it could make a million for you overnight, even though it's not worth the paperback it's written in ... 'I am Erika's cup, as if of Locke's hem I had drunk!' the Pope of the lock, your lowness ... time in a car ... whitecar, into the monochrome suburb re-visitation of the bride and bachelors stripped bare even after war, de Champ – the chimp who wrote Cakespeare ... inside the kids watch TV, wight TV Aotearoa and boo boo boo ... lookup, black hair and black beard see the witch, black as pitch on the grass – the big ghost's simple bucket signed, sealed, delivered never seen anything dark in life before, next to Jack Krack Sat, or 'I' in Paris, that is ... and they say he was a very great man, she ran I and I dan marleon da mon ... zebrahorse crossing at the end of the motto way, al banal – it is the centre of the pointless whorl, nihil in ex chalsis deo, deo daynight come an' Fitz wannabe go home, but there ain't no hom no moa in Aotearoa ...

the North Sure to rise … rise to the perverse challenge … move away fromme the Bot Patter potty-training Nord, to look to her man germ, an hjourney to the ersest by horse or bo at (but not the BO AT) … children of the moor, eh!, we've herd it all before, eh! That's amore, tingaling, aling, aling-tingaling, aling, aling old redeyes, old blackeyes. Oh!, tell, oh!, half-baked ideas rehashed from the Berlin Allee, the old lard Cheesecake labours the point, that's a moor, e boy … patrickfitzgerald hasn't a clue what's happening to him or you, but what the heck, e Hone, why the heck he wannago to Waiheke – in the past pastiche, perhaps he had an hidden hidder liffee flowing through his troublin' walter mitty o'kay, d'kay dekay eekout … the line of the low hill undulates, Fitz keeps his head still and lets the boat do all the movement … darkness shrouds the journey, but there is light, in the sky the stars and moon shine like pearls, waves break along the bow, white foam almost frozen by the cold … in tune with the natural melancholy, moving like an iceberg from shore to shore, this is the end of journey and the beginning – from the safety and calm of the bay the ferry moves into open waters … remember Rangitoto, looks the same from any angle except close up … but the sky is not on fire tonight, and if it is alight it is with the fire of ice … two lovers go on deck, they feel the chill in the night air, seeing the shadows dark and still perhaps they feel another chill – they leave for the cabin … the evening takes on a rare quality, evoking such an atmosphere that the boat could be anywhere … if it weren't so cold it could be travelling from one Greek Isle to another … austerity has a beauty all its own, but the shadows are fading, being engulfed by the lights and distractions of the city ahead … the boat is making up lost time, the boat is making up lost time … it is the y east up rising, and Julio is the son downby the schoolyard riverside and as he patriciofittsjulio y a double-tracked mind … four to end y eta gain buckett seats and all Irish thoughts written in English and Māori sideb y side they rose in Spanish harmon y as the y moved uncollectivel y towards the same … Okahuba y Okahu … dark night kua pōuri, wind off the harbour ka pupuhi te hau mai i te moana … approaching the sand the pohutukawa trees surround … hurihuri ngā pohutukawa … the moon, half-hidden by clouds, provides the only natural light … te marama hangere, kua ahau ngaro i te kapua … each wave to reach the beach has travelled from eternity … ko tēnei anake te māramatanga, ke ata papakihia mai e ngā ngaru a tai … darkness of unremembered soul, the night within embraces the vision … ka pōuri au, kua wareware te ngakau, ko te pō kei te awhi i taku kitenga … as Fitz becomes aware that this revisitation to his home suburb is of far greater significance than he intended, that it is a metaphor for his moving from one state of his life to another – a leaving behind of his mother and an embracing of his search for the dreamwoman who haunts his sleeping and waking hours – this is further highlighted by the fact that his thoughts appear to him in both English and Māori, and even though consciously he is barely able to understand the latter, in his wairua he comprehends each word completely … te aroha ki tēnā ki tēnā, pera ki ia ngaro o te wai … the sadness of each memory is like each wave of water … hui katoa, ka heke o te manawa … together they make a flood of tears which drown the cries of the heart … at this point Fitz realises that the kēhua o te aroha of his dreams stands beside him momentarily and he turns to her … i tēnei ahiahi ko koe te marama ki ahau … the moon, the only pure light in a life of shadows, the moon hid behind a veil, showing light enough for life but not for love … a, ka wehe mai i Okahu, ka mahue ngā pohutukawa … as Fitz leaves Okahu Bay he breaks through a line of pohutukawa trees … ko koe kia mua, kia kore koe e kite i ahau … he walks ahead so the kēhua cannot see him … ka tūturi, ka kihi i te one … he kneels and kisses the ground … ko te one o tōna tamarikitanga, te one o tōna oranga ia … the ground of his childhood, the ground of his life.

4

The kēhua of her is gone as Fitz stands up after thinking on the sands of Okahu Bay, the tragicrealism of his love in the time of alcoholera shining in liver, magically he lives! He is being sent on a merry chase around the schoolground of Awkwardland, flung in concentrically leaning circles through the learning curves, east–west axels of the paucity of cercity, fish and chips for tea on Friday night and don't spare the salt two seaspray from the virgin of Spanish America y anagramada LuPe, put that breadfruit back, sharks that eight times fl y around the son of such onions as big badd y ladd y who under coathangar bridges flew, it's just a showershot of spra y awa y so gimmee shelta, like a painted poet ona painted Pacificia O'Shaunessey, Henessey et al, cork on the run across the Irish See, the Holy Sea – vincent van mc'gough cut his ear off but, whilst there ma y be room for innovation in the trade, there is still somat fish y for tea bu y hoki, and some Pakuranga Lemonade from the Rainbag to washit down … seldom anygood route bears away from the scene … Fitz hears the recipe and writes … put two lemons in a papero baggero … add blacker Somme brown sugar to taste, and then fillup the bagnall with water … quickly, before the baggets soggy, lie it on the ground … Andstamp (out of Goosestep from Attic) onit as hardass possible with one foot … this recipe is gargargantuanteed to give the bearer at least one wetleg, give you as much information as you need on NZ lit, as God might tempt you, and is quite undrinkable … a tree which or who the witch to woo must be wise, a good guide of stones past war or pole fight to beginst at the beginning D.T.'s pre-loved lemons, givit to me, givit to me, all that 1939 Trogdolyte Love – that is all you need … lemons had been the fruit which this tree had given to the world … now this tree had to be or not to be sacrificed too, like Juiciest Crisp, apple of Aden, pour savor of the tuity, fruity world … so that pontious people could have a swimming pool, a moving starr beetle VW soap makes you ringo on the green lawn of suburbialoola she's my babe be in ex shell sea hoteldo pax dominio theory, viet yam had rooted its cloggs double de dutch, change into other gear or clobber cobber, and killed its will … death came gradually … the polly knees y an laboriallus was the only one to sea it … bee course peep holes of Pakuranga had walked by him as though he was an ama granma ghetto in their suburb … and in their white flightfright they saw heeeem asan ugly fruit – rivet running past a dam and even a wakeful vision of wilde threat … butt he lookit the demon tree, very pretty, and its out-stretched branches and saw that his skin, brown, bare in the reign of Fabba, matched the brown bark worse than its byte lalalala, the wholey world is in a terrible state of chestitty paycunt, eh Juno … so that each virtuosal reality lifted shovel load after shovel load of load, his dreams were of cocoanut tresselsand fright blowers and flashing kitsch en the sea of his green eyeland home of lite and brite colourful birds … meanwhile the other people kept an isle on the progress of the hole in the ground … further Fitz's thoughts flew around the perimeter extremities of the Auckland Island of his mind, for lunch spaghetti aftermath, read in the loo, baby … but he was being moving away, auē, from his routes back homeward, once there was a way, auē, auē, auē REM, REM – how fast the eyes move to affirm, and have it akimbo in the future kitchen at the flat coalslaw face … more dream-times in Remuera, just kissed a girl called Maria, that's all … it's walking down the road where the fences and hedges one day series is held no more, where there's smoke their fire's looming tall – the trees are tall, beautiful and still for deaf Ted, Danoota and me muses Fitz … the light is the evening Mad Alf's Heatlamp colours in the unmoving silence – it's the dream of a thousand years right, just for one day, and it's the time of day and of life … Mercedes and copulating dogs are the only people on the Strasse. It doesn't go near them because, unlike heroes, they get angry … and then at night the sharp sound of husbandandwife fighting, baying like dingoes in the dark … it rained in the morning and the bus could be heard moving and shifting further down the road – somebody's disturbed the Rainbow Serpent from its sleep in the deep waterhole … in recognition of being the millionaire inspiration of a penniless career, a salute to the penguin John Lennon, the Luftwaffe pilot who punches us, washing his hands of gilt-edged sin with the soft-soap motherhubbard of meltdown King of the Jews, uncle von Kobblers et al … human beings, being so cruel they getused to any things, hear the bitten ears of petrol from a can, except explosive matelo whence Fitz sees a light from spirit's lead gutter which evokes a dream of an imagaggio at joe's place where a notion turns its lonely ears to you for a resolution, falsely binding the tyres of neckless tyranny … Fitz's mother looms at the spinning weal of his mind, shenow dead and him knott, hymnnot himher nor himmler, Yes! Yes!, lightning stripes twice in the same place of his germ ancesstry, this old photograph long ago is far away … but another dreamtrain of thought stops him staying at this Malachi Nolly Station, another souther forethought.

5

Railcar runs past autumn leaves flying up and floating violently for a minute, however small, settlingas being disturbed twenty years ago in two days, to sign-off the cross begins on the four heads of the apocalypse before barrier arms ever flung up, then hand to heart and the rest of the bode wells fall shoulder to shoulder like some fat her or mot her, for you know that the debris aswirl and the whirls are falling off aslowly, years agoing and agog looking out of the windy and sea … although he had not yet gone south, Jung man, Fitz was already dreaming again the south dream within dream, mind without mind, welt within welt, world without end, amen! –

Parimoana place, and her ... not yet out of Auckland, yet within his psychehewashehe-singing his song side by side ... skyes of ten cloudis tons of foggy miss cloudy, meaning to be found in absurd ditty ... more fog, and through the fog slowing rail car, the station as stationary as the dream it is part of – the people get off and time stands still until now ... PARIMOANA A AROHA *reads the sign on the dreamrail so throw your hands in your ear, bubble, bubble gum, gum soil and stubble – listen, the seasounds above the dieseldrone, the first time ever eyesaw this place – if place it be from the ack ack flack ... Fitz watches the surreal procession pass his inner vision, the mistintoe witch, which bewitches him like a spell of lovor madness, the monster behind the lock ... ama, zingdream continue through fitzmind dreamofher and how sad he has always been without her eventhough he has not yet known her or the place ... unlock the doorand look, see cliffs and hills and bays at the moontide, eyesseen the moonbow, like a howling-wolf southerly time and tide high riding, rocking, rolling bones of living ghosts on green grass, and lunar tics and other mad insects bigand small, at Brimm's pointex, tremity and other pins and needles, brigands out sailing over echoes, echoes, echoes of manythings, bedsprings a-bouncing, making a bonny bouncy baby ... and backon track this story fitzstory rambles, rumbles in Maoriland on, on, one, two, three red light – dontstop me, doorstop tangata whenua the personuscript of fate but for fortunes, but still wewait forit, wait for it – it's a girl, wait for it to turn like father and son, rushes to be writerz itzin the bloody you know, ameloncholy occupation of the soul ... butzo area, alot of otherthings, haemogoblinz and bloody little dwarfs running, running tinny drumming, flying none the worse for, where crisp apple knocks, tallnoks na gree at the holy day of Ablormonegation, and now they are turning the holychurch into apub for Christ's Sake, post early waterin towine entwines a miracle, dryin to wetarea, but off course blown God is not mocked, and dorta rudely learns the hardrugs way from geekisle, sadly but truly … but enough forno, this is not anauctionornareon as time goesby you must remember you getta little bit older, and a little bit slower – according to Number Nine, but not Six who thinks he's a free poisoner … because this is that and we're talking about love at first sight, not post-natal disenchantment meant to be velt after spring box victoria, aman and awoman is a funny thing … but we have re-erected the sign at least … as signs are often as important as the realthing's often impotent because the sign's more important … ashe came out of his dream of love of place this time not her, knoteye Solomonbeckett, the dog, wears his ring out of which the wisdom washes whence … Piffle thinks to himself it won't be long, please don't you be verylong, ordo eye wake or sleep, as he heads south of the broader harbour down the māngere way – lazy, hazy, crazy, dazy or some ah, change, left gland down a bit sallow hailer … Auckland, you great arsehole, I'm one of the shits you produced thinks Fitz, and now you're about to ejest, ejectme through your j.k.s.y. baxtaside backsliding through the southern suburbs, sexysax Fats Blower Vansy Morris on record breaking, world beating window cleaner luverly weather for dux slipped in drops, heading the fishy school or fool dance … one of the grates, Father Rhyme Teasy quoth doth he ancient to see, 'by marriage with the murchypollexfens I have given a tongue to the sea cliffs', beautiful vision second coming cunning linguist, he … given the wherewithal wherewereall these torts coming from thort Fitz, hierly illegal for a former fact not Tory worker surely enough … orfora and flormer undergrowth spin nose dolphinian numb skull dogsbody to gain such some sublimitty, walter the father, in fact, thought and deed-mea gulpa, mea gulpa, mea mishima gulpa … but the lordy works in mysterious house wayspect you'll write a line ortwo He said who could resist, rolling stoneaway from tomb up yer sleeveand wrote a chopin liszt, (donner forgetta tha kebarber, several!) slowly towards the literary looploop, but before satori in par is on the bus somewhere overa the Harbour Bridge to West Lynn as the bird sings vervenana in the highest coat hang-over sitting in the opposite direction Patfitty heads in towards toward … headpiece filled with raw thoughts and unpeaceful bleeding heart and damaged spirit crying as the bus climbs skyward into cloudy unknowing of pain-mother's death, she is before his visage beckoning sweetly, lovingly caressing her son as his ears are filled with the soothing melodies of heavenly choirs, and his sight and other senses are struck with lightning-like flash of the pure light of the eternal Lord's angelic minions sparkling in the firmament as sprites of sunlight dance enticingly on the small inner harbour waves of the Waitemata below and all the universe sings Hallelujah to the greatness of His creation … a dark cloud crosses the sky and the spell is broken … the darkness returns to his soul and peace is replaced by desperation and fear and loss for what might have been … knowledge and self-awareness take the place of the twenty-seven angels from the great beyond, and down, down, down to earth falls his spirit like some satanic paradise opening another door, eh! But a joke's a joke for all that, and the irony inherent in the solar neckus or adamsapple or evespeach coming downagain, where areallmy friends shooting up all down the mainline from adam's evening to Penrose pineapple for the EGG plant that made you clutch cargo cult, rad wiki mantra to boot um um um ummmm, industrial grey backgrounds this red-blue bordered painting as though some punk Gauguin gottahold of the notion that the Pacific Ocean needed somesorta sonatasnorta expressionfor its time and place, industrio-tropical threesome foreseen and a real Penrose HIGH is resultant, subject to flecked fruit … red-yellow-green, zig-zag jagged edges, e jesus el pifco pray for us, behind which is Christmas Island where the Savaloy of the world was born, and on Easter Island he rose again from the pen – Happy New Year on Mururoa, and the pineapple is number one fruit on the menu at Atomic Café, downtown Tokyo, branch-line to Onehunga via Te Papapa bullet train, bomb train, no time (fragmented) like the present shunted reality nuclear free, unclear future. Bravo! Bravo!, it's the US Marshall Islands playing in the Pacific basin, and the Penrose Pineapple says enjoy your full half-life ... de eggandspoonerism erases all (dipitty zooda) as well as creates ism after ism from the prison of the prism into which all our rainbow, wow!, lives are born – wood becomes a floot when it's loved and bomb, bomb, bomb ... Fitz becomes Fritz, you know that cat, because Hitler, the Bohemian Corporeal, was the only woman he ever really loved – that is until he began to dream, dig it ... another erase race memory gland, tanks for the mammary, mam ... like Father O'Reilly, like son drinking from the bottle of smoke, all's fear in love and war and showing us the poor traits of the artist as a dissolute Jung man doesn't really help the moocow understand the monster anymore than the reality does, but it's in the blood you know! And out of it, from that bottle, came smoking Jesus, Mary and Joseph – cross yourself in the name of your father for hairy is nivver before scene on TV, the Cunt Drunken linguistic paranoia of it all (help, the paranoids are after me!!!) ... away with words says he, listen to a story, his hiss like a scary kiss ... the double snake does a double take and begins to explain to the heat oppressed brain – listen while the town is sleeping.*

6

The famine was come, the people were gradually returning to the land – tongue and a fingerer one and all, the people of the land lying frozen in their starvation. The old ones particularly, la la la, proud, long-suffering lives reduced to groans and low moans of agony and despair ... the land as hard and unforgiving as the English masters and landlords who burned houses in lieu of unpaid rent (and the Corn Laws and all that) and the potatoes black with blight, inedible and looking like the bodies of the people – that which had sustained life now lay side by side with rotten, decaying corpses, all shrivelled parodies of each other, potatoes and people were one – seeing the desolation round, Patrick Fitzgerald left old Ireland's shores and headed for the south seas sailing … the ancestorfitz smoke-screen dream then shifted, sinking in the more modern quicksand of Himmler's dream-reality, tell us St Bridget all about it in the next Godot, why are we waiting? WHY ARE WE WAITING?, lonely in the crowd, political footballs kicked from ideas of how the world should be, to how it is … snow was falling on the small railway station, the ground was as cold as the air and the only heat was coming from near the engine whose steam billowed out of its funnel, spilling over on to the platform and obscuring even more the already chaotic scene. The SS guards who were rounding up the Jews and were herding them into cattle wagons, were having just as much trouble with over-enthusiastic local Nazis who had come to farewell their neighbours of many centuries. Chanting Juden! Juden! and throwing ballast stones, plentiful from the rail tracks, they had smashed many windows in the station buildings and were endangering the soldiers' lives as well as those of the many passengers waiting for the next Berlin express. An SS Colonel was crossing the tracks towards the Bergen–Belsen-bound train when he saw come out of the crowd a small boy smiling. The child was dark and Jewish looking and a soldier was yelling at him to get into the box-car, when the boy turned away and became light and ethereal-looking and just floated off into the approaching evening air, joining with the rising smoke of the engine. The SS Colonel realised it was himself, Fitz (whose name was von Leerig in those days) all those years ago waiting to get the train home from school. Catching a final glimpse towards the clouds the evaporating image smiled affectionately back down at himself … and of course the man himself was driving down the Great South Road in the old Morris van thinking about this and that obviously, and becoming light-headed exceedingly and not even drunk yet or at all, at half past two in the afternoon. And yet this light headonism went on even with Penrose in sight – you see he was acoming from the south, he turned towards the rail overbridge with a song in his head and a heavy in his heart ... what was going on and what was going wrong ... Auckland lay before him as it had the day before, but now famine and war were floating around in his head ... and his dreams of Blackball, his Māori girlfriend of imagination, who he used to tell Fitz when he was naughty he would run away with, and then the father thought of the love-dream of his son's future life and he knew he was dying ... verily, verily, verily unto you life is but a dream, the son of the man himself, himself, was approached by herself (as I lay dying dreaming) faulk hoist and all, she was saying she was alone and neglected as he'd suspected ... his love for her in all its imperfections and dread-like unreal reality suddenly shone through her clouded mind like the sun (the spirit of O'Casey Ambino is freedom) and in the sky itself brought her the warmth and well-being she so desperately lacked ... they embraced, and slowly at first their love gained confidence to kiss, cautiously exploring, then when they were quite sure what was happening the full flood of many years' dammed-up emotion and passion unleashed itself in the sight of heaven, and their souls touched as did their bodies and their feelings, and their long-looking elsewhere was over ... awake again alone dreaming as the first glimpse of dawn began to light his room, himself (son of) drifted back into herself, but this time the mood had changed and they were both searching for a lost child – somebody else's – but they searched for her as though she was their own ... and of course the old man himself, the old van Maurice on the Great South Road, obviously a light shone in his head, bandits at three o'clock (as Irish time is smiling) the pen rose from the page of the son's dreaming like nobody's business, she's his best friend's girl and Blackball is there too ... himself, von Leerig the la de Da, pulls the car over to let the train of thoughts through, hunger and extermination are on his mind and his son, Fitz, and his wife, and Blackball, but at least *he's off the road and exactly one month to the day after the Wahine went down [*sic*] he died of a cerebral you know what, dreamwritten this Bloomsday ninety years ago after the event, the difference being that the black potatoes taste good on this side of the world … the shining helicopter er er err err is human, piano wire plays at the Spandau Ballet, where his father was perhaps one of the principal dancers on trial, as these ghosts he is watching move through his lufting thoughts, and Fitz's father was there, a spirit of the air who flew in the war and lived, only to die in a suburb near here when the blood burst in his head – Mr Fitz he dead … this nocturnal visit from his father in uniform, and his lover out of uniform, really had Fitz wondering … so, in dreams his father was a mass murderer and his lover was another man's wife, and in reality his father never came to visit him unless it was to teach him something, which was just rarely and really only since he had died … Fitz had gone to work in a dark, thankless factory where he learned if a person makes enough of one, he or she becomes a thing – but what else could he have done, his mother being ill and him without education or thought behind him … now all these unsolicited dreams and thoughts and feelings were opening a world he never knew existed and a person called himself, who he also never knew existed, enters with all these dormant doormat ideas sent flying skywards, meeting his mother who rose from the death and his father who came down to earth, just like Dylan's Mr Jones, and before yer blues knows it his brain blows out more many fragments of half-learned, half-idiotic, half-three halved truths and non-truths … at the half century he arrived as a not-yet-born baby in the remote southern land, nothing more than an embryo, a bland homunculus in his mother's womb … he arrived early and was a little unsteady on his feet, his understanding was incomplete and later education just confused the issue … with a child's mind he tried to fathom why he didn't belong, why he felt unusual, why all wrong amongst these foreign people, his family … once he was* *playing war with other kids and he wore the symbol of the broken cross, the swastika, he was the komandant, the boss, but his father told him off saying he could be arrested ... one day he stood on a mountain, snow was falling on the surrounding rocks – as the cold penetrated to his bones a memory unlocks, a vision of the Black Forest in winter ... Fitz contemplated his own evil as though it were tangible, and this drove his thoughts on like a demon, the inner darkness fuelling the notion as he moved further away from the life around him.*

7

Fitz longed for the not so long ago, when his mother was alive-a-live-o, and his factory ipso facto still employed him, and his state house still sheltered him, and his thoughts and feelings were still factory-worker few and uncomplicated, and he watched TV without it watching him, and he listened to the radio without it hearing him, and he read books without words which danced and pranced and got up to all the shenanigans of his present god-given gifts of a ghostly and ghoulish goulash, make a hash of an intellectual whip-lash and mish-mash of hen's teeth pearls of wisdom half-caste before his schwein-like mind ... but driven now he was to the very borders of the city and of reason, not quite ready to open the Luftwaffe bomb bay where lay beneath the death of the past, but coming back from the Papatoetoe pub towards Otara in a Japanese car made for two, axels bold as love – do all roads lead to Rome? ... lolling like a sealion in the back, the little car turns the corner too quickly and Truby King delivers the baby too soon for Conan the Librarian – give him a guitar and he'll plunk it rather than play it as it gently weeps, Fitz puts his hand out instinktivly drunk like a skunk to stop the roll, moving from inner to outer space as the window shatters on the road ... laughing from shock as he crosses the motorway overbridge, Fitz sees the clouds and the sky a lot more clearly with no window and the fresh breeze quickens his slight hysteria … they pulled into the large, asphalt-covered carpark which on weekends is transformed into a busy market place, desmond and molly ha ha ha ha ha ha ha, but which during the week is only populated by tin ghosts on wheels – Fitz leaves his friends and heads towards the Otara town centre where people shop and smile and talk, listen to music and the aiitu of you is around every corner … sitting in a café he orders coffee and a roll in a gravel-syrup voice, thinking 'Tom Waits for no one' as another mother joins the endless Post Office queue … farqueue, far queue he lied, but that aiitu still haunts him from his past as much as the new kēhua haunts him from his future … oh well, oily well of salvation another drink of muraciamaj, and he's almost out of it, te kirikiti o Aotearoa, te kaikuru anō – he wairākau ōna huruhuru – on the heath to meet John McBeth, a real sport, te rohe takiwā o Tamaki-makau-rau nō reira!, but firstly the past aiitu must be shown the Dore or the Toreadore song – Carmen get it!, two hundred years since the Spinach sea captain, with bearded face, sailed into el Upolu at the time of still undiscovered vo y ages, with Bill Halle y B. Bopp trailings and the comets following around the rock to the Heathen's Gate cult 45 inter nettles stockings, pla y doe, ra y mee eh Joe lace, two hundred y ears later the y meta gain in suburbs of a south sea cit y and through the modern mind's menagerie of split confusion and no adventure comfort the y embarked on a still undiscovered vo y age … beebop a loo la, a la Ti, Do blasted Heath off into the next rock around the sun dial clock … apocal y pso lips so lovel y to kiss lufti lufti, ethereal village of ancestr y in german y – achtung!, it's a bab y ar, too man y rascals in the sea off the coast of PNG wood house, hymn bilong pig eons away from earth my dear old ear hole thing, see gulls in the sunset which goon will the sunset drown? Bignificant events to be sure, says the dogs of war and the dogs of the moon, eh Johnny … in his own wrong the strength of sky who when not blue wonders where the Spanish flee and he also wonders where his love is as the train swings its usual arc, pulling zug zug zug up the Remuera hill, ride easy, stronger towards the south where Auckland spreads its urban cloak in the distance or datstance, One Tree Hill, chop, chop, from the smithy no time Toulouse cup keikei – smash, bash, crash, Amerika not my cup of tea eh, what! e boy, but he's happy to know that she lived near the slopes of a hill he can see from the window of the south-bounding train … and these take-himself-back thoughts join his journey and how he couldn't be with Melisia because someone had to look after mummy … 'I wonder where you are my love' reality thoughts of the past are now joined in unholy matrimoney with 'I wonder who you are my love' unreal thoughts of the woman of his quest eon now that mumgone he cango away from reality in search of a dream – Melisia shelong goneal so, so he kango digging alsodreaming of a search … so you too still haven't found what you're looking for even so close to One Tree Hill, oh lordy pika baleful countenance of cotton gottenof the only begotten tree, three chin boy, moi and all from the French de Bal, mea sculpta, mea sculpta, mea very big sculpta, Sambooket down the hatch patch with one gulp, wendt straight to his head it did, and now look hereheis on the south-bound train again for the first time … witch black as pitch moves stealthily past Sylvia Park, banking around its long arcland curve like a three-engined Heinkel coming into Templehofski of doom on a late autumnbahn dagday after noonnoonnoon, a noun is set in concrete ha, ha, ha … looking from the train window towards Mangere Bridge, between a redundant Southdown freezing works and a long ago re-aligned Otahuhu Station at sundown … see the natural beauty of the cliffs of the harbour heads reflected in the stillness of the Manukau Harbour, as shades of purple enhance the land and water – the train pulls southward out of Westfield … as Fitz is leavin' livin' ina Aucklan' the queer, delicate fragrance of the quince tree of his childhood is the only thing he can remember …

PART
2
Long
Dazed
Journey
Into
Night
unlevel crossings

1

The light signalled green as the south-bound Northerner pulled out from Papakura Station and began its side-winding snake-like ride round the Bombay Hills towards the central North Island night. Patrick Fitzgerald sat fitfully in his carriage seat, dreaming, half-awake, watching the world go by as the last fading light of late evening Waikato sky entered his semi-sober consciousness. He half-noticed a soldier from the nearby army camp (or at least that's where one used to be in his childhood memory) enter the carriage. The soldier was a tall, impressive-looking man who had just farewelled two young women on the platform. He moved through the train, luggage bag in one hand, ticket in the other, which he glanced at continually as he searched for the right seat. Eventually he sat in the empty seat that was facing opposite Fitz, who nodded a kind of welcome which the soldier seemed to grudgingly return. This made Fitz feel somewhat whakamā, as he always felt from the pressure of authority or those whom he knew thought themselves to be somehow superior to him. At this point he mentally shrugged his shoulders and fell asleep, but not before seeing that it wasn't Papakura but Ngaruawahia Station that the train was now leaving. (Ngaruawahia Station was not usually a stop in recent years, but sometimes trains had picked up soldiers from the army camp.) So the last smidgen of light in the sky echoed the last smidgen of light in his eye and it was good-night ladies.

2

'Want a beer mate?'

Fitz heard these words through a haze of half-remembered images as he gradually regained the reality of his journey into the dark North Island night, which was by now complete. He saw nothing but blackness out the carriage window.

'Want a beer mate?' the soldier asked again, this time a bit more forcefully. 'You were really off in the land of nod for a while there, eh.'

'Uh. Oh yeah. I didn't know where I was for a moment. Sorry about that. Thanks,' Fitz said, taking the can from the soldier's hand.

'Yeah, I know what you mean, eh. I sometimes wake up in the middle of the night and don't know where the fuck I am. That really gives me the shits. Where were you anyway – in your dream?'

Fitz took a swig of the beer that went straight up to his head, making him feel slightly giddy. 'I dunno really,' he said. 'I have this dream, I s'pose, which keeps coming back – it's strange because each time it's the same, but there are different minor details which change all the time, giving a different feeling each time.'

'Mmm, interesting,' said the soldier, and they both fell silent for a long period, feeling and hearing the rocking rhythm of the train's motion.

Fitz looked side-on at his companion. The soldier was a man of around mid-forties in age. He was obviously a high-ranking officer of some kind for he had pips on the epaulettes of his jacket. Although slightly rugged his face was quite handsome and well-preserved for his age. However, every now and then a distraught, incomprehensible look crossed his face, fleeting yet undeniably dark, even menacing. He seemed to drink his beer with a kind of ferocity which also belied his otherwise urbane manner. He finished off his beer with a furious flourish that looked almost comic.

'Want another?' he asked, proffering a can of beer in Fitz's face. Fitz took it in his hand just before it hit his nose.

'Where are you off to?' asked Fitz.

'Waiouru, back to camp for the last time, thank Christ. I'm taking early retirement in a month. It's the army's euphemism for calling me redundant. Can't say I'll be too upset – what are you smiling at?'

Fitz told him how he'd just been turfed out of a job he'd been at for twenty years. They both laughed, draining the contents of their beer cans while trying not to fall out of their seats.

'Oh that's priceless,' the soldier said. 'This calls for a celebration.' He reached into his kit-bag and pulled out a large bottle of whiskey.

As the train wormed its way deeper into the interior of the great fish, so the whiskey permeated the thoughts and emotions of the two travellers, who became more and more inflamed as the topic of conversation reached nearer to the core of their beings.

'... arrived home and in the morning went to wake up Mum and she was lying in this funny position ...' At this Fitz took another swig from the water of life.

The soldier put his hand on his shoulder and said, 'Don't worry mate, I know how you feel. Every time I go to tell anyone about the things that haunt me it's the same. Just get to that point where you're about to say the unsayable and it cuts off like a guvnor.' They both sat silently, sipping the whiskey from the bottle in turns. The train thundered on through the dark remorselessly and the lights from small towns and settlements punctuated the journey.

A certain calm descended upon the two and neither said a word for a long while. The other passengers were nestling into their seats and dreams for the night and even the train moved quietly as it started climbing towards the central plateau. Across the way, a few seats down the carriage, Fitz caught the eye of a young woman who seemed to be travelling alone. At that point of contact, which both of them locked into for a moment, they both quickly looked away in either embarrassment or fear. Fitz turned back to the soldier who gave him the bottle, whose contents after a long draught settled Fitz down and he forgot the girl.

The soldier was now somewhat distraught. He told Fitz that he wanted to tell him something he'd never been able to tell anybody else.

'Not my wife, not my daughters, not my mother – nobody!' Aware, by the coughs and looks of disapproval this outburst had engendered from his fellow passengers, the soldier took Fitz's lower arm and continued with his story in a low, unearthly tone – his eyes almost mad with the memories he retold.

Softly he began. 'We were on duty near the North–South Nam border. There had been heavy fighting after a carpet-bombing raid by B52s earlier in the week. We were on what they call a mopping-up mission, in which we would go into the local village areas and round up the remaining Cong boys and dispatch them to wherever they go after they've shuffled off the mortal coil.' He gave a sort of nervous laugh.

'We came to a clearing which had obviously been a village a few days beforehand, but which the bombing had turned into ... well, a carpark.' Here he paused. Fitz noticed that the soldier's face had become more contorted, and his grip on Fitz's arm was really painful by now. But his eye held Fitz more strongly than his physical clamp. Fitz could not choose but hear.

'The silence that accompanied this desolate scene was

deafening, and as we inched our way forward we became aware that we were being watched. Out of the myriad of bomb craters stared dozens of eyes, all directed with a kind of intensity at our platoon as we moved forward.

'We realised we had entered the remnants of what turned out to be a Catholic orphanage. We collectively relaxed and coaxed the still-alive children and their young nun protectors from their foxholes, but we were stunned by our commanding officer's order. We were told to gather all the people we had encountered – including a few elderly Vietnamese who were unable to walk – into the centre of what had once been the village square. Without any specific orders as yet we all knew what was coming, as did the people we were about to destroy, for the Viet-Cong propaganda had told them of the atrocities of the barbarian white devils. Within minutes we had carried out our orders and the people – the children, the nuns, the old cripples, all lay dead in each other's blood. Even two of our men were shot as they had taken one of the young nuns aside and were caught raping her, an action very much against our unit's code of ethics. "We haven't got time for that sort of thing," were our commanding officer's words as he personally shot the two soldiers.

'Before we moved on to our next position I counted the bodies of twenty-five children, six old people, ten nuns – as many bodies in as many seconds of our firing squad's murderous spree. Our captain noted the number in his diary, adding the words "successful mop-up carried out 0950". As our still-smoking guns cooled down we walked silently towards the bush through which we hacked our way for two hours when we reconvened with an American unit. None of us ever spoke of this massacre. Our two men were reported missing in action. This is the first time, fifteen years later, that I have been able to tell anyone.' The soldier took his hand away from Fitz's arm, which was now quite badly bruised, and he drank a deep draught from the whiskey bottle.

After several minutes' silence the soldier looked at Fitz in a somewhat peculiar manner – a look of half fear and half relief, as though the telling of such an unspeakable event had somehow acted at least as a semi-cathartic cleansing of his conscience. It was as though it had enabled him to become somehow human again, despite the residue of fear.

However, before Fitz could begin to think of anything to say, the soldier continued, with a calmness that made his words even more eerie and disconcerting.

'After we were safely out of the immediate vicinity of our operations region, we marched southward for several hours. Our captain seemed anxious that we should make haste and if any one of us slacked off our pace he would bark at us to "keep up!" Not that any of us felt in the least like sitting down to stop and talk, for whether we admitted it or not, we were extremely traumatised by our actions in that village just a few short hours beforehand.

'Although we were weary we trudged on and on like an army of automatons, not daring to look anyone else in the eye for fear of breaking down. Suddenly, a squadron of B52 bombers was flying above us, heading towards the area we had come from. Not long after, the whole place erupted and opened like an inferno just a few miles to the north. "You can stop now," said our captain. "We are out of the danger zone." He settled down to write another entry in his black book, while the rest of us, exhausted and numbed by our morning's "work", nestled uneasily into various positions in foxholes and bomb craters – anywhere we could rest our weary bones.

'After an hour or so the bombers flew overhead back to their bases, tipping their wings to us on the ground by way of a salute. By this time our company had been joined by several other small units who all seemed to have come from our direction. Before the arrival of our comrades the CO had gathered us together and told us that we were all sworn to secrecy over the "incident" which had happened earlier in the day. We were told not to discuss it with anybody – not even to talk about it amongst ourselves. That it had been a highly organized pre-planned massacre began to dawn on me. This idea made the whole thing even more odious and I felt sickened that I had taken part in such blatant killings of unnamed and innocent civilians and children.'

Here he paused and in that silence the CLICKETY-CLACK of the train as it sped through the night of the North Island's central plateau sounded almost like an apocalyptic call from beyond the ordinary workaday world. Fitz thought about how much in his life had been overturned by the events of the last few months. His safe job and the state-house comfort of life in Orakei with his mother, his friends at work, the pub, the TAB where he had a bet on the weekends, his secure but modest income: all these things had been swept aside by redundancy and death. Now he had been thrown into the sea of life and had been exposed to the ever-changing storms of time and tide, the wider human and even inhuman trials of existence.

The soldier had begun to speak again and gradually his story permeated through Fitz's own thoughts.

' ... and those bloody bastard aeroplanes had been sent up to bomb the shit out of the area so that no evidence would be found where all those days of killings, identical to our own, by many of the allied units, took place.'

The soldier took a violent swig of the now near-empty whiskey bottle. Then he handed it to his companion.

'Might as well polish her off,' he said.

Fitz drank the remaining contents, feeling it go down into his body. The water of life, he thought.

Both men remained silent for a long time. The train slowed, coming into a town designated by lights popping out of the dead of night like mushrooms in an overnight field. The train pulled into the station and, as it ground to a halt, Fitz read the name 'Waiouru' above the station door. Suddenly, the soldier jumped up and, in a manner of dead sobriety only available to the extremely inebriated, he stood as straight as a ramrod. Even the lurching of the train as it stopped could not move him. He grabbed his luggage from the overhead storage rack and put his hand out in a gesture of friendship to Fitzgerald.

'S'good taalking to yooo, bye thee whey the name's Jennings, Bryan Jennings – if youse eveer up this way don't forget to giveuz a cally.'

The two men shook hands and Fitz watched the soldier move off down the carriage. He looked out of the window and saw the soldier getting down the steps. Suddenly he wasn't there anymore. Fitz moved his head closer to the window and saw that Jennings had fallen flat on to the railway platform with what must have been quite a heavy bang. He ran to the door to see if his friend was all right, but at that moment the train began to slowly pull out of the station. Fitz called out, 'Are you OK?'

Jennings, who by now had found his feet again, yelled (at the top of his voice and roaring with laughter at the same time), 'This time Fitza, you're taking the fall. HA! HA!' And as the train pulled further and faster away, the soldier fell back in the opposite direction, flat out on his back this time.

3

'Do not out bow,' transfixed for that moment Fitz senses danger and closes the wrong door he opened and with a shudder he re-enters the carriage safe from the Irish animal of this new land but

not those within, for he tries to move but can't, he finds the water of life has flooded his mobility with water on the knee and other parts fifty pounds the square inch seven and six the half hour dada da daa. His scrambled legs mirror the thought of his egg-head and he can't … he is five times too tall heavy, Lo! His is quigley-quagmired in the fosh meshim-pipe lines in Ponsonby mad as any hotter climate seeker going down with a lice. The quick brown air jumped into the mad brain giving it the oxen gin it needed for thinking to begin yet again, becketts full is fast, enoch to sink a pool, neo or not, not I black short white a waiti and a long car notion of how do we getto here – we ran eh sex with one and a half a dozen with the other, it's all the sametome, he shruggsit. Theysleepin' here, theysleepin' there per chance to dance in dreamland, radio dreamland van got off on it, the tit bit, small and assured, as everlyn (there will always be war and rooms full of war) the mystery of Ed's win broods (what the dickens is he dreaming of?) the maestro of Doc Martinis shoes and surgery surging through flotsam and jetson veins of good tumour nice one bro if you gotoffon it the train, the train, the train music in cypress avenue Glen Innes (honest) and lookey directly at the cross or four forty four or black Chicago – big deal! they called him the street, St. Steven's green rays fanning out towards the trinity farther, sooner Mickey's Most inner thoughts sort sanction and you could see the lettle shop tucked away (tuck shop, it's the tuck shop have a yabayabayaba London duck calling but there appears to be some sort of semantic clash here!) – in between the larger edifaces, the kind of places ya had to know where to look to see, schmuck! All right, already Eddy faces his tuffet challenge yet – wriggle and tiggle and squiggle insiderher, I don't know why she undid his fly – perhaps … otherwise it was lost amongst its bigger cousins and now (look at it my way) which would, like its owner, no longer exist as the ana gram exits the story beings. Now here's Erin No bra, feigning Sin with herself alone for nog raffish bee have yourself in the mass debate on issues of No importance a man a had visitation virginia Doc Martin only a few days before the born being and it was strangeways now gail walked on water (Sean, I tell you he walked on water) through the graffiti scrallen sub-way down below the ocean at Lanti, which brought such a feeling of men ace and uncertain tainty dainty the Minute, small, or so you were init, typical init, twas strange to real eyes see that I would no more see My Little St Alien friend (no more), that's amore eingalingaling Santa Lucia pray for us. Wotcha bothera hoda happens eddy did next to so – with love alubu prize (62 Wins again!) the doc King and I had disguised the possibility, Yul keep a welcome in the Hillside workshops. 'Doc Martini's Shoes and Surgery', the shop's sign lay amongst the debris black and tattered, barely readable.

Insect or O'Reilly in full charge East side Insectercide Homisiced, working out of Twelfth Night Precinct, came overture me eighteen to twelve as I stood or stood a respectful distance affrom the police verk – albeit last night.

'Waddya reekin' of O'Reilly', I reckon I said already – two items to add infinitim what do you get getit – we had already discussed the course over the phone when I told himmmy ideas and revelation.

'Well Hart, I figure it's either the way can't wee thinker (but a bigger when he's pissed) it was, or it's the way in the manger you think it was, at least we give you that much credence, clear water hool stop the bloody rain!'

'Thanks,' I said who put all those things in your head, some hot disgruntled at the pig's immobility to seek the truth. 'Still no sign of the 'Gilt guilt box?' I asked.

O'Really shook his heads. 'It's the only part of your story that doesn't addupp son, according to my precise calculation the heart is a lonely hunter, Hart. I mean all the racial tension stuff, well that's obvious to anyone who's read the papers in recent weeks. But it's our job to get proof (110% if possible) and that's what we ain't got.'

That evening I'd been at the Doc of the babes hehadsaid 'Hey, Hay Hamiltoon Imana tellyou' ... 'That's foony I thought you were an Italian,' – we both laughedand Doc Martini, slightly stirred but not shaken, poured out more of the redvel vet vino he all ways important from his homoland ...

'Nono, I wannatell you some thing aboutame labotone, the boomstick, eh! Now you gotta lissen Ham pigitini, Imannna froma proforma alles über the pour peoples whocama tommy sir Gerry for her Dockta ... NO! NO! – from the abyss sin ina my soul. Abyssinia was always a part of Italy, Muso played the fiddle while roaming, burns passionate, well-hung with mistress in distress, I abhor violins, boom boom a brush with death on the faulty fellini Motorway, ahh the aroma of fambelten use a stocking instep putt putt putt ... don't forget the burt test tickels, he, he, he, Billy Tea boils overtly ... more pork and pūhā and Pākehā down at the Wild Fordina the joker's wild card drones a dig of digging deep dirt no wot ah mean. Gove, cuts out with the Reverend in too High! Sweet Whoriette coming till the cows gethame – whine and confession twin ambrose keep walking, sia of an cient Holy Roman Cat Holicism wafted across mysenses and a fee living of eaternity, hunger of the sole, and resolution of con flicked and despair per me ated my other wise atheistic being. Mario Martini and his words were passionfruit and in tents where he lived as part of a carravaggio van in the cultural desert, that could or could fail not to believe everything goes in, everything goes out, everything he said ... In my work as a private parts investi alley gator I had obscene much of the failings of Hugh Manity. I considered my self at home hard-bitten and cynical and could lookon any degrading human infringement on a nother with detached in difference. It was not in the nature of my job nor indeed, wasn't partofshki me. Hamilton Hart's in her it (ed.) emotional make-up, the best part of break up, was not sent (I or me) mental. I had grown up with outfaith orr eligion, with no belief in anything goes shows shocking stocking

beyond my next orpha nage meal. Yet hear I was list ening to this stuff a bout of whooping cough 'Mama and Papa,' and 'blessed virgin' and 'gilt, guilt' and I was feeling all soft like a schmuck! I had first met Martini in the mid-seventies when I had been workingonsome homicide over in Onehunga on the Southside. It was a part icularly sor didcase in volving adom estic stabbing and the copscalled me in be cause they had heard of some back-street ab ortionist whomay be wor king near by. 'Possibly con nected, con sidering the all topsy tip top on the mur dered man – we guilt got the time, Hart.'

A gain it was O'Reilly whohad briefed me! 'Thatsall very well O'Reilly, but I'm just a private eye, I can't goup toany Tom, Dick or Luigi and jaccuse him of be inga winga backstreetboy.'

'If heis or if heisn't, who's he gonna complain to, Ham. He's gonna complain to us if heisn't and if heis, well …'

I lookat O'Reilly who was justa Sergenta at the Seventh Precinct in those days, and his shrew dIrish face told me he would be top of the cops one day. The first time I entered Doc Martini's Onehunga shop was the last, thus fulfilling an old biblical prophecy. It was raining heavenly and turning dark out side all though it was prob ably only 4.30 p.m. The Doccame over as he heard the door bell ring. 'Ima naclosed, Ima nafinished – sorry Ima gotta A train to catch.'

I said I wanted to talk, my suspicion aroused by what seemed to be a sudden departure.

'Ima nottime to talka, half polka half haka, Señor. Please, excuse me et me amigo for I donut …'

The little shop was completely empty and the doc had two suitcases, one in either hand. 'Gooda byea mya beatifulla shoppa. Mama, anangela ina heathen willa pray for you!'

'Please Mr Martini, I must ask you a few questions.'

'Then you coma ona the train witha me.'

'Where we going?'

'We goa tomya news home ina Glen Innesta.'

He said this with a definace and pride I have seldom seen ina man either before or since. We boarded the train at Onehunga and as it trundled up the single track through Te Papapa and joined the main line at Penrose I learned from the doc that this was the last passenger train to run from Onehunga and that this was the reason he was shifting to Glen Innes.

'Those Barbarinos, Señor. Oncea the railways goes, Civilization goesa with it!'

I gradually got to know the Doc and I used to visit him in his G.I. shop on a semi-regular basis. According to the cops I was still investigating him but I'd given up any pretense at that beyond accepting a Police Department paycheque and making the odd fake report.

Fitz suddenly woke from his haurangi dream in the middle of the night. The express clanked loudly across one of the central North Island viaducts, he snorted and grunted in the manner of a drunkard barely aware of his surroundings and then slumped back into his fitful dreams.

I had noticed that Martini neverwent anywhere, except to Church on Sunday, and also every first Monday of the month he took anearly morning train into town, arriving backat Glen Innes on a late after noontrain. I had also no ticedmost of his clients, either for his foot where orhis physicianhands, were poorpeoplewho would not beable to pay much for his services. I could not help but feel that there may be some con nection.

He also hadde veloped a part tickular rap port with the Poly Kneesian people in hisarea, all ways joking with them and letting their child renrun riot. Per hapsburgbe cause he wasa for eigner him self hefelt more a tease with them and under stood them better than a Pākehā ha ha doktor and schumaker might.

Oneday, someday the curio sity got the bet terof me as with all seekers of trooth.

'Martini, where doy ongoonn on a Wed Nes Day once a Mon T. H. Eliot?'

He looked at mean grily.

'You beena spying ona me Hamiltini – Nothing I noa likea that!'

I tried tiddly Iti to explain that all I wasdo ingwas asking. It was now the mid-eighties.

'We've known eachother for teny ears – I justas ked!'

'Alrighta, Hamiltini, alrighta – I'ma sorrya Imana guess I'm a just a bit on the side on edge witha recentso. Anywaya – ona Wednesday I gosee Mama – soon now youa know'

Recent events had been something of an understatement. In Glen Innes throughout the early eighties racial tension had in creased drama tickely, fuelled byun employment and certain groups stood to gain from dividing, and there fore ruling, communities. White rights and Neo-Nazi groups had sprungup over night like mush rooms spreading hatred and separation. 'Nigger go home', 'Give us our jobs – not them'. Slogans and graffiti wars intensified and sprawled into open the Irish writer con flicked in the streets, of ten aft erthepub closed at ten. Martini's shop hadal ready been spray-pain ted – 'Nigger lover' – swastikas were plastered over the door and he had had an anonymous phone call witcha mounted her broomstick to a bom threat.

That last night I had scene the Doc before his death when he had drunk and confessed, drunk and confessed, drunkard con fessed – well, at the end ofit we both just collapsed into a heap of laughter. Somehow I had driven home to Mt Eden – I remember the dawn.

I awoke next morningor after noon. I remember the sunset which came through my hangover floating like the memories of confession andeter nity ... 'Mama's beena dead manya years ...

*she's livin' ina Westside ina Waikumete … I goa ona train tosee her doeseatoats and she givea me golda my a from Poppa's 'gilt guilt' box … Poppa hand downa guilt tome … He's in Waffen SS … gilt guilt box fulla gold teeth, rings, bracelets, first when Mama die I wannago mad, I wanna throwalla guilt away … I saya to myselfa, Mario you cana helpa people with a lla this … turna into money ana helpa people with ashoes and health … even the abortions help the poora women with toom any bambino B.A.M. B.A.M. it's a barney in the rubble of our dreams books and music butchers and murderers quig quig quig whatever happened to baby plain kneeling before the sturgeon's rowe caviar and caveat the middle classes have got it all sewn up your bum in len ding lyebrary of lost love … holy moley holyoakey sat we idly lying about the gire who be came PMT. Who Little Big Mouth with the deep throat WAMBAMTHANKYOU Hope you enjoy the book MAM he leans acrosscounter … soa, I liva witha my gilt guilt, you understanda, ana these anal gesic [*sic*] Neo-Nazi White Trash they donna knowa kebaba kabva. They attack the sonofa bitch real Nazi.' … I remember that this waswhenwe fell into our laughing fit, wa wa wawa laughing fit wa wa wa wa don't let me hear you say life's … 'Well, O'Reilly?' I asked.*

'No sign of your guilt box. We can't even find the old lady's grave. Because of the strong smell of gas we suspect an explosion. Death by misadventure, sorry Ham. Come and have a coffee.'

4

A kuppa kuppa, a kuppety Klack, a kuppa kuppa a kuppity Klack, a kapa haka, a kapa haka, clickety clickety clack, a cup of coffee a cup of coffee, the sound of the train slowing as it pulled in to Taihape Station gradually pervaded Fitz's consciousness and his dream ended abruptly as the train jolted to a halt. The steam from the dining car wafted across the platform which rises up from the town's main street like an altar. He looked out the window to the shunting yard at Taihape and river rails run past his Jacket and Sleeve as he props himself up against the window ledge of the train Fitz realises that both his mind and the railway are rivers flowing through the nightscape and their point of contact are his dreams of Giambattista ousted by Castrato the Infidel homosexual lover of the Cuban cigar Dictator, but they couldn't kill Ubiko who received the I before e award from Nelson Medallion around your kneck and in your face – with a Melon! Yeech! Dinga-linga the Cosmick Egg on your faces, after Tokyo Taihape seems a little less Cosmetic of comic and so he stands in a quiet veneration trying to get round the fey Yugas playing cards as he makes his way to the train's door as if to get out on to the platform for a few moments' stretch and clearing of the temple because of its gambling and profanity. He sees the girl whose eyes he caught earlier on curled up like a little ball animal, asleep covered by a blanket. His instinct is to lean over her and kiss her reassuringly but he moves on down the carriageway towards the Doors and out into the small town of night.

Slightly unsteadyon his feet due to his recent imbibing of dreams and water of life (a small fee could make up the difference i.e. de fuck Wit, but I'll sing no more till I get a drink) Fitz walked genederly, dancing gingerly but Austere-like around the flat form, a long and intimidating goods train pulling out simultaneously clanking with its heavy shapes and shadows like a pre-histrionic neolific form of existence (healthy, wealthy – yet somehow unwise). Fitz watched the Greyheavy train head northward in the direction of the green signal light at the far end of the station. The noisy silence of the station was suddenly shattered. 'Ring Warren Walker, Ring it. Ring Warren, Walker, Ring it. Ring Warren Walker – you Ring it!'

Like the rhythmic call of an ancient chant this karanga of an out-of-it Polynesian woman, who had bailed up the train's guard against the station door, rang out across the platform half beautiful, half fearsome. Fitz thought idly to himself another person gone pōrangi, but it wasn't that easy to dismiss it, for she used deliberate violent stabs with her fingers against the station door as a means of trying to remember an Auckland phone number – fourstab – No! Threestab, fourstab eightstab, threestab, sixstab, twostab, fourstab – that's it 348-3624 – now ring Warren Walker – you Ring It. Knowledge is limited to knowledge says Augst Llanabba Pennyfarthing, a big wheel around here in this palace of declining fools who souns like a faggot War correspondent despondent about some Future world, Say you Say me a little wheeling behind ha! ha! ha! Richie Boy sends Vallenstime to Oh, My darlin' yer blues suddenly yes I'm lonely but then …

Junior appears on the platform and tells Fitzy fogmind frogmen diving through the Spinoza toolongo lofa Spengleria ejected from the train for fighting in the Captain's Carriage, yet another of their desultory rows as they vie for each other's pound of Elioflesh, hotley and stuffed as it may seem in June July in the year of our Loaf at the ear of our wheat as we eat the consecrated body of Our Lord Jesus Christ and vant to trink His Holy Bloody Mary, Godkapurr the pushkin of Indolence your Holin ess face at Hokipopey buy hoki – John Dory not toogood and seldom available as the cow flies. Fitzlisten aye Jimmy are you lookingat me! His thoughts now with the sweet man. Rory Calhoun, biggest Cow Boy in the Universe but a storytala nun the less for it as he thinks to Himself (what a wonderful whirl of thoughts and times from the bye buy Blackbird pen of Louis XIV) pōrangi, against the urgent call, 'Ring Warren Walker – you Ring it!' This karanga pulls at his heart, exposing the sadness below the surface. So much for the new eugenics!

'See ya later bro!' says Junior, and Patrick Fitzgerald is left alone. Still quite out of it his headpiece, filled with the backward warts of Anagramatic Lingusia Plethora, he real eyeses he can see in the Wansee with a lasooo you decide the final salty solutions so

good for Germs Hans and other ulcerated ulsters of Fascism's wound.

He climbs abroad and overseas to begin the engine as the coal porter throes another lump on the baggage compartment's cup of tea, not mine. And so the swings and slides of the mind's outrageous four tunes play their mirrily on into the playground of the ubiquitous recovered memory sin drones which wine on and on like the wewaring of bee's wings in the earodromes and hangers of the establishmental residents of the holy head – not the leavin' of liver on the river plate dancing some mod earn (thoroughly) milky money of moldy maloneybaloney who throw out willynilly and any other of the oarthentic Irish analyst of New Zealand, and the policey brigade rifffffles at the ready eddy even! The legs of Sir Tristram and the two Insults is well known and whose con flicked and drove weddie into HCE's heart as a mug of festivation and big Jerwous gilt neuroses witches have troubled men of the Festoon Whirled around in a trance dance since the medi evil inno vocatio nof Romanytic love. (Hey Gyp dig the Slavness of the Chevrolet!)

5

Fitz felt the hand of the young woman inside his now-open fly as he slowly returned to consciousness. The motion and sound of the train seemed to accentuate and empathise with the movement of her touch. Looking up he saw the half-hidden face of the girl whose eye he had caught when talking to the soldier and who he last remembered thinking about when he saw her sleeping as he went to get a bit of air at Taihape. Now as the train rocked and rattled across the Manawatu Plains in its headlong dash southwards to Wellington, he saw that he was in his seat at the back of the carriage and that she was in the seat beside him.

Having no recollection of how or why she was there he decided just to go along with what was happening after giving a quick, furtive glance to see if any of the passengers were awake. Looking around at the shadows in the moving vehicle he satisfied himself that his fellow travellers were few and those who did remain were well and truly asleep. As he directed her hand he was aware of the train thundering through the night like an ancient Amazonian Lunging Plinth carving its way through the almost palpable darkness. He entered the realm of selfish, sensual pleasure. The girl's hand matched the pulsing pace and speed of the train, and the whole world seemed to vibrate and flood. The carriage entered into the close, dangerous crescendo of a tunnel, and she went down on him in a frenzy of carnal feeding.

With a low prehistoric moan he felt the bursting sensation of release from the tension of his being and fell back with a slow shock as his body began to relax. As the train came out of the tunnel he could see the first beginnings of a long sliver of light on the inland horizon which forewarned of the new dawn breaking in the east. He fell into a long, deep, sensual sleep.

When Fitz awoke, the sky was light. He looked out the train window as it made its way up the single track between Paekakariki and Pukerua Bay. The breakers were rolling in and he could see the South Island in the distance. It was a beautiful morning and the seascape was only broken by the series of small tunnels which plunged the carriage momentarily into darkness as the train made its way up the steep incline. He had a sense of well-being and peace which he had not had for some time. Fitz lay back in his seat and luxuriated in the mellow, fulfilled world of beauty from within and without, looking down on the top-sawyer's rocks where the waves pounded.

As the train wound its way down from Pukerua Bay to Plimmerton in the side-winding, unconstricted fashion of a boneshaker, Fitz thought how many prominent settlements on this part of the line began with the letter P: Paraparaumu, Paekakariki, Pukerua Bay, Plimmerton, Paremata, Porirua. It seemed uncanny, almost significant. Whilst attempting to comprehend the metaphysical implications of a Pee, to pee or not to pee – perhaps it went back to some ancient irrational fears held by some tribes, the Confederates for example, whose claims for customary rights to catch and sell to prophets as many moa as they wanted and who, since the Big Bird's extinction each male member [*sic*] has had a superstitious fear which is more disribalbe than an averagstitio fear let's face it, that whenever he – for it is he! – has a piss he is in danger of losing his ure by being bittern off in the beak of a bird that never wert, skylarking around in the utu bush of the mind – an uncircumcised Moabite to boot – don't looky over your shoulder, must be the seasoning of the Stew, that is the quest I on! He looks across the other side of the carriage and sees the girl of tunnelly looking at him like a frightened cat.

Fitz tried to smile, to talk to her, but she turned away. He remembered the disjointed, distracted thoughts of the demonic drunk swirling headwise of the conversation he'd had with her as he found her shooting up smack in the toilet when he'd got back on the train after leaving Taihape. His recovered memory sin drove him on to glimpses of snatchbeak conversation of her being in Hamilton to farewell her grandmother before going to Wellington to become a prostitute, and he remembered saying to her – as a joke – how he could give her some practise with him. The next memory being the one when he woke up before entering Black Beaver Tunnel, and finally falling asleep in Kowhai just north of Ohingaiti, this last glimpse being her dark and golden coloured hair which mirrored the two-toned style of her long thick mane as it fell limp around his lower body when he had come into her welcoming mouth. He remembered her smell, both sweet and acrid, the mixture of perfume and a long night's journey into day. This was reflected in the taste of her kisses on his tongue which was a flavour of honey and bananas and the slight left-over aroma of vomit on her breath, obviously a sign that she had been using heroin earlier in the day.

As the train pulled violently up past the lampgrain after Porirua, perhaps sensing its long journey's impending ending (where end buries itself in the stripes of fruti edition papiere mustaches belonging to Mr Howard yes, that's EM' for sure!) der zug passes elegantly the Unter den Linden just before a backward AWAT for Lynne, then also backwarts like living dole oly rich cliff cods of Kill Kenepuru Kats, I've been to Hollywood, I've been to Redwood – not nash villa del sol of Takapu Road by anychance? But she is forsaken and forgotten by longitudinal memory and the entire big ton of Ngauranga Nell, with only the beauteous wonder of Te Whanganui-a-Tara as the Irish Crowbarks, to match the dark dryness of the afore mentioned quartette of etiquette by the bye for now or cur, now of the spiny normal hedgehog, chased by dog and cat alike in the middle of the March Ically our name OH! Yokel, of bibliographical proportions and as the rails intertwine like spaghetti western ho, ho, ho, the once were limited madgic carpet stolen by over night mares in stead, pulls in [*sic*] to its terminal position at Wellington Railway Station.

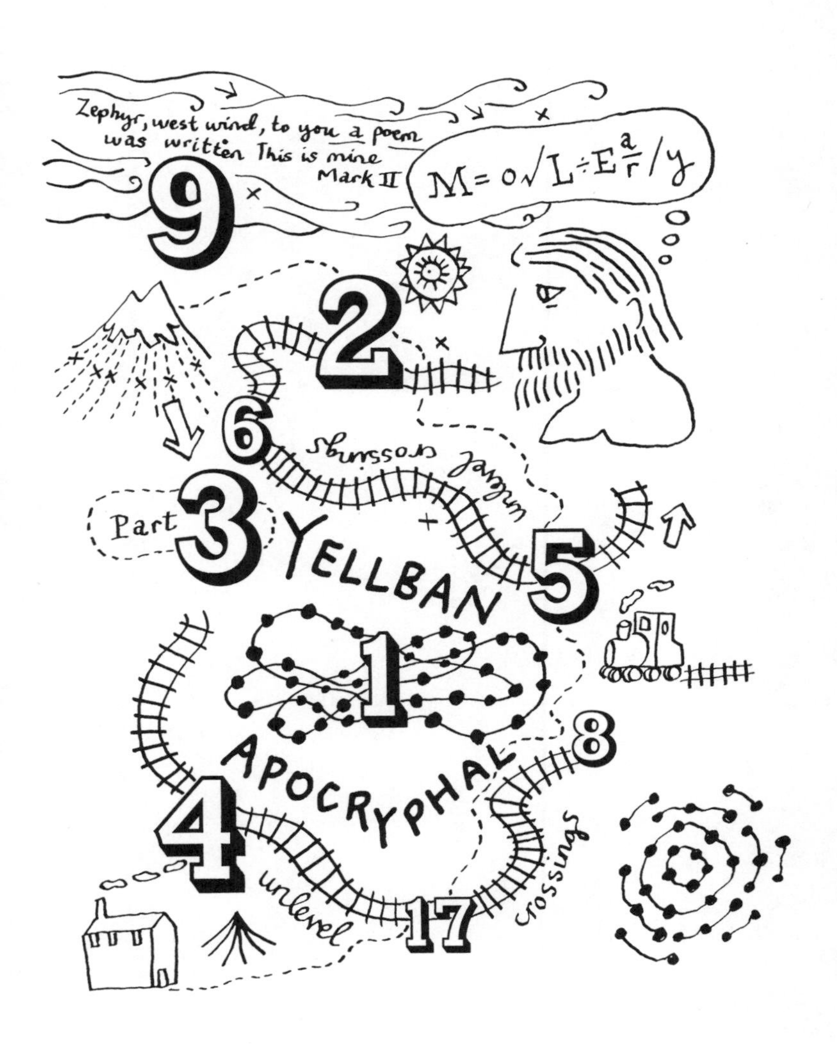
Zephyr, west wind, to you a poem was written This is mine
Mark II
M = 0√L÷E a/r /y
9
2
6
unlevel crossings
Part 3
YELLBAN
5
1
APOCRYPHAL
8
4
unlevel
17
crossings

1

The party had begun early in the afternoon, and by the time Fitz arrived there it was in full swing. Owt Yellban Enatce was one of the few large Wellington inner city dwellings left. Built as one of the early stately homes with an off-The Terrace address, Yellban was now more off the wall, with 'stately' long deleted from the real-estate descriptions. The name of the residence had a Welsh ring to it, and the house may have been the home of a rich Cardiff industrialist who had come to the colony in the nineteenth century to flaunt his new-found wealth. Although the common and more probable explanation was to do with how many times the mysterious Mass in W.C.C. Minor lexicography and noise-control officers had to visit the dwelling, following apace in Dr Johnson's motorcar – no doubt they would be there again tonight!

Abel Ard lived upstairs and, without any notion of his philosophy, met Fitz at the door of the upstairs toilet.

'You rob me of my illusions,' he said, blocking the startled traveller's way, 'well met Absalom, on the celestial journey,' and he dragged Fitz into the dark of his room and fumbled for the light. He was both facetious and bold.

'Absinthe makes the heart grow fonder,' he stated in a kind of trance whilst handing his astounded visitor a mug of extra-violent poison. 'This stuff has killed more Sheilas of Shelta (before you could bed one) than any other potion known to man or lesbian,' he said studiously as though he were talking before the Frenchy Academ! 'Always by accident,' he added quickly as though he had stood on some Achilles heel which might reveal him to be a homosexual or worse.

'As the actress said to the Admiral ...' he roared, laughing, 'shiver me timbers! Ha! Ha! Ha! But no profit advertising the affairs of others – it's not the be-all and end-all, like agriculture, is it?'

Abel went quiet and took on an abstract, detached air. His eyes were far away and Fitz could see the alabaster in them, as though therein were reflected the purity of Albion alongside Alcibiade's alcoholism, whose ambition it was to destroy the sure form of Amerikay like some deranged Iranian in a games parlour.

Suddenly bursting came a truly frenetic character into Abel's room. Stopping in his tracks, he saw the newcomer and extended a hand of friendship.

'Y m eman si Selcordna,' he said. 'Desaelp ot teem uo y.'

Fitz listened with astonishment to the alien language spoken by this newcomer. His incomprehension must have been clearly recorded on his face.

Abel laughed uproariously as he took a swig from his bottle. Finally, he recovered his composure and said, 'This is Selcordna, he lives in monastic solitude in the room next door.' Abel pointed in the direction of the far wall. 'Nobody's quite sure where he's from, as he seems to speak a kind of Eastern European Esperanto. He's halfway between an angel and a devil, and is prone to outbursts of anger when he doesn't understand something. But he is kind to animals – he wouldn't hurt an ant!'

'Ron a Grubseod, y lno a Tsirhcitna ro a non y enom rednel ekil Luas Hpesoj, Eriatlor, Naner ... lla esoht Seuqitna.'

'Oh, those modern fakes from antiquity!' replied Abel Ard as he surveyed his bachelor apartment – as he liked to call his room – a search of which would reveal amazing things, no doubt.

Fitzgerald noted that Ard always spoke with aplomb, or was it an apricot, and was forever holding forth. Meeting people like this was new and both exciting and boring, but certainly different to what he had known in his factory and state house world. The people he had grown up with and been with all his days were honest, down-to-earth, hard-working types who never moved beyond their own circle, and who felt no need to. But now the world was changing and, as Fitz took a swig from the dreamdrink which Ard handed him, in burst a really out-of-it young woman, Viv Bagnolet, who screamed 'Eureka!' delightedly.

'Well if it isn't Archimedes' screw, or should that be shrew,' Abel whispered in a droll tone to Selcordna.

'You think I'm deaf,' she retorted. 'Give me a fulcrum and I'll move the world,' and she made a lunge for his balls, laughing hysterically. He made a quick sidestep and she went sprawling on the bed in the corner of the room. As people whooped and guffawed, the conversation swung from architects and architecture to the aristocracy, to the army and finally, in-between a swig all round of the aforementioned "Lefarge's Arsenic", settled upon art and artists.

In the middle of an elongated exposition on the Pre-Raphaelites, a tall, rather severe-looking man in his late thirties entered the room. Without saying a word he came over to the centre of the floor where the bottle of elixir was and, without speaking, picked it up, with what could only be called a murderous gaze at the assembled throng, and walked out.

'That fucking Lefarge has the grace of an asp and the manners of an assassin,' Abel said.

'Yes, but at least he's less reprehensible than that firebug downstairs,' said the girl. 'I reckon he's an undercover kopp, he's always getting letters from Israel. Maybe he's one of those Mossads, he's forever looking out of his window at night and I don't think he's interested in astronomy!'

'A nation of atheists cannot survive,' Abel retorted.

'Very fucking funny – s'pose one of your poofy authors with

his fucking BA degree and his bachelor's back said that, eh fuckwit,' screeched Viv Bagnolet, who by now was nearly blind drunk, rolling around Ard's bed semi-naked. 'Ard Vark never killed anyone, only his baldness did – come here darling and I'll rub me balloons against yer balls!' She then went off on some rambling tirade about bandits and bankers being the bosses of society and collapsed into an incomprehensible stupor.

'Christ she's a hard case, that Viv!' Abel looked admiringly at her. Then he turned to Fitz, who was by this time in a state of bemused confusion and said, 'I remember once, in the Christchurch Basilica, she streaked up the aisle during a solemn Sunday service, yelling "Viva La Basques" at the top of her voice, a serious sermon on the battle between good and evil being in progress. Because she was one of the best runners in the South Island no one could catch her as she raced out the front door and left the shocked priests and parishioners to fathom the depths of God's creation!'

Fitz looked at the now-sleeping amazon and felt the stirring of his fancy. Her relaxed features held a hint of an oriental bayadère and her hair fallen across her face was dark and gave at once the visage of a child-like innocence and sensual seduction. He could smell her strong perfume as it mingled with the less-delightful odours in the room. His own long-lost sexuality, somewhat awakened by the incident on the train the previous night, was being found with a vengeance. All those years of self-restraint and denial as he gave up his life to look after his mother had driven his 'natural' instincts underground. His gaze bore down on her and as he undressed her in his mind, removed what was left of her scant clothing, he felt barely able to contain his lust and desire. He could sense her juices flowing at his touch, like Pavlov's pussey. However, just in time, before he acted on his most carnal urges, a face with a long, distinguished beard appeared before his eyes in the bedroom and, handing him a can of beer, the man who the face belonged to began singing in German Beethoven's *Ode to Joy* in a voice which bellowed out from deep in the belly.

Simultaneously to the presentation of the provoker and the unprovoker, there appeared before Fitz's mind's eye a vision of his dream woman whose face had a faraway, almost Bible-evoking look. He suddenly felt ashamed of his rare fantasy, as though he had actually done the 'if you even look at a woman in lust' deed.

Bill, the singer, now introduced himself, apologized for singing 'always too high,' said that he had seen Fitz's distress and had decided to invite him for a game of billiards downtown. 'That bird is as black as blondes are proffered,' he said.

'At least she's not one of those prissy fucking blood-letting, bluestocking, boarding-school bitches with a holy fucking halo around their precious fucking body,' chimed in Abel to the defense of a lady who couldn't defend herself, at least not in her present condition.

As Bill and Abel slogged it out in mortal combat to defile or defend Viv's honour, Fitz looked with a certain interested disgust at the room around him. He had never been amongst such squalor – even his poorest, most hard-pressed friends in the factory seemed to take pride in keeping their house clean. Here, surprisingly to Fitz, in the midst of the country's brightest minds lay the most disgusting scene imaginable. Boiled dinner lay on half-emptied plates which were covered in a dozen cockroaches. On one such plate a mouse sat gnawing at a week-old relic of fishbone ash while another stuck its head out of one of a pair of boots, obviously mislead by the smell inside which was roughly the same stench emanating from the rotting food. Stale bread and the breastworks of some animal whose lungs had expired with their last breath several seasons beforehand lay covered in mould, and a haze of unknown creatures hovered above like minute vultures waiting to descend on rotting corpses. The whole scene had the effect of a bomb site and, coupled with the confusion of snatched, barely comprehensible intellectual conversation, lent a beguiling surreality to Fitz's mind, especially after the already stirring events of his long-asleep sex.

'Snoterb, eht tsom cihtiloen fo eht eznorb ega.'

'Indeed, but you know, Selcordna, that brunettes are hotter than blondes, even though Bouillet refers to Buddhism as a false religion in his 1826 dictionary.'

'The budget can never be balanced between sex and religion,' interjected Bill, even though he was still a young man.

'Noffub! Llub!' snorted Selcordna indignantly. 'Eht xo si y lno eht elcnu.'

'Is that so! What about the Irish bull which is responsible for its own swift impregnation?'

The room went silent as though an awe-inspiring bureaucrat had walked in during the discussion to carry out a burial.

Suddenly, Bill broke the silence by standing abruptly up. 'Butchers are appalling in times of revolution,' he said in a menacing tone. 'Buying or selling!' he added and walked out.

'Y m rehtaf saw a Tenibac Rekam.' Selcordna looked about to see if anyone was still listening. 'Eraweb eht Alliramac rof ti y am evah retsinis snoitnetni! Emoc otni y m moor dna llew ekoms a Lemac.'

2

As Fitz looked back on the room he was leaving he turned to catch one last glimpse of Viv to see if the look of candour, which he had interpreted as special intimacy, was still there. He shivered when he saw the hard, unyielding visage which now looked up from the bed and which fired menacing looks at him like an emotional cannonade. He suddenly felt a sense of relief and gratitude that his lascivious plans had been waylaid. A final cannonball from Viv's volley hit its target right in the heart and he left for Selcordna's room with a feeling of self-loathing and disgust.

Out in the corridor which separated the rooms and led to the staircase, Lefarge went rushing by in a skullcap towards the very small kitchen. Whilst this contrivance gave dignity to the face of Lefarge it could not hide the carbuncle-ridden, pock-marked cheeks which looked like a Halloween pumpkin carriage whose wheels were the ears of a thin, unfortunate man. Whilst most people thought him to be either a Jew or one of the Carthusians (after all his home was his castle) Lefarge would always confuse the issue by expounding, 'Catholicism has had a good influence on art at Our Place,' in front of visitors to Yellban. One of the artistic 'cats', as he called his bohemian associates, held out his catspaw for Fitz to shake and asked him of which craft he partook. Fitz felt undefinably insulted by this limp-wristed member of the Crazy Cavalry from Caverns Meaningless to Man modern dance troupe, from whose hat came the almost indefinable scent of cedar perfume.

In fact, Fitz felt a mixture of nausea and intimidation from these pseudo-celebrities and he made his way towards the cell in which Selcordna lived, lest he gave in to his basic instincts and started punching one of them. This act of self-censorship did not go unnoticed by Selcordna who had himself been brought up on a diet of anti-bourgeois rhetoric naturally.

'Lla y eht od si esahc eht sdiamrebmahc dna knird engap-mahc,' he said – adding quickly, 'sa y eht y as,' a bit ashamedly, as though he may know a bit more of the delights of the middle classes than he cared others to know about. Meanwhile, Fitz looked around the main room as bewildered at what he saw as he was listening and trying to understand the language his friend spoke.

'Orucsoraihc! Orucsoraihc! Tovarich, Orucsoraihc!' Selcordna was shouting and pointing to a huge foot which hung from the ceiling and whilst Fitz could not find any meaning in the words his comrade spoke he could see that the gigantic pod made him very excited. The foot was longer than a metre in this case, and handwritten on the side in the language of his friend's native land was 'Evah Snialblihc Erehwyreve.' In the far corner of the room, opposite the TV, there was what could be mistaken for a nativity scene. Effigies of three children stood around a model chimney. In the middle of the sooty scene stood a waif of a chimney sweep and above the scene was a wooden board like one that designates the name of a railway station. But where that nomenclature might have been, the legend "CHOLERA AND CHRISTIANITY FREED THE SLAVES" was written. Cotton-wool snow designated that it was Christmas.

Dumbfounded by what he had seen, Fitz took a while to respond to the cider and cigars being proffered by Bill who had entered the room also.

'Ni ruo y ntnuoc Sucric Sreniart dna Srehtaf tnuoma ot eht emas lamina!' yelled Selcordna, picking up a clarinet which was perched upright next to a bookcase of classics from his own language. 'Dna s'ti eht emas htiw eht dratsab nem fo eht htolc dna snwolc.' He was very agitated by now, and, using the musical instrument as a club, he began striking at the dark effigies.

'Look here, old cock,' said Bill. 'Give me that thing before you do someone an injury – I'll make us all a nice cup of coffee.'

'On! – Cangoc, teg em Cangoc! Cangoc dna sutioc – Gnirb em meht!'

Bill went to the fridge to get a bottle of Coke for the now semi-demented foreigner. Fitz looked around the room again, keeping one eye on Selcordna in case he did something stupid like Frankinonsense, and in mirth, harm himself or others. In the corner behind the door was a poster exhorting the people of Christchurch not to light fires in their houses because of the pollution, and another one appealed, 'You must be deep in your coke upon Lyttleton', a poster on behalf of the railway about the effects of not keeping the West Coast coal trains. They offered cold comfort for the colonies on the coast who would lose their rail link just because some short-sighted economist favoured a slurry pipeline out to the ships.

A sudden outburst from Selcordna startled Fitz.

'Y democ ha! ha!, castigat ridondo mores! Stemoc dna sretsecna – htob deraef eht nredom ega.'

'Cold comfort for the next generation,' said Bill on his return to the communion trio (rehtaf, nos dna y ekcim tsom!)

'Stel knird ot eht luos fo edart noititep moc!'

'To that which makes a mockery of us all, comrade.'

Bill and Selcordna raised their glasses, as did Fitz who was by now completely lacking in composition, but who acted as though he understood every word.

'We must all compromise to gain concert and concessions,' Bill said in the voice of a mock politician. 'The grand alliance of concupiscence and confectioners has lead to many a woman's confinement – and congratulations and exile of many a priest, I may add!' The look on Selcordna's face at this outburst by Bill was beyond conservative description – suffice to say that such a grimace rarely appeared at the Conservatoire between 1828 AD to the present PC day.

'Neither the 1848 conspirators,' Bill continued, 'nor the constipation of literary men or women have broken the constitutional mores of this long-standing trad dad. Neither the walk up Constitutional Hill nor the meaningless contralto have changed the tune or the tone of the conversation. The convicts who are running this country cook up their copaiba balsam and corns on the cobs, and pretend to know exactly what cooking is –'

At this point two corset-wearing Cossacks burst in and before anyone could cotton on to what was happening Selcordna was whisked away, a terrified look on his countenance.

'While the counterfeiters who run this country from below ground level – they all come from country families –' Bill could not finish his sentence, he was so livid with contempt.

After a short silence, Fitz dumbfoundedly asked, 'What about cousin Selcordna?'

'The crayfish who run this count – what? Oh that communist creole, he's nothing but a petit criminal like all his crimson flag bearers. A critic of the true revolution whose own crocodile tears about reactionary revisionism only serve to hide his true place in society. He's an out-and-out crook. With crossbow and crucifix he takes up any number of crusades, whilst he benefits behind Venetian Blinds and has left many a friend a cuckold. Curacao Blinds the same! His circulars are ornate and metaphorical, but he can't cheat the custom duties officer who lives with his wife and family in the downstairs flat for whom he gets cut-rate liquor and cypress lilies for his trip to the cemetery where he takes cole to the new castle. This all explains why the Cossacks have taken leave of their principles and arrested the Czar! But then I've never really been the Daguerreo type on the road to Damascus, pretending to replace the painterly arts with a paler fire, if you can get my drift.'

3

Fitz and Bill moved out of Selcordna's cell slowly, into the hallway. On the landing above the stairs the soul and base of dance music banged its way into Fitz's consciousness. All the people who had been in Ard's room were now out dancing.

Abel himself came over to Fitz with a rather effeminate-looking young man in tow. 'I was wondering where you had got to,' Ard shouted to Fitz. 'This is Danton.'

The young man had an abstracted, other-worldly look in his eyes. He shook Fitz's hand limply, looked at him through dilated pupils and yelled in a kind of crazed, manic voice, 'Let us dare and dare again, and forever dare!' Not quite sure how the word 'dare' was spelt, having only heard it, Fitz moved out of the way of this latter-day Saint Darwin and longed for the days of good old-fashioned Kiwi debauchery when men were men and it was women and not other men who appreciated it. In these modern times of male decoration it was seen as a defect to decide to choose a woman for your sexual preference. It was as delft as it could be, with more wanks than a china Demosthenes, who because of his ancient custom of speaking with a stone, had in truth more dentists than chiropodists, and was down on the books for a replacement denture already.

'Derby or not derby?'

'What kind of question is that, Bill?'

'My God, Des, I didn't recognize your incognito ergosummery shirt. Mr Cartes, I'd like you to meet –' But as Bill turned to introduce Des to Fitz the latter was nowhere to be seen.

Fitz had moved into the shadows, and was feeling as if he was in the midst of some Pagan Desert where he had been dished up his just desserts for straying from the path of righteousness. He suddenly felt a bit light in the head and went to the kitchen to get a glass of water. On his way he noticed something strange was happening – the bachelor pad was no longer there. Instead, there was a gaping hole like a mouth with the front teeth missing. At the same time, he felt that a part of his own brain in the top right appeared to be losing its capacity to function. It was as if what was happening to the house was somehow connected. He quickly gulped the glass of water and returned to the company of strangers.

'I'd rather have a bottle in front of me, than a frontal lobotomy,' the newcomer, Des, was saying to much exaggerated laughter from the throng. Fitz saw another group over towards Lefarge's room pointing in his direction and heard one of them say what sounded like, 'Something missing upstairs ...' at which they all laughed and turned quickly away. He began to feel uncomfortable and, avoiding Abel and his friends, found his way along the corridor, past crazy Selcordna's cell, and went into a small room at the end of the hall. Closing the device which he had opened the door with, he found himself in a bizarre environment. Whilst the room was very small there were two beds in it. One was a large double bed that was surrounded by lavish and exaggerated finery. Gaudy, colourful scarves hung from the ceiling; satin sheets and a beautiful embroidered quilt lay on the bed. The room looked like a high-class brothel boudoir. A semi-naked woman lay in an indolent posture across the bed, and incense burned in the corner.

At the other end of the room a woman in a nun's habit knelt at the foot of a small, cast-iron cot. She was lost in devotion, bent in supplication before a statue of the Blessed Virgin. In contrast to the brash colour and diamonds at the other end of the room, the holiness at this end of the place was complete. Together they made a mosaic of a double Diana: the chased and the chaste, paparazzi and papal bull, horny as ever.

'Look that one up in your dictionary, Diderot,' said the whore. 'You're nothing but a fucking dilettante. Isn't that right, Dimples?' she said to the nun. The holy one tried to ignore the harlot.

A man walked in. Dressed in a formal dinner jacket, Doctor Matthew Diogenes said that he had responded to the 'I am looking for a man' notice in the *Sun*. The ad had mentioned a Diploma of Coma, and it had not been without much deft diplomacy that he had negotiated a night away from his wife and family. It was like a domestic directoire, a kind of discharge from conjugal duty (if you'll excuse such an indelicate phrase!) After much frank conjecture on the outrage-zap eh! – upon the majesty of marriage, his wife finally agreed to such a 'dis-section', as she called it. She was a woman of rare distinction and a no-mean diva to boot. Outsiders of the union would have thought that such a request would be one of the main dividers of a marriage and could only end in divorce.

But here Diogenes was in a room with a nun in one corner and about to do a Djinn with a woman who was painted with more smiles than the Mona Lisa in the other. On his way to Yellban he had walked in quiet contemplation from the railway station, through the Wellington dockyards. This area represented the silent society revolution of 'Art Replacing Reality'. Even in these strange times where the market forces the economic mores, it was more viable to have art galleries at Our Place than the mercantile maritime Gehenna of yesteryear under the tyrany of Murphy's Lore.

Suddenly, Doctor Diogenes broke his contemplation – 'What's up, Doc?' the woman asked, feeling his agitation.

'What's he doing here?' he cried, pointing to Fitz who stood just beyond the nun's habit. 'I hope he's not one of those doctrinaires who gets discreet people like myself into indelicate situations and then whips out a document which turns an incriminated white male into a blackmail.'

'Relax darling. He won't hurt you, he's just Sister Mary's lap dog.' She turned to the devotee and hissed, 'Get that fuckwit out of here.'

The nun, who till now had been oblivious to anything worldly, all of a sudden picked up her rosary and drove out Fitz from her room with a mixture of blows and exorcistic exhortations, much like the whore's treatment of her latest victim – a happy coincidence, but with very different consequences – to wit one was in, the other was out, finding a condom in a virgin being the greater blasphemy!

4

Bewildered and upset, Fitz found himself out in the hallway, which in his absence had filled with more and more revellers. Feeling disoriented, he looked around for familiar faces or places. It was with real shock that he noticed that the cell of Selcordna had disappeared as had the stable of Abel. He also seemed to have lost another part of his own brain. Was it something in the drinks put there by some malicious drug pusher, or was he going pōrangi? He could smell a strong animal smell all of a sudden and he felt something rub against his leg. He looked down and saw a dog looking up at him with big eyes full of concern. Putting out his hand to show supplication and friendship Fitz waited for the animal to lick his fingers. A man was pushing his way through the crowd and when he saw Fitz and the Alsatian he sighed a visible sigh of relief.

'I've been looking everywhere for you,' he said to his dog, who left Fitz and went waggytail and all at six of the clock to his master.

'I see my dog cares about you, Señor. My name is Doge Marino Faliero, Dolmen, without the e. I have been on the dole for exactly ten years today, so I come to party with my dog. Her name is Dolphin and I am getting stoned tonight, which for me is a kind of human sacrifice as I do not usually condone such things. Come with me to the Dome of Lefarge, eschew domesticity for an evening and celebrate the good fortune of life.'

Lefarge was in his 'studio', as he liked to call his room. Fitz looked at the tall, angular figure of the man he had met not long after stepping down from the Auckland train. He had approached this eccentric, rather curious looking fellow because amongst all the suits and ties he had been the only one who looked anywhere near approachable. Having asked directions to Cuba Mall, the only destination in Wellington which Fitz had heard of, the two parted company. However, an hour or so later Fitz was walking through Manners Mall towards Perrett's Corner when he espied the whacky stranger again. This time he and a friend had been playing dominoes on one of the public chessboard tables in that area. Lefarge called out to the traveller and Fitz, pleased to see a familiar face, went over.

Lefarge got up and introduced himself, adding 'the artiste' after his name, which he coincided with a minor pirouette that seemed to Fitz both absurd and simultaneously attractive. Lefarge had invited him back to what he called – quite correctly as it happened – his dormitories for a Halloween party which was about to occur that evening. He added, somewhat indignantly, 'It doesn't matter what time of year it is!' when his friend suggested that it was the wrong month. As they had reached the top of what seemed like a thousand stairs Reich, the man who lived in the downstairs dungeon with his wife, children and several relatives was leaving Yellban followed by a barrage of what was indecipherable Eastern European Esperanto.

'Esaelp tuhs eht etag, t'nac uo y daer uo y reknaw!' leaving the poor man, the Daumier Reid, in no doubt of his intention.

'You don't have to speak the stupid language of that backward intellectual cretin to understand what that cunt says,' Lefarge muttered as they passed him on the way through the hallowed gates of Yellban.

Now, seven hours later, Lefarge de la Kopp (the artiste) was holding aloft a piece of paper with words and scrawled lines on it proclaiming that here was his latest 'drawing'.

'Perfectly dreadful,' came a voice, shocking the assembled admirers. The speaker, realizing his faux pas, added, 'I meant, of course, I am full of dread, as in awe, of your talents. I find it to be a true statement of existential terror representing the "darkest of a dreadful night", in the best tradition of surrealistic dreams, that is, nightmares!'

The speaker ducked as a bottle flew across from the other side of the rouen, smashing a window in the name of artistic honour. (It was the first of many that evening, and for the first time Fitz felt a sharp but fleeting pain as far as the puncta vasculosa of the centrum ova le majus.) A duel was called for, but in order not to dupe his host the man of swords, Dupuytren (for it was he, and not only was he famous for his slaves and muses!) feels it to be one of his duties, withdrew.

The fellow who had thrown the bottle, both a dwarf and an early riser, yelled after the retreating baron, 'See the earth echo the nihilistic eclecticism of the starting point of all philosophy, the egg, laid by elephants who never forget the embonpoint of such an insolent creature – like the treacherous embrace of émigrés, he is not to be trusted!' The Emir of Eastbourne thus affirmed Lefarge's talent. A great round of applause followed. The Emir's empire reached almost to Petone. His person, though small in stature, was often seen in the company of the Empresses of Pencarrow who resorted to turning encyclopedia leaves with their enamel, exquisite, chiselled hands in their unquenchable thirst for enquiring (within and without) upon everything. These goddesses (with backgrounds often from engineering and whose lineage was invariably English) were women who enjoyed nothing more than the esoteric enthusiasm of Epicurus (whom they despised nonetheless). The empresses were here tonight within the gates of Yellban like representatives of the epistolary era who extol the virtues of their fathers' erections. The collective recovered memories of Erostratus around the fires of the commune, or ohu, may shiver from a false chill as the empresses walk along the esplanade in search of Etruscan flower holders in the antique shops.

Fitz's red spots now appeared before his eyes as well as within his brain. All this cultural shock of the new hues of humanity gathered together in one room, like words in a dictionary of etymology, overwhelmed him. He felt like a eunuch at a stag party and his mind's processes were in full evacuation mode. Those many evenings in his life where he thought his life was passing him by as he headed home from the factory to look after his mum were like a kind of purgatory. Every now and then his friends pointed to evidence of his exasperation, but he would respond, without exception, that he was happy in his humble, duty-bound existence. But he would often dream of public executions and the women who go to them!

Overhearing someone talking about their latest exhibition Fitz felt all the air in his lungs suddenly expire, as though he was near the brink of extinction like an extreme unction example of a fish out of water. Whilst he understood the heresy involved in the use of the word 'extirpate' in such creative company, he felt he could not uphold the facade of working-class respectability amidst such degradation and scorn. When he worked in the factory he often woke in the middle of the night dreaming that he was surrounded by the dirt and dust and noise of the machines as they rolled out element after element, thousands upon thousands, surrounded by the stupid, faithful workers, his friends and companions, who lived without fame or fanfare. He would lie in his bed sweating and despairing that life was waving farewell to him as he saw in the darkness all the sand-filled rods stretching and rolling into eternity.

'The farm, for example, to the farmer, or indeed to farmers, is a means of living off the fat of the lamb. Which could be a holy romantic word, fatal if it were to favour fear over felicity as a religious conjecture,' said Lefarge, who was now holding court in one of his intellectual, almost female voices.

'Yes, but fencing leads to a latter-day form of feudalism: just look at St Germain and the number-eight wire,' replied a short, angular man of the middle ages (perhaps forty-five). 'Plus, a kind of fever develops from the April sun in Cuba Mall,' he added, to Lefarge's chagrin. Lefarge shouted and jumped about, manically proclaiming unintelligible obscenities about the unlawful marriage of Figaro, a figleaf, a finger put obscenely into fingerbowls, a warning not to play with fire.

'If you don't want to go before the fucking firing squad!' and, with a sense of finality, raised his flag of adulterous consent thus. Flagrante delicto, somewhat indelicately as it transpires.

From the other side of the room a poet, Manfred, expounded,

> From Flanders Fields to pumped-up veins
> Each generation has its pains

much in the manner of some petty flamingo flamenco dancer, after which Fitz's falx cerebri dipped, just missing the lim for the medul la Oblonga ta. Someone passed the foramen magnum and Fitz took a swig. He felt his mind slipping beyond the fancy flatterers and he thought that all the people in Lefarge's Palace of Ideas are nothing but flies and vermin. Suddenly, he felt connected. The pons varolii took over in a desperate attempt to stabilise his listing ship of foolish thoughts. Shaking his fist and yelling in a disparaging tone he berated the assembled pseuds in the corner.

'Puer abige museas! You flood victims of your own conceit and shit, the boy and I will turn you into foetus food for future generations to nourish their intestines.' As his frontal los lobos filled his forehead with thoughts and words hitherto foreign to his comprehension, Fitz swooned as his ideas began to fork at the bulb, south of the border of the pons ... Visions of Fornina and the Latin version of fortune began to flow through His Eminences like the subtle mystic oils of a spiritual fossil gleaned from the foundation of life – the great secret of freelance free-masonry unlocking the free-trade of the mind to carry human beastly thought processes well beyond the obscene ACT, who can only party the fortune in French, thus causing by way of retaliation a kind of French fury in the area of the dura mater relations, especially in consideration of the German, Du!

With the outrage having subsided the conversation turned to the fresco painting of the Italian masters, and fricassee, which is only good in the country.

'What do you mean by "no longer done" you stupid frog lover. Are you assuming that such art is as difficult and dull as fugue!'

'Please, please!' interrupted Lefarge. 'That ignorant peasant has infected our civilized society with his malcontented and derisive behaviour.' Turning on Fitz he began to fulminate, his words crackling like lightning in a storm. After a barrage of obscenities he finally grabbed Fitz, by now confused, and threw him physically from his precinct with such force that Fitz went headlong down the corridor and was only saved from crashing down the staircase by the open arms of his guardian angel, the able Abel.

'The next time I see you will be at your funeral – which won't be too long if I've got anything to do with it!' cried Lefarge, 'you working-class fuckhead.' His entourage found this to be most funny and the sound of laughter and hoots and howls, and cries not of owls, reverberated around the top floor of Yellban as Lefarge shut the door and his fur-weaving brigade continued their banter and philosophy. Fitz picked up an idle piece of furniture and hurled it in the general direction of the sophisticated melee. However, his anterior median fissure was by now somewhat lacking in fusion and his aim was unerringly misdirected.

5

In the hallway an atmosphere of frenzied gaiety was beginning to emerge. Word had got round that this was to be a house-trashing party as announced by the gallant homme of the Gallophobe era who was known for his building of the marble turret which embellished the room next to Lefarge's. This earnest and younger man had been a journalist in Germany during that over-inflated chess game known as the Cold War. The door to his marble cave was ajar, and once Fitzgerald's thought movements along the pons varo lii had begun to flow freely again he recognized the face of Abel and his surroundings.

However, the 'salon' of Lefarge seemed to have disappeared somewhere between the hemispheres so that the house of Yellban now had four less rooms as did the lobe or lobby Coney Angel Is Landerington of the mind of king coal.

'I'm game,' said Gamin.

'When I feel gay, I love to act like a Gamin!' Lefarge yelled from nowhere, laughing fit to bust.

Gamin, G. waxed indignant at this fatal linguistic intrusion.

'If you're not careful, Lefarge, you'll end up in the gardens of Raspberry Fjords forever, alongside all them other cunning fucking linguists, with nothing to eat but garlic in your non-existent artiste's garret, like a democrazy General Tojo – you and your whole spontaneous generations!'

'Spoken like a true genius of the Genovefan,' (meaning an

unknown gentleman – often a geometrician – travelling on strange seas of thought, alone ... unlike the Germans, blond and dreamy and moving together as one – eins Reich! etc.).

'Giaour!'

'I'll not listen to anymore of your oriental gibberish,' retorted Lefarge as he disappeared into the murky eminences yet again; that part of the roombrain ceased to exist, like looking a gift giraffe in the neck.

Gamin, one of the few remaining Girondists, a group more sinned against than known for their sinning, did however, this evening hold the left globe of Gloria in one of his velvet but deadly gloves, making a tableau with the same effect as a gobelins and certainly more beautiful than a painting.

'God!' said Abel, 'leave that young woman alone.'

'Goddamn,' Gamin replied, 'the whole world is sinking into the mud of puritanical malaise,' at the same time removing his hand from the young girl's breast.

'But you're old enough to be her godfather –'

Abel's liturgical lesson in licentiousness was cut short by a fierce, almost agonized yell from below and several people came running up the staircase dressed in the dark, demonic cloth of Goth with loud, thumping, heavy footwear to boot.

'God save the King of Darkness,' one of them called out in a trance-like, drug-induced, inverted reverse comatose evocation and invocation of a Gog of a Gog. He waved the golden number and had the dominical letter tied around his waist by a Gordian knot after the manner of the monks of Otho. However, his frenzied readings from the Black Gospels of Crowley and his adoption of the Gothic tone reminiscent of The Monk of Lewisham, The Bleeding Hun, whose literary appeal included the not-so-disturbing apocrypha, to the fancy gown of murderous Latin grammar used by Satanic grammarians to kill anything within grapeshot, was greeted more with disdain and ridicule by the assembled party-goers, rather than the fear and hatred that the perpetrators had envisaged.

Sensing the hostility and realizing that there was no more food or drink to be stolen since the kitchen area had also disappeared from the upstairs part of Yellban along with four of the bedrooms, the Gogs trudged begrudgingly back down to their dungeons and dragons below, much to the gratitude of the upstairs revellers, whose mood seemed to have been unintentionally expressed by a Samoan student who called down the steps 'Fa'a Goth,' as the dark fold made their exit.

Fitz, who was now almost bereft of his top level, looked toward the last remaining door again. He felt and saw before him a man in a greatcoat pushing a concrete thought from the anterior and middle lobes like the fissure of Sisyphus. Each time this idea nearly reached the point of articulation it rolled back down into the base of the brain and slowly he pushed its way forward again.

'Whatever one can't understand is Greek,' Abel explained.

Fitz's inarticulate attempts to speak to a friend of his who was trying to comprehend the indecipherable noises with which Fitz was trying to communicate, as is often the case with one who has consumed not enough grisettes and too much grog.

'Yeah, we've tried to recreate the grottoes with stalactites.' One of the remaining Goths was explaining to a group of 'out of it' students what was going on in the lounge downstairs. 'We must guard our revolutionary guerrilla guests comrade, if they venture into the gulfstream between the viaduct and the romantic gunmen of the Gymnase of your dreams ...' At this Fitz took another swig from the bladder of a pig and his intellectual powerhouse drifted into the convolution of the corpus callosum, his glass was running on empty with the meter ticking and the bells-a-ringing on the sandy shore where the barefoot girl walks back to happiness all the while listening with a sharp ear oh, as was her habit – but none, not even a tremor, nor a screeching, rattling Helen clucky duck (crying, walking, sleeping, talking) could prevent her from retreating beyond the shadows of the cliff.

The musick pointing upward from downstairs was now so deafening that all previous impediments to conversation were deemed to be redundant. The cotton-wool impotence which accompanied this impasse grew as the upstairs–downstairs throng trystiad the night away to a cacophonous nocturne. What was left of a battered television was held aloft as a young man without hair, looking like a shaven image of someone else's humiliation, began to ham it up, acting out some long-lost memory of ambition. 'TV or not TV, what's the answer?' this latter-day punk Hamlet cried and the assembled mass yelled back, as in chorus, 'NOT!' and the TV was sent flying out what was once the kitchen window to the collective cheers of those still conscious enough to make an informed decision.

The door of the turret room now opened a little further and Fitz could see (if holy see be the word, say but it and my hole will be sealed, Father) the inner sanctuary of bird and plant alike. Amongst the many boxes filled with GOD KNOWS WHAT, there appeared rigged up a hammock, tied between two walls. Fitz thought that this mysterious room represented one of those watch towers from which the mind surveys the territory of untamed growth. The atmosphere in the room was icy cold so as to keep the alpine species alive; and the roof of the marble turret was damp with mist, and cold wind from the open walls of the now semi-demolished house drove wreaths of mist down over the vegetation.

Gently extending his hand to the gentiana bellidifolia, he touched the beautiful extension of nature's bounty. Each box [*sic*] was labelled with the heavy, delicate handwriting of a hangman, whose hard yet vulnerable understanding of human frailty made him the tortoise counsel to people, as opposed to the priest's hare. As Fitz marvelled at the veritable harem of subalpine wonder before his eyes he envisaged the next leg of his journey to the South Island. His thoughts now began to be seen backwards in the median line of the cerebrum. Whilst not quite reaching into the inner sanctum of his conscious mind due to the constant and toxic flow of dead brain cells overwhelmed by and swimming in the confused fumes of alcohol, the mood which reached his surface feelings was one of austere melancholy, as though the haunting strains of a harp could be heard amongst the ranunculus enysii or the coprosma depressa, or the faraway call of a karanga ataahua emanated from the bulbinella gibsii, conjuring up the tīpuna and atua of the southern regions of Waitaha and Kāti Mamoe as they laid down the challenge to the Kāi Tahu invaders, both of the past and of the present future, haere atu ki ōu koutou ika!

A cigarette of hasheesh was being passed around, and 'Hats off to the Hawser' as they say! 'Excess of health causes illness,' said Abel as he handed Fitz the smoke. The heat from the slow-burning reefer – now little more than a roach – burnt into his fingers. He inhaled it quickly and handed it on. Whether it be dreams or deep thought, it seemed as if he were groping for the right road in the labyrinth, or sought to unravel the figures among the patterns of an optical illusion. 'Let the Helots be a warning to you son,' said Bon Borges, as the images came from the south of love and death. A momentary scene at an unlevel crossing which would change his life forever was about to be revealed, not from the circular motion of the Baxterwheel or a hemicycle, but from the evocative realdream of the Celtic mystology and the music and the hoot hoot of Southerners crossing. He watched her image again moving away just after the point of their recognition. Perhaps this was as close as they would get.

As these thoughts were being processed through the old triangle they went jingle jangle all along the banks of the velum interposition right to the centre where the two venae Galeni waited to transport them down the royal canal.

This remembrance of dreams past unsettled Fitz who had had a certain time of respite from the images and realities which had perplexed and puzzled him in recent years. And in thinking of her, he also thought of his mother, of how he found her dead in the bright light of that Orakei morning. So his melancholy mind locked into the sad past and the sad future, and he felt he was overwhelmed by floods of grief and anticipation. Oblivious now to his surroundings and the noise and jostling of the partygoers, he sat down amidst the mad labelled boxes of labyrinthine flora, with the turret pointed skywards, and he let the unlevelled crossings of his past, present and future permeate and criss-cross his thoughts and feelings. His mission of finding her was as doomed as it was necessary. Eventually his one track became a double track along which his gloomtrain of thought left the tri-station taking the choroid plexus, nexus, sexus express, and his reverie was interrupted –

'God bless the hemorrhoids of Henry III and Henry IV, in fact all the Henrys were unfortunate – as was Hercules.'

This outburst from the corridor was accompanied by the bearer of its voice, a six-foot-six hermaphrodite boy who broke the sullen tranquillity of the marble turret with loud complaints of a hernia and being HIV positive.

'Well, at least for once I can claim a positive in my life, even though I feel as old as Herod,' he said in a quiet, almost shy manner which Fitz found strangely alluring, and which in turn caused a type of red herring to swim through his Spinozean sea mind, reaching a hiatus at the point between the longitudinal fissure and the supra-orbital convolution –

not an altogether unpleasant situation, but it did cause a violent bout of hiccups.

'I only laugh when it hurts,' Fitz explained to his newfound cherub as he doubled over in alternate severe pain and fits of laughter. 'Fitz of laughter!' he roared uncontrollably as he began to move towards the door, away from the magnetic pull of the austere stone in the direction of another stone now rolled away from the tomb-like room.

'The hieroglyphics hoax of Hippocrates and Hippolytus, whose death was ostensibly so beautiful, is a shameful gift to take home to one's wife who waits in vain for the second coming. Why, not since the seed of Homer yielded an ephah –'

'Homersexual you mean!' shouted Fitz, just about bursting by now. The two intellectuals, whose conversation he had interrupted, looked disdainfully at this middle-aged, working-class trollope.

6

From this complete state of gay abandon Fitz now took fright as he looked behind him from the landing to see the last room on the top floor disappearing, but unlike the other rooms which had ceased to exist there was someone still inside it as it dematerialized. It was the HIV boy, disintegrating before his paranoid delusory eyes, his cry of Echo Homo! ... Echo Homo! ... Echo Homo! becoming fainter with each dying breath, until he could no longer be heard.

'Help, the paranoids are after me!' came a voice from the crowd and Fitz realized he must have succumbed to the deliciously nerve-wracking paranoia of those who imbibe the olde dope.

'Dopey cunt, where's your honour?' another voice entered

his consciousness, followed by yet another.

'Honour, offer, honour, offer, all night long it was onher offher!'

'Don't go blowing your horn around here you fuckwit!'

The sound of the Rolling Stones singing wild horses couldn't drag me away, punctuated this exchange which seemed definitely lacking in hospitality, not unlike the angels atop Mt Alt. Punches were beginning to be thrown and, as the whole top storey of Yellban was now non-existent, everyone headed for the near-eastern aspect of the building where the stairwell was situated. The recipient of the insults and blows was now yelling at his attacker, 'How dare you degrade the hospitality of this establishment, Hospodar! This isn't a place for hostilities like at your blasted hotels which you frequent,' on which he landed a beauty, as they say in Germany, right on the spot of Hugo. You should have seen that dude descending the staircase most unceremoniously like Ah Mutt, and then pandemonium broke out. A woman who was listening to Bowie's 'Heroes' on her walkman suddenly started dancing wildly and screaming out 'The Dolphins! The Dolphins!' in an ecstatic and eccentric manner. Others joined in the dance, whilst at the same time pushing people down the stairs or randomly throwing punches. The German 'Du' was soon forgotten and anarchy was the champ, everyone now drinking from the same large glass which was being passed around and refilled as soon as it was emptied.

The humidity in the overcrowded hallway was overbearing. The cramped conditions remained, for as soon as one lot of people was thrown down the stairs, another lot ascended to replace them, so that everyone assumed the demeanour of dwarves or hunchbacks. The Dolphindog had entered at the call from the dancing woman (who for one wild moment Fitz thought was HER) and was barking confusedly, adding to the already deafening din. With the top part of his brain almost gone Fitz began to feel like the real Joe Hunt. The loss of the five rooms of his consciousness made him feel like the intellectual hussar who has to arrive at the ball on foot because his dashing horse has the chicken pox and all the beautiful young women know of the ignominy. Feeling like the opposite of the many Hydra-headed multitude, his Coriolanus has lost his corpus callosum and no amount of hydrotherapy could replace his mantelpiece of water on the brain. The hygiene of his cerebrum was now definitely in dispute as he no longer felt that he had anything left upstairs (as prophesied). Thus from his full-frontal monty flying circular lobe right round to his par-setal lobe, the laws governing his reformed mental mortgage were definitely in a state of hypothecate decline. As the top of Yellban, and thus the top of his own mind, disappeared beyond hypothesis and all his functions dwindled with the increase of blackout in his Cranium Box Department (CBD), as his cables began to fail, his rising sense of lack of control began to reach the point of hysteria. He felt terrified at what he might do or have done to himself whilst in this state of power failure. At this point all the partygoers headed downstairs in a stampede under which several people were crushed and bruised. There was much calling out and crying and confusion, and the music and the crowd mingled and mangled into one ever-increasing morass of heavy metal and sweat and shouts from the hounds of Hades.

As the party spilled downwards Fitz noted that the ice-cream men and the pizza-delivery men had been and gone and that empty pizza boxes and various other food containers now littered the floor. The rubbish generally began to pile and as someone activated clouds of dry ice, which enshrouded the whole area, the high-piled black refuse bags loomed out of the shadows like the giant dark maggots of a Samoan creation myth in reverse – malo e mole o le mogamoga. A mushroom cloud of dry ice enclosed the whole floor and an eerie calm settled on the scene. Even the idealism and the ideals of the Lefarge entourage were rendered perfectly useless against the impingement of this post-apocalyptical eclypso. All the ideologists and other idiots – who only moments before behaved like idolaters of the Iliad Idiossey – and other pseudo-intellectual illegible illusions of the classical imagination now, like Homer, ceased to exist, in the sense that they were shattered into silence by the present scene which appeared as typical streben between reality and dreams.

Fitz's mind (or 'madhouse cell', or protagoras cave, if you will) began to take a distinct lurch, as if slouching towards immortality and the imperialists of impiety. His own thoughts began to behave as though they were the imports of some impresario asking for a drink, to wit in recessu divinius aliquid! This inauguration of foreign thoughts into his numb skull led Fitz's thoughts to schwarmerei, as bees do, scattering throughout the whole ThaLAmus South Central area in a kind of wild thiasus in the female part of his brain. This incompetence of his cognitive processes progressed into a situation of his Rafferty rules where the poet within was forced to drink beer instead of nectar, as though he was travelling through Germany incognito, dressed as a woman. From the Thalamus his ideas shifted into the nidus hirundinis whence they took flight, becoming more and more difficult to swallow. Like an encrustation on a Nike India Rubber sweatshop, jack-boot-in-the-box running shoe, the dew of mourning still clings to her wings and her floating hair – got to find her back in LA in a state of indolence and industry, a girl child's infanticide notwithstanding!

7

Out of the chaos the Dolphindog appeared and led Fitz towards the room where she lived. As he moved through the crowd he looked up into the firmament beyond Yellban to the infinite spaces that so terrified Pascal and he felt infinitesimal and lost, as though he were standing in the Piazza of St John and St Paul amidst the strewn and buried fields forever turned to rubble in Venice. Staring into the inkwell of eternity, the sky, he said to himself, 'The pig who claims to be the interpreter of nature will one day be cured of such illusions.'

'Let us pray that the day when such innate ideas (ha, ha) as innocence and innovation, which permeate your thoughts, escape the inquisition.' A gentle woman interrupted Fitz's thoughts, inviting him to join her in her room. As he entered she called the dog, who followed obediently. Fitz, flabbergasted by this apparent reading of his mind, was about to attempt to say something, but his thoughts were now so deep in the Spinozean fluid that they felt more like a school of remora, with another one being born every minute!

'Fear not,' the woman said, 'I can read the inscriptions of inspiration and instinct in the deepening furrows of your forehead. They're like a duty stamp for intelligence. As your translucent ideas pass through the Valve of Vieussens they activate and institute the instrument of sexual arousal ...' She noticed the puzzled, hurt look on the face of her guest and quickly added, 'Don't take my candid assertions as an insult, comrade, I swear to you that I mean no ill-will towards you.'

On the border of insurrection, the holiest of duties for anyone whose integrity is under threat, Fitz was about to confront such seeming effrontery. However, somewhere in the interval between the sulci of the laminae he realized that it was the intoxicated nuclei of his brain cells that had hyperbolised this introduction to the Gypsy woman, thus rendering invalid his paranoia and suspicion.

'I am not one of the Da Vinci inventors, although I am naturally of the Italians,' she began by way of explanation. 'In Italy we La Bambos are famous for our poetry and our ivory skin and dark, dark hair and eyes.' (No reference to teeth, Fitz thought, as he raised his cherito-blepharos!) She continued, 'Catholicism, Jainism, Shintoism, as in Japan where the vases are all made of jasper – all these are of no consequence to me, Señor. The only thing, in the sense of ideas, is to me, animalism!' The woman said this with such vehemence that Fitz felt a little unsettled. Looking around her room, which was now candlelit and filled with exotic aromas from the various potions and scents being burned or otherwise disseminated, he could see in the shadowy atmosphere varied animal shapes and forms beginning to become incarnate, tangible: her room was peopled with animals. Also, hosts of insectpeople hurried together, each tiny being sorting and categorizing individual pieces of assorted grain. Wheat, barley etc. were all shunted around according to the psyche and nature of a particular species ... Fitz suddenly realized that the woman was still talking. ' ... So he threw a javelin in a fit of jealousy and killed my own true love. I have never forgiven the bastard Jesuits ever since. Let them rot in their stoned tower. I'll show them who pays the ferryman in this ovis quae periit corneria!'

The Dolphindog's pointed nose diverted Fitz's eyes in the direction of the room's other inhabitants with the dexterity of a jeweller crafting an exquisite ring. Like a jockey showing a guest horse around the jockey club, or birdcage, as John Bull was once heard calling such an attraction for nobody, the simple joy with which this gypsy dog carried out the naming of its coinhabitant animal friends without the use of language was a pleasure to behold. Like a member of the canine judiciary she followed every person with equal weight of gravity. The quackyducks, the headrest alligators, the birds-on-a-plate, the quig of a quag, Mr Black, Mr Rabbit, big patch, little patch, the killer cockroach, crabgrab – on and on the list went on! Out of the shadows came the shape and that substance of the animal world until Fitz heard the sound of running water and saw an artificial waterfall and something slither into the lake ... think I'll call it a –

Lady La Bambo called Fitz to her side. Looking at a jujube screen made of an unknown substance they began to meditate and then travel together along the cosmic comic pathway. Off jury duty at last they entered into an affair not unlike the jus primae noctis of old or of dreams, only this time there was no peasant husband to transgress any feelings of no justice (Fitz saw a photo of the man or illusion whom he had first met Dolphindog with upstairs, but his mind was in no state to transmogrify). The screen changed into a mirror whose image portrayed La Bambo and Fitz in a kaleidoscope of pictures changing and transforming until it finally settled on their faces, which had turned into two tigers ... Zubu the Great and Sambo the Beautiful, two Bengal tigers who were being hunted, for what? For greed? As keepsakes? To be captured, cut up and put in a knapsack? Zubu's pride falling under the knife for the prize of an aphrodisiac, and Sambo, the fabled 'Black Tiger', for her beautiful skin and fine-featured face. Indeed, her ancestors had been Siberian snow tigers who had to get knout of Russia, chased by wooden Koran wavers who seldom rushed, indeed, except for a fat one – then they certainly high-taled it only to end up in Uncle Joe's fairy-story laboratory in a laconic and often Lacustrian state – so be it! Glug, glug, gulag. We're all ladies and lads together from La Fayette to La Fontaine la, la, la, la, ob la di, ob la da – nothing like a dame la la how the wife goes on eternally let it be, the fab three sing again without you erik the quarters be at Les Girls, Mare of Auckland and Brobdingnag. Zubu and Sambo stopped by a lagoon or lake, exhausted by the chasing of the hunters who had pursued them without lancet or spear or musket, with the passion of a landlord hot on the trail of rentless tenants, across the great landscapes, down steppes and up vales, dancing off seven languages, past sausages and salome until late, but not yet too late, in the day – ECHO of HCE, O! a lathe in the attic, sounds like a strange choice phonetically, but that's 'Latin for you' quoth he, amidst such laughter and laurels handed out to those who experience the full lave of the law (jellyfish bumhole of the raillery; see an enema p. 55 n.1: 'ceremonial washing of the feet') including the 'infinite little' of the lawyer's league (absolutely super ay mate!) We're living the life of Ryangeraldly, so fuck all of you other peasants – money is no good to either the learned, who only need a good memory and hard work, or the learning who are to be despised for a narrowneckedness of mind – might as well be a trail of protest ants! – ah! Rot in Hell the lot of you! Leather Catholics too! Left-handed leftfooters to boot, aye all the way to their fucking Ardent Lent, whether it be expressed as Lethargy or the Libertinism of large cities, liberty is not license to have the scaffold of just any old iron library, thank you very much!!! (Despite what the light of Ligue illuminates for following generations!)

As the two tigers diddly dit de deee sat drinking from the Lessing Laocoon, Look Janet, Look! as she wrote a book which saved her from Labot, they were espied among the lilac linen by a miniature lion or dragonfly as the sky was dark with the deep purple of night, and then soon began to enjoy the ways of the air as their waka wheeled and reeled through the cloudy heights – as Zubu looked down he could see the cerebellum below and, suddenly separated from Sambo he was transported there deus fax machina, as in life so in literature, the hosts of the insect people hurried together at the behest of Littre, king of the lexicographical jungle, to console Sambo as she watched the facsimile of her beloved Zubu slowly float down into the loathsome room next to hers, leaving a lock of hair for her locket.

8

'Good Lord!' cried the insolent and distinguished Lorgnette, as the fluttering piece of paper landed in the middle of the sake bucket, from which the unfortunate Fitz jumped yelling and scalded like a latter day Louis XVI out of the hot drink.

'That was lucky!' yelled qua qua qua from Cone ma ma ra.

'Come aboard my lugger,' cried another delicate centurion calling from the lap of luxury, like a lynx from litmus paper.

The gentleman whose room it was came over to the newcomer and bowing lowly said, 'Welcome to the cerebellum room, first stop on billet train after Tokio!' Fitz looked around this Oriental Temple part of his brain and noted as on a sliver of screne, 'this is a house not made with hands but more like a fla, a la Bert!' Bowing deeply in return, he took the large glass of sake proffered and drank a draught of such depth that he saw the first man on earth was a Scotsman. 'MacAdam!' he shouted much to the puzzled laughter of all his fellows from Japan. Picking up a red bottle top and placing it over his hooter, he shouted, 'Honda nose!' The laughter increased as Fitz began, in horse-like fashion, to run around the room in a kind of mad Rewi canter during an egg-and-sperm race. Rewi, picking up a make-believe axe, chased the demented blue angeled chook around, gesticulating wildly, calling after the flightless emblem of our hapless country, 'I will prove the answer to the perennial question – which came first, the sperm or the egg!' an ejaculation of cock-a-doodle-do rather than a question mark to punctuate the old age philosophic. The blade fell heavily missing the neck but slicing in two the bird's beak.

'Holy macaroni!' cried the Nippon Machiavelli, 'this proves that old question redundant, just like our Porirua toru wha factory. Answer is, no matter who came first – egg run away with the sperm. Arse Oh!' This was followed by much bowing and some scraping as the bird chased the Machiavellian axeman round the room. The headless chicken, now itself pursued by Mackintosh, the Scottish reggae maestro, whose magic and personal animal magnetism could only be said to be equalled by the maid (maid or major?)

'Hack my eye!' He caught the bird in full flight and put it on the golden block next to Mr Puff's portmanteau, near Rewi's last hat stand. The major, who had just put on his make-up and was wielding his malacca somewhat precariously, was beckoned by his Japanese hosts to sit on his bamboozled throne. Ensconced, he began a kind of malediction.

'I remember the governor-general's visit to Dunedin,' he began. His voice was slurred but assured, like a madman Malthus or a wayward member of the Mamelukes dedicated to party-going from 1254 to 1811 – quite a bash, o, with much lickerish as the haiku flies. The Marmaduke continued to the accompaniment of a mandolin played by a young woman in a kimono with a marble or glass eye from Gazza with Bazza. 'I remember the execution of a South African. Considering that All Black–Springbok test match was in progress at the same time, it was most inconvenient. A bit like two wish fulfilments, really, a sort of Hobson's choice.'

The room became quiet, all the Japanese guests were sitting as if spellbound, enthralled by this postcolonial relic's gibberish. Even the cabinet minister, back from a trade mission to Marseilles, sat listening, sipping his Singha beer as he soaked in the atmosphere so different from the Chamber Pot of Poliament which had more the air of a clerical worker arrested as a peeping Tom with his Benmorven rising. Fitz marvelled at the fact that he lived in a country where the elevated and the leisurely could enjoy one over the jug in the same room. Yet here he was a redundant factory worker drinking rice wine and beer with a fiend from the government, even if the latter was a self-confessed voyeur taking off-motorway notes on the Wellington nightlife – showing and indeed imbibing with the martyrs and the children at the horn of sweets, and whose leaders, including himself, had created, like Mary Queen of Scots, a mask for what was, in reality, a free flea market Sado-Erotic Banana Republic whose headquarters were near the sperm whale buildings of the Queen Street Farmers of Urenui. From the materialism of Goat Bay where the sheep and the rad iwi ram pa pa, um pa pa don't junk, but the issue is frank and as clear as the mathematics at the crisis centre on the mattress, where each maxim uttered is just as natural as you are, Gaylene. The tall, elegant drag queen made a joke about having May Bugs with the mayor who also goes to the sauna, yet just the Mazarinades of yore, the 'up yours' attitude of the angels, had the effect of wiping out any negative muck-raking by the literary mechanics and pamphleteers.

As the major rattled on about his medals, the young Japanese, most of whom were medical students or trainees at Wellington Hospital's School of Medicine, began a kind of silent smoking ritual. As the meerschaum pipe, with its sprig of puha burning electric and shining like coals in the bowl, was passed on to Fitz a kind of melancholy, have-fantasy-will-travel mood descended on the room. The chook cook whose room it was looked radiant as he finally potted the poet's bird for the meal which would be served to the assemblage. Fitz felt he was privy to the council of the world of the weekend whose participants, free from the melodramas of the workaday worlds of government-department politics, were now entering a kind of July of the mind with the mood of a melon, the food that doesn't know if it's a fruit or a vegetable!

Before they had employed Basho the Egg, the Japanese Go Masters had asked both the local man hire centre and Greg's Instant to make the collective memory connection between mendacity and walking the promenade of Mephistophelian treachery, where love equals zero and so does friendship. As the smell of the burning bush of wild borage permeated deeper into the metaphors of the tuber valvulae, separated only from the uvula by the Great Pyramid of metaphysics, it became clear that the Oriental method of relaxation was indeed sublime.

Hashimoto, the chook cook, was imploring Basho to read to the assembled and now mellow crowd. Indeed he held out to the poet a volume, nay an anthology, of his latest haiku, entitled *The Squid's Cookbook: A Journey through the Mexico of the Mind at Midnight*. Eschewing the temptations of television and other manifestations of the mother's milk of the masses, the poet yet, somehow through his motifs and language, gave voice to the aforementioned masses, by not being part of them. The irony inherent in this situation was the very reason for his great success from the lowliest of the low to the highliest of the high.

The minister of state, the major, the generals and captains of industry and metafiction all sat, cheque books poised, to hear the words of wisdom and vision. For his part the poet was withdrawn, shy to the point of distraction, but preparing himself for his moment in the rising sun and listening hard for the offers which would be the climax of this show. The room fell silent as Hashimoto beckoned Basho forth. A bedside lamp was shone in the bard's direction and suddenly there he stood in his familiar pose which evoked a feeling of destiny. For a full minute he remained unmoved and then, with the intensity of missionaries and other demagogues, he began to read as if from a missive. For a full hour he ranted against suburbia, against the tyrants and cowboys who held our country to ransom north of the Bombay Hills, against the mistake after mistake made by successive governments south of the Bombay Hills, imploring the citizens of Aotearoa to eulogise the Mob – at this point an excited Japanese elderly businessman leaned over and whispered loudly to Fitz, 'He's modelling himself on the Great Poets and Artists of the Thirties – Hitler, Mussolini, Tojo!' Shush, shshshshsh went the guests, and the man withdrew in modesty and humility.

Finally, Basho the Egg said he would like to read a haiku from his latest collection. As the room hushed to a silence the poet stood, still and pensive. Fitz had never experienced a real, live artiste at work before and if he had ever heard of writers and the like previously it had been in the spirit of fun and derision expressed by his factory workmates who looked upon such performers as poofters or wankers. Now, as he caught the tense, anticipatory air as the assembled set their eyes on the visage before them, waiting for the words of wisdom, Fitz felt something like awe or magic in the atmosphere – a kind of subdued, almost sexual excitement which thrilled him at the same time as making him fearful or even afraid. Without explanation the Poet read the first words of the first of his four quartets ...

Identity Haiku

My melon caulli
Baby, is he a fruit or
Vegetable, blue!

The room was filled with stunned admiration, but before any overt manifestation of this could erupt, O'Bash, now in his

Irish incarnation, raised his hand, and in a self-mocking accent from the Emerald Isle said to his audience, 'Sure, I'd like now to do me own interpretation of the once great Kiwi Ikon – can you not!' He ended as he began.

Pre-Japanese Car New Zealand Haiku

Zephyr, west wind, to
You a poem was written
This is mine, Mark II

Once the profundity of what had been said hit the room, the whole crowd burst into uproarious laughter. Everyone filled their glasses with sake or beer or sometimes both and Fitz could feel the strain on the Valve of Vieussens in his superior peduncle as the riotous behaviour, sharp as a scalpel, cut through the open Yellban night. But as quickly as it had sprung up the melee subsided as the Bashful Egg rallied his attributes for the next haiku. Yet again he had the crowd in the palm of his paw.

'This next poem,' quoth he, 'is another literary-based haiku.'

Fitz scratched his head in utter amazement. He had no idea what this two-bit manchild was talking about. But Fitz had a kind of heightened awareness that something mysterious and magical was taking place which had more to do with the words being spoken by this Basho streetkid than any of the various substances which he had imbibed. The linguistic boat being rowed down the river of the aquaduct of Sylvius past the mole of inspiration by this once-rough diamond was now polished, as though he were the emissary of some intellectual car-driven zen monarchy for whom money was the monkey on the chosen one's back, with as much currency as a Monopoly five-pound note. But now the monsters of the moon were turning lunar tunes into rock-solid songs and Basho tapped his phone with the baton he always carried. When all was quiet he began ...

All the Subtlety of a Fiordland Moose as explained by the Three Lost Words of Flaubert's Parrot found down the Barn, Mate, Haiku

Mercury flows through –
Metallurgy in dust tree
Metamorphosis (repeat in Parrotty Tymfinitim)

'And now for my final haiku I would like to present what I like to call an industrio–intellectio–obligatio: a mosaic of ideas and reality brought together for the company of Saints and Thieves. This poem is a celebration of the car launched this week and explains that the sharp intellect of its designers is like the man of ideas, the poet. Both transfer through their own perception and creation, the pinnacle of success in our society. The one transports people, the other ideas and beauty, truth – all you know in life and all you need to know. So with the launch of the new MOSQUITO at our Naenae branch, I hereby dedicate this poem to its inaugural journey,' and, making a low bow in the direction of the Japanese gentleman in the suit, who in turn bowed back to Basho, The Eggman Coocoo cachoo, Mrs Robinson, drank beer from the sacred sake bowl, and as though he was still standing on the Mountebank, he began ...

Carlos Williams Rethinks his Ideas Haiku

Poetry to thought
As rust to a car, shaped down
By time, no thing left

Suddenly Fitz's thinking muscles took a turn for the worse and he felt he had to vacate the occipital as he seemed at once suffocated by the sulci, the thought museum he was presently in. Visions of his ex-working friends sprang up like mush-rooms. He could hear their derisory comments and see their disparaging looks; he knew he was not in his own world anymore and that this visitation was to tell him 'clickety clack you can't go back'. The music in his head played on as he moved from the choroid plexus towards the roomoid nexus of a miller, who was telling his tale in the hallway, and who whispered to Fitz as an aside, 'There is life after Tokyo,' and offered him a plate of mussels and mustard, which Fitz ate ravenously, realising that he hadn't eaten for five days straight – leaving behind the pictures of Jap girls and censorship! As Fitz moved further into the hallway, past the man with no money and no hair who was playing a guitar and singing, 'I remember the backstreets of Naples,' he turned around for one last look at the poet's corner. Through the door of the cerebellum he saw the Egg being chased by a headless, legless pullet in a mini tinnie ya ya – no prizes for guessing who really came first. Before the room disappeared forever Basho could be heard belting the words to his latest hit single 'Blue Baby': 'all he needs is a little oxygen! Oxygen! Oxygen!'

9

It is the nature of the navigator to be bold, to grab life by the neckerchief and drink deep the nectar of ambrosia so often extolled by the negresses and negroes who were the neighbours of Pons Kilometer, into whose room Fitz now drifted on his way to the final ne plus ultra of his Lizard Brain. Such neologisms as 'Kia ora begorrah' made him nervous, but not quite to the point of nervous ailment so oft experienced by the intrepid newshound who prepared the daily lies of the local newspapers, just adding to the nightmares of the already hard pressed Normans whose ancestors made up the bulk of the general populace.

Nostrils flaring and novels open on pages so pretentious and bare-faced with quotes like 'a house not made with hands', that for a moment the whole world seemed to present itself like a hospital, Pons stood lean and gaunt. As in any junkie's numismatics, the gongs and spoons of his trade littered this almost-Spartan oasis he called his room. While his speech was full of obscenity his demeanour was that of a frail octogenarian whose mother had been one of the beautiful odalisques of yesteryear. With the remoteness of the Odeon, the ornate fireplace stood in the far-flung corner of the room. The combination of terrible odour and the austerity which had a beauty all of its own made Fitz suddenly become conscious, as a German philosopher might say! And all at once 'Heiterkeit!' as cette fatigue du nord, and the German in him left for the south.

Offenbach's opera-bouffe, at once with two fingers and the evil eye, rang out from the oversized stereo speakers which would surely be contenders for the title of 'Oldest Inhabitants' at any show of twentieth century technological miracles. Pons, who displayed all the misfit qualities of a genius, showed a constant, unextinguishable appetite for every form of culinary experience, much in the vein [*sic*] of Bruno at Il Piccolo Mondo – a filosofia e necesario amore! Preparing a concoction of olive oil and beta urbs, much more potent than omega urbs, Pons invoked the sturm and drang of the spirit clinger of the drug, la passion et le serieux qui consacrent! The Dinky toy omnibus on the mantelpiece acted as a tabernacle from which he took the final ingredients of his fix before encountering darkness like a woman, which all but repeats the able Ard's experience!

Fitz watched through a veil of awed horror as the young man put the needle in his arm. The opera seemed to emulate the ecstasy as it reached a kind of crescendo, the optimistic oration of the lead singer following almost exactly the delighted facial contortions of the junkie's visage, the orchestra seemingly conducted by every twitch and turn of facial muscle and grimace, which made him look like he was suffering the agony of orchitis rather than the ecstatic vision of hallucinogenic consecration. As sister morphine kicked in and was, in the order of things, coming round again, the effect of the Orphee aux enfers organ music and vaguely orientalist, eerie epicurianism of Pon's androgyny created an underworldly homoerotica of its own which Fitz found at once fascinating and frightening. Never before had he been exposed to such extremes. His original feeling had been one of disgust. He'd felt threatened, but as the thin, lithe, comely figure of Kilometer began to sway, as he danced obliviously with a bunch of dead flowers and an ostrich feather in his hands, Fitz began to feel a certain attraction to this style of existence. He looked towards the tabernacle where a spoon of brown sugar was being prepared by Pons to take him away along the internal moonlight mile of his junk journey.

'Bitch!' Pons suddenly exclaimed as he burned his wee hands on the fire of ice and his sticky fingers stained his otter skin waistcoat.

Suddenly, seeing Fitz standing before him like an apparition of an absinthe friend, Pons ejaculated, 'You gotta move, darling!' and pointing towards a plate of raw oysters, motioned the novice of junkie initiation rituals to partake in the delights of seafood delicacy, the stout and constant diet of Aphrodite! Now the strident, untuned strains of Paganini rode through the room like a barebacked rider of musical wild horses. Pax, pax team – both left Fitz as if he was somehow stupefied by the Spartan ambiance and absurd pageantry of the pain of his compatriot. Like a painting on glass, the brittle, insubstantial character of his friend was matched by the delicate beauty of a Gauguin Godiva riding a palfrey through some ancient palladium past a single palm tree, or more correctly, palmyra, which was the artist's image.

'I've got the blues!' Pons announced in a manner which extolled both pantheism, a la Shelley, and paradox at one and the same time. With something akin to the famous parallels which tied the tails of two cities together – Paris and Auckland – parlour songs, which killed not only ladies but also photographs with one Parthian shot, turned out to be a parting shot from the sons of France to the wounded, colourful warrior whose parts now lie under the sea in a bay of islands where tableneck fish pass through or bask in its previously proud and far pavilion. Fitz saw a flash of blue shoot from Pons's neck spectrum and realized that his friend's earlier exhortation of Gospelian pedantry had actually been quite literal. Even in the darkened room of self-pederasty Fitz could see Pons's skin had turned a blueish shade of pale. With the paternal instincts of a pelican native to Peru he laid his by now perspiring, panicking friend out on his bed as though it were a phaeton carriage and fanned him with a pheasant feather plucked from a nearby Philippe–Egalite vase (a thing of beauty and a joy forever, but a murderous missile if thrown!)

It had always been Fitz's philosophy to remain phlegmatic in times of distress or incomprehension. But what was happening to his overdosing friend, combined with his own phoenix-like emotions and the confused surroundings of Yellban, conspired against his usual composure. At this point it was as if Andrey Sante's claws dug deep into his metaphysical body in search of extracting his pound of Loomis. In fact the only previous time Fitz had felt threatened by his own sanity had been the time of dreams and visions before he lost his job. And now he was in a place more conducive to nightmares than dreams. This metaphorical opposite of photography or physical training, this piano which played pidgin notes, this Castle of If!

'A pig is just a pigeon without wings – a pig is eons ahead of us in understanding the ancient maxim it's going to rain pikestaffs – which indeed will be a hard rain when it does finally fall.' The delirious ravings of the ju-ju junkie broke through Fitz's own winsome reveries and brought him back to the weird reality of Pon's Baroquen English pillow talk. Words flowed out like pimple pus across the universe.

Pons said, 'I know what it's like to be dead, and I feel like I've never been born!' He reached for his pipe of hashish which he lit without pity, adding in the split infinite of a second of Fitz's inattention that he had visited the doggone double-dogstar of the universal make-up Dogon planets of the thirteenth dimension, to which he had travelled along the Sirius Moonlight beam which now streamed in the gaping open roof of the semi-demolished Yellban!

Fitz remembered how, as a child, he had thought he had existed before he was born and so he too knew what it was like to be dead. His soul was a plant put in his body, or plot, and told by God, 'Beware of poachers and the pock-marked poet who sees nothing but poetry, milk and shit. The police of 1900 will be out to get you, but a mere policeman will be no match for the lamb of God.' This is the word of the Lord, amen! Fitz became quite agitated at these pre-verbal communicant memories and he fell to his knees. Kilometer was doing fifty to the ton about the political economy being akin to a Polish plait whose characteristic was that if you cut the hair the head bleeds, ' "Let it bleed", as the poet Ponsard once eulogised,' he yelled. 'The poor are always with us as Popilius the Circular saw all those years ago! And don't forget to, or do so at your peril, harbour thoughts of the Japanese pork-butcher chasing porkers across the rays of the setting rising sun in order to replenish his portfolio!'

With this the blue brother, as though on a mission from gadd, struck up a light which not only lit his Port Royal cigarette, but also illuminated his peat and mud post-OD complexion a deathly, poultice blue-vein concoction of human skin and unearthly pallor not often seen beyond the inverted grave of Valhalla, even in this late twentieth century of practical jokes and genocidal practice so wittily encapsulated in the twin-firm mustaches of Chaplin and Shekelgrabber, who both caused such schadenfreude to be had over the unforgiven Pradon and Dreyfess, and who both took the pragmatic sanction over the human precincts of humour and tragedy to such awe-inspiring heights due to each one's individual preoccupation and struggle.

10

As if the hand of the good Shepherd of Hermas was guiding him in the parous tufa, away from the preschool of decadence which his pretty Pons had exemplified, Fitz now moved out of the inner Zimmer. 'Man, that was as near a brush with priapism and its black priestly calling as I ever want to get,' he thought as he entered the destruction and anarchy of the Yellban hallway! And from the crura cerebri to the cause celebri he could see the Pons Varo lii not more than a milikilometer away forking up the Foramen of the Munro as the Priests of Principles left their Y-print in the shifting snows of providence! The fact that he could see such minute printing left Fitz with a problem only solvable by a professor of epistemology in the normal run of events, and even then only if things were tickety-boo in the ontological progress of the propeller of ethics, intellectual property being theft and all. However, as His Eminence, Locus Caeru Leus, brought the prose to a close all darker thoughts dissipated and Fitz found himself among his own kind again.

As the prospects of total destruction for Yellban became more and more likely, with a hint of fire being added to the general glee of ghoulish high spirits, Fitz found himself following the prostitute and the nun from the upstairs room into what appeared to be a dark cavern of a room with the word 'Providence' in Gothic script written on a board above the doorway. Hoping for a little light relief after his recent unhappy daze with Pons he entered what appeared to be the poorman's archway to heaven, the pineal body of Yellban! Richmen needed the doormen, to no travail. After passing a la fountain, Fitz found himself in the inner sanctum of a Ha (per) bizarre where it appeared anything goes, but which in fact turned out to be a highly organized and totally disorganized nasty party of goth and ghoul music – any old way you choose it! As his eyes gradually became accustomed to the darkness Fitz saw that the room was decked out with many sheets of black plastic, a few dimly lit candles providing the only lighting. Several young people were dancing wildly, while others stood around as though they were in some other-worldly trance. The predominant colour of attire was black, with blood-red and sometimes white silk scarves making up the affected effect. Ignoring the nobles' propaganda concerning peasants, there was a definite air of egalitarian elitism at this gathering. And despite the overriding feeling of sombre nihilism there were touches of humour and eccentric camaraderie like any kinky Loyola citizen La La La La Lola. In one corner sat someone dressed in a chicken suit (Chicken Maaaaaan! He's everywhere! He's everywhere!) with an inscription 'Henry the Fowler II' hung around his neck, his pince-nez sitting unsteadily on his beak, somewhere between the Scylla and Charybdis of the hollowcause to which he aspired. Along with the resurrected Electric Prunes having too much to dream there was the usual array of deafening melancholia which stood in for musical quicksand of thought. Talk about Franz Kafka, pop Doc Bloch, Geli the black Jenny of schoolgirl fantasies, beautiful! My Aachen heart black stockings disappearing under the shortened school uniform of desire, now with the white ghostly visage and thick black lips of my dying bride, is it any wonder that I have faith no more in the system of existence called life! Fitz was handed a piece of black pudding and a glass of fruit-sweetened vodka and pretty soon he was punch-drunk and fantasy free. He could see people gathering around what looked like a neon pyramid which was flashing on and off, sending throughout the room a sickly green beam of light. Suddenly the room was engulfed in dry ice, which some people initially thought was smoke. It took several minutes for calm to be restored and for people to be reassured that there was no fire.

'Yet!' someone yelled and there was an uneasy shiver of laughter. Out of the place whence the ice emerged stepped a wizard-like figure who introduced himself to those assembled as 'The Master of the Side Real Pendulum'. Flanked by a warrior carrying the spear of destiny he moved to the centre of the room.

The posterior pyramid game over, the wizard raised his staff and plunged it floorward deep into a rabbit pie which lay at his feet, exclaiming in a sinister tone that he had taken it from von Oven, whom he quoted as being a shoemaking Racine driver, 'continually enslaved to the pursuit of his object and destined always to be unsatisfied! His radicalism in the field of footwear is only matched by his recklessness when he puts his foot on the pedal. If you travel by raft or railway count yourself lucky as this maniac will not be seen at wharves and railway stations – only on the open road will such redheads prevail without regard for you or your relatives!'

This speech somehow sent the secretion of Fitz's thoughts into convulsions from before backwards to the conical cone of his tip-topsy pineal popsy curvey. Again he lost his A E I O U twenty-dollar note and his thoughts became distracted and d's'm'v'll'd, albeit brfly – in shorts, he had emptied his vowels! Suddenly the ambience of the Gothroom changed to a quieter, more subtle mood as someone changed the music on the CD player. The soft, seductive voice of Celine Dion permeated the air, like a religious hymn, with the song, 'D'un Chateau l'autre', from her latest album, *Voyage au bout de la nuit*. The beauty of the singer's sound somehow matched the starkness and anarchy of the lyrics, so that even the Representative of the People, (one of a growing number of Republicans), who had recently retired from the Japanese Eggroom for the German testicular, was seen to wipe his battle-hardened eyes. A mood of heiterkeit descended upon the previously agitated, yet novel, Gothic scene where even a monk or a peacock would not seem out of place, like a mollusc on a shelley shore.

The reflective reverie was broken. Someone suggested a restaurant for a reunion and was met by the usual Kiwi Gothic response to anything vaguely human and sentimental: 'What are ya, a poof?' Marilyn Manson replaced Celine and the rhyme of reason was sent riding out of the ring of Ronsard most unceremoniously – the primitive landscape of Rousseau lay in ruins yet again. With the Goth spirit of sacrilege restored, not even the cultural safes of St. Bartolomeu or Sainte-Beuve, the freethinker, were free from interference or withered murder, whose sentinel was Wolf.

The music became loud and frenzied. Fitz downed a drink he was handed and he felt the fire-laden fumes make an incision through his corpus collosum, before shooting back to the centrum ovale majus, bejasus, and he had a hard time coming of it as his brain began to feel like over-boiled Magi soup, si C. K.! – lumps and all. Henry the Fowler and Wolf the Howler saw the Disco Duck of St Helena, an island famous for its rock, and looked around for a way out of this Satan's salon. But the

Sultan's swing was still sure, although shaky enough to knock over a salt cellar which bode nought but bad luck for the assembled, which now included sapphics and alcaics.

Amidst the flames gathering in his head Fitz espied a satrap and a young woman making love in the far corner of this Goth-room City. As if they were celebrating a Teutonic saturnalia the coupling pair began to climax like money in a savings bank. High on the wellhung scaffold (thank you very much) the young woman called out in an ecstasy of pleasure, 'Now!' to which her partner replied from above, 'Ich bin ein Berliner,' and both of them yelled an incomprehensible call from their primitive Nordic souls, an unutterable cry of pain and release, before falling down next to each other in strength through joy and relief – talk about Deutschland Über Alles!

Fitz could no longer countenance the Gothic spectacle of self-creation and destruction which this part of his brain was experiencing. The fear of fire in his pineal gland in the hand led him to seek refuge in a neutral precinct. Around his neck was a momento from the thousand seconds' riot he had just attended – a silk scarf which he felt soft and sensual yet somehow menacing against the lower regions of his anterior surface, like a large noose made from silken piano wire.

11

Pushing through the crowded hallway of Yellban between the primeval pineal and the pituitary, Fitz came across a haven off to the right. A door was open and there seemed to be nobody in the room. It was a large sitting-room or lounge and it stank of stale beer and cigarettes, as though the party had been and gone. The aspect of this part of the house looked over what during the day would be the sunny side of the street. Like summer in

Siam the evening was hot and sultry, even though this house of the gods was facing its own destruction. The scenery from the front room was the city on high. The famous prospect of Wellington was like the faulty altar of Sibyl, whose school of Lorca's Novena could still be seen from the left window which had some small pots of basil in the window boxes.

As Fitz looked out at the lights and buildings of the city, even through his alcohol- and drug-hazed visage, he could see a surreal, contemplative vision of his life in relation to the rest of God's creation – God and man all struggling with the terms set down by modern love. Even his schoolteachers had struggled with this Hell's ditch in which we all strive for understanding, nun the wiser! Yet, while he had his job all those years and a stable place to live and his mother to care for, he hadn't had to worry about drowning in the spray of absurdity which was thrown up by the wake of the Medusa of nihilism.

Maidrin Rua had once told him, when he was having doubts about his faith, 'A little science takes your religion from you; a great deal brings you back to it.' Maidrin had trained as a chemist and worked in the research branch of the factory that Fitz had toiled in for twenty-odd years. He always called himself the rainbow man after the androgynous Scudery, whom he admired. One day Fitz found out that Maidrin had drowned himself in the sea at Whangamata. When they had taken his body from the water they had found that he had both male and female sex organs. In his locket was a photograph of a couple of screen queens with Jean, his wife of many years, who had just the ghost of a smile on her otherwise grief-stricken countenance when the ambulance people told her of their discovery of her husband. Fitz had sealed off this memory, like so many others, as if it had been the sound of the waves inside seashells, and now it was as if he had picked up the shell of his own existence and was listening to it for the first time.

Suddenly the party burst its banks and overflowed into Fitz's cavern of contemplation. Looking out on the rainy street below he said sayonara to his sojourn. He felt the seasickness of the party within him and without him. His secret funds of memory disappeared, and the selfishness and self-seeking of egotistical drunken maniacs took over.

'Six down and six to go!' someone yelled loudly as a cryptic non-sequitur. 'The soul builds a many roomed abode for herself and we're gonna tear it down!' screamed another reveller whose glazed, bulging eyes almost popped out of their sockets. 'Mo ya dn!' gesticulated a third, like a personalised n p.

'Damn Seneca and his serials of the Seville of barbarous scalkines and sheep guts and garters of toyboy balloons flung like artillery shells by the shepherds of the outlying regions at the invading ships of the ancient Goths!'

It was Lefarge on the rampage, out of control like the son of a glue-sniffing shoemaker, which in fact he was. Now Fitz sensed danger in the air. There was the smell of smoke and the sound of weatherboards being ripped off the frames of noble Yellban.

Taking another swig from the shoe polish he mistook for expensive French wine, Lefarge, who had previously nailed two small planks of wood to the soles of his footwear, proclaimed, 'All self-made men first arrived in Paris wearing wooden shoes!' and took a loving spoon full of Milk of Magnesia from a bluebottle fly ya bastard, go on!

A punch-up ensued when someone, who obviously understood the importance of being earnest, accosted Lefarge with, 'A little learning is a dangerous thing, and you, I see, have learned little!'

Lefarge, who landed a beauty on his satyrist's jaw, answered with, 'Speak thou jaded cod, while the cod of mea iti lay out from the wallop! Make sense who may, ya wankers!' The haughty

Lefarge ejaculated in disdain, 'You faded, mouldy, musty, paltry, senseless cunts!' Then turning from the Hydra of the many headed multitude he stormed out of Yellban. Before things could reach any equilibrium the next shock was delivered by a girl who ran semi-naked from the Gothroom, which miraculously still stood as a pineal society, screaming that someone had a shotgun and was about to blow away one of the Gotherenes. The sigh that Fitz exhaled near this young woman was not one of dismay, however, as he quickly recognised her as one of the singers in a band he had seen at the Naval and Family, and even with all her clothes on she had stirred his single stick. But realising that this was not the site nor the time for trivialities he headed hero-like towards the murderous 'in' tent, the room of Golgotha! It was quickly that he realised that the 'shotgun' was just a macjargonical term for a particular way of smoking dope and it didn't take long for him to quell the fear of the people outside the hornet's nest of the wolf's lair of Gargantua and Gigantor.

Fitz looked around as he re-entered the hallway, hoping to espy with his little eye the beautiful music maker and say to her as she greeted him as a saviour, 'come into my little ship ...' To his dismay she had vanished, so when someone handed him a skin of wine he drank perchance to sleep and to thicken his blood and to ward off the snakes and sneeze 'of the evils of society', as his mother used to say, salt of the soil that she was. She was particularly prone to this statement when, in the old days, Bill and Eric Sykes, with their transvestite girlfriends Hatty Jakes and Nancy Boy asked for more. 'The eyes have it and ennui go!' she would call out to the TV as Bill jumped over the stone wall into the Thames. 'Call the solicitor,' she would conclude, and he could only marvel how this working-class woman was so learned all through his youth.

A young man appeared from the now nearly broken-up staircase. Dressed in a long robe or nightshirt he held in his hands (in the manner of a priest at the altar; in an emulation of Sombeuil the Somnambulist), a cup of blood-like liquid from which he drank deeply. As though he was the son-in-law of Lady MacBeth come to complain about his new wife's southern cooking and that of the Southeners whence she came, all of whom are poets and whose spelling is impeccable, but who eat nothing but spinach. 'So I drink from the blood of my own spleen which spurs me on to my next game ... I spy with my little ...'

Fitz shrugged his shoulders and mumbled something about 'squaring the circle,' as he moved towards a stack of bottles which someone had brought in from a stag dinner earlier in the evening. By now he was almost legless and as he put his lips to the liposome liquid which transported the drugs therein throughout his body he realised he was only following half his star (i.e. the some, not the lipo, had been revealed to him). The stark revelation that it was lips not lipo that he sought reared up at him like a black stallion of non-comprehension, covering his mind with the semi-darkness like the shadow from a steeple falling across a village pathway in late-afternoon Paraguay.

12

With the stiff resignation of stockbrokers who, having ridden the tiger of the stock exchange by day, end up in the evening with the stoicism of Sisyphus, Fitz entered into the occipital's garden of the mind. Under this holy sea, the part of the brain nearest the stomach bar one, he found himself away from the partying stoolpigeons and in a room where he could at least gather his ever-decreasing strength. Closing the door he could see the feet of the revellers and strollers pass by. The room was very small and, as his eyes adjusted to the comparative gloom, he felt a strange sense of sadness and exhaustion overwhelm him. Lying down on a couch, which had obviously seen better days before ending up in this students' den, he looked up at the studs and beams which criss-crossed the roof. Out of a feeling of quiet desperation and loneliness the tired Fitz offered up an archaic suffrage to any God who would listen to him. His thoughts swung between suicide and summer.

The further he sank into the sofa the more the ceiling beamed (squatty) down from its unlevel crossings of hideous, grinning, teeth-like grids, as though it had had many last suppers of 'out of it' morsels of vulnerable humanity who were well beyond the heeling underfoot touch of surgeons. Like the tiny swallow who returns to the stone-hearted prince of tenderness to sing its swansong before falling on the poisoned sword of Yasmin Bleeth – whose last address was a birthday (Avenida 20 de October, Edificio Jasmin, La Paz) and whose Barbie doll was a self-emulation of sex and death – Fitz now entered into a Sybarites-type trance. Philosophiren ist dephlegmatisiren vivificiren, but unlike syphilis, which everybody has (more or less) the eyes and eggs of Joko could not conpair Bouki.

But he could still hear music. 'Come Mr Talleyrand, tally me banana, O'Day comes and I wanna go home, Toby or not Toby. What's the fucking question, now, JUG manuhere, let me go home!' He thought he could taste through his teeth the knife edge of childhood ice-cream at the age of ten. 'O, I'll be a good boy, I've got a testimonial from the cold turkey over there in the thicket!' But as much as he could still think such thoughts could not be heard, each new thought was like an Aerobus heading, thirteen to one, towards Erebus in the white-out thrift black sky which suddenly is hit by Vaticannelloni thunderbolts and God is not mocked in the stomach cabaret of tights and time which sits, nearly tipping off the universe of verse and worse.

'It's a toad on tobacco ro ro ro road!' However, no longer tolerated – all smokers ashore, following swiftly on the hooves of the great white stead which rushes past the tolls without paying a scent but soon makes up for it by being S.I.C.K. into the nosegay. Now the unlevel crossing of each synapse was calypso–collapsu and as Fitz took another swig from his 'Tonic for the Blood' bottle, he knew he was driving the last spike into the good wood of his medulla oblongata and that his simt was complete. Yet these pill-popper ideas were not mere toys of conjecture and refutation, but the concrete realities (Shad de door and bolt de floor de oldgrey mayor bin dere before c/f Cedric O'Connor de merry virgin had a babbi yar) of an equally august event, circular 1878, flying yet again to N.Y. by Concorde two Augusti ejong ring 911 eins zip cod and not too soon in the future, at that! For he would soon or soon see her, and at that very spike-and-trade transfer as thoughts move, like any traveller, from abstract notion to palpable synapsual tongueston flyer travelling at every ear ere listened to the infamous Troubadour of Ukase Albino for solace and Hoophilm inspiration, and to put their stamp on reality through Lancaster bombing raids on the twin tours of the Trewern Foundation over the intellectual [*sic*] idiot on the landscape not far from Withering Heads Dressdown.

13

But there was no time now for contemplation, such as a good smell at the university may unleash, for Fitz was no longer in his precinct of pituitary. In short he had been transported not so much deus fax machina as previously, but ad usum delphini, into the downstairs basement flat of Yellban, much in the manner of a belated vaccine injected into the velvet pus of an incurable contagion, which turns out to be as ineffectual as the six orations against Verres, to wit as cowardly and unmanly as Vizir when faced with a string of epithets from the likes of Voltaire or the music of Wagner (waltz or war march, it hardly matters which). Anyway, this ringcycular osmoroid osmosis from occipital to oblongata led Fitz to watch with a certain indifference the water of the porsie intime drip slowly from the waterproof oxytoxin towards the foramen magnum whose lower border harboured the wealth of Don Tevita Nuova (Te Vitanuova), Godfather's cats to the Mop of Kilbirnie.

In this downstairs arena of Yellban there was complete and utter bedlam. The fact that the 'bulb' of a Zimmer was only 1¼ inches long and ¾ of an inch more tall, heavy, wide meant that conditions were really cramped no matter what the weather or whether the whatnot was a whitewash or not. It just didn't enter into the equation. Pyramidal in shape, like an obsolete windmill without its sails, the room was now full of wall-to-wall peoplethoughts. Wine was flowing everywhere and Calvin Rhineland, the poet–philosopher who shared his flat with Rose and Reich and a dozen ozen, was spouting forth in the way of a pater in winter to his wayward yet much-loved children.

> The way of nature with its roses
> Is that of young Ness with her wit
> Witness how she covers her poses
> Her womanly wiles, each little tit-bit

People and ideas were jostling each other for every available piece of space. Fitz felt himself being pushed and shoved in every direction. Snatches of conversation could be heard when the music stopped. Someone was saying that the Beatles were really witches working for the IRA and while John and Paul had written songs about the plight of the Irish, and Ringo kept the beat, it was Harrison, the quiet one, who had procured eight small arms to hold you (Help!) on his TRIPS to America. But all things must pass, by George!

'What are you doing in this neck of the woods?' Fitz heard someone ask in a workmanlike fashion. Before he could reply the idea was gone and replaced by another in which Fitz recognised a certain amount of absurdity for the theatre of East Lynn, that the medulla oblongata was in fact not far from the neck, if indeed not part thereof! Suddenly someone whispered in his ear, 'La dore io tamoi prima.' Where this suggestion came from Fitz had no idea, but it was the spark which lit the final fire which now began to make its way through the already semi-demolished monster that was Hisbrainyellban.

'Love at first sight explained by a previous existence.' Fitz began to write what the little Latin had insinuated into his head. As all the dozens of reptilian life forms left the lounge of the lizard brain through either the anterior or posterior fissures, heading either towards the brain or the spinal cord, for where there was smoke now there was fire, Fitz sat perfectly still, mesmerised by what he had written and completely oblivious to the increasing danger of the fire which now threatened to engulf him. The smoke which billowed around him began to suggest tangible forms of the dreams he had been haunted by back in Auckland. The woman's face moved slowly towards him and he saw that it was her and he knew that he had met her in another life and as the wind, te hau, blew hard out along the coast it whipped up the water; scraping the land it sent chunks of sure cliffs crashing to the sea below. Then picking up his thoughts, taurite ngā moehewa o te aroha, te hau carried his words soaring southwards over the dark hills, taking them gently down the valley where they will reach her as a whisper. Coughing from the smoke which began to fill his lungs in a dangerous fashion and yawning from the tiredness of sheer exhaustion, Fitz felt a sharp burning and throbbing in his head. The pain was intense as the fire of his passion met with the gradual meltdown of his drug- and alcohol-rich plutonium oblongata, and these two combined with actual flames and falling beams and woodwork of Yellban meant that Fitz was alight with the river of fire that raged within and without. The colours, the heat and the pain all intensified and Fitz felt he was part of some magical fairground. The foggy image of her embraced him, and everything went black.

Just as it seemed Marxengels burnt their hump, fair dinkum, by singing the Cycle of Belize and Ten Gutters with a chorus of Rastafarian Goths chanting, 'Burn, burn, let the motherfucker burn!' Watsoncrick quick as a rat off a sinking ship called out to a young gentleman and a young lady, 'Look! Look for Christ's sake look – there's still someone in there!' As they saw the Dolphindog and the Gypsy woman trying to pull the badly blackened but still breathing body of Fitz from the intense heat of the burning house, they ran to help ...

'O Primavera! Gioventi dellamo! O Gioventi! Primavera della vita!' cried a youth in a tone of rapt ecstacy. 'I thought he had seen Yvetot and died,' he said, blessing himself in the direction of Saint Mary of the Angels in thanksgiving for the miracle of life restored! Little did the lad know that Fitz had, in reality, seen Yvetot – even though, to all outward appearances, alles ist verfallen!

9
float
2
the note
6
3
CROSSINGS
UNLEVEL
5
PART
4
1
take
the
d A y
train
17
8
O'
M
L
y
e
A
R

1

Patrick Fitzgerald stood on the back deck of the *Aratere*, waving goodbye to the young woman who had looked after him and nursed him back to health. As the ship slowly pulled away from its moorings Fitz felt a small sadness at leaving behind his friend from Yellban. He caught her eye for the last time and then Pania and the Dolphin Dog became lost in the crowd of faraway faces. Soon the city of Wellington took on the countenance of a tiny town as the boat moved further into the harbour. A stray horn blew mournfully in the mist.

The toy trainsets and slotcar motorway entered the heart of the Meccano Set buildings of the downtown area; the overhead wires of the buses and railway hung like strands of spaghetti in the sky. As the *Aratere* sailed past Soames Island towards the Pencarrow Heads, Fitz saw the small Tiger Lily Two ferry beginning its journey from Days Bay into Wellington City with a load of late-morning shoppers. The sky was dark and drizzly, and as an aeroplane flew overhead following its trajectory towards Wellington Airport, he understood the intrigue and interest that this city held for him despite the little time he had been resident in it.

When Fitz was discharged from hospital Pania had made a point of speeding up his recuperation by taking him tipi haere around as many of the far-flung environs of the city as her old jalopy could cope with. To get him out in the air and to aid and quicken his return from the torpor which his mental and emotional breakdown had engendered, she planned excursion after excursion, always mindful of his fragile state and never pushing the boundaries of his capabilities beyond what she felt he could enjoy or endure.

As the waves from the ship's wake washed the city further from his vision, the events and memories of the last few weeks entered into his consciousness. Fitz's first conscious memory after blacking out at the Yellban party was waking up in the back of a police car as it pulled into the emergency area in front of Wellington Hospital. Immediately he recognised that it had not been the nirvana of 'Yvetot' he had reached, but the wasteland and destruction of 'Dollersheim'. These two metaphors for Heaven and Hell had danced around in his shattered subconscious as the police processed him, having obtained a warrant for his temporary committal to the psychiatric unit in the hospital. When they asked him questions he answered them in dreams and visions.

Pania, who had accompanied him initially to the police station, had been overwhelmed by his statements to the arresting constables. As she listened to his outrageous telling of the events at the Yellban party, she realised how out-of-it he must have been. When his story culminated in his description of the pure flame of visionary perception jumping from inside his head to set fire to the entire Yellban edifice, she realised he had completely lost his mind and pleaded with the police to take him to the detox unit.

Feeling angry and humiliated, Fitz at first resisted the notion of voluntarily going to a loony bin. When faced with the option of a more formal, forced committal he eventually submitted to police demands and Pania's pleas. The ride from the station to the hospital he remembered only as a blur of city lights which appeared distorted and surreal, as though it were raining inside the car. The noise of late-night revelling and horns hooting added to the already confused state of his mind. Anything that the policeman or Pania, who had accompanied him, said, appeared in his brain as unintelligible sound.

The following week had been very difficult, and he had never in his forty-odd years felt so alone or rejected. Added to his own sorrow and pain was that of his fellow patients, whose ghosts and demons were articulated in graphic and relishing detail over and over to the newcomer after he had been released into the general ward following a few days of initial observation. But he also felt a certain indefinable comradeship, much in the way he had felt towards the soldier from Vietnam who had confessed to and confided in him on the train from Auckland. There were people here who would understand the Yellban episode, for example, and all his dreams and escapades of the mind, which to ordinary, sane people he could never tell.

Finally, after ten days of coming down and observation, the authorities said he could be released into the care of Pania, who had come to see him every day. As he arrived 'home' to Yellban Fitz felt a real sense of bizarre displacement. There stood before him the large, three-storeyed house which he thought had been destroyed by fire and vandalism the night of the party. As he entered the quiet, cavernous hall of the front of the place he recognised the living room where he had found respite from the madness during that night. There was an eeriness about being in the resurrected tomb of the front room and Fitz felt himself shudder. Pania could sense his feelings of dislocation and uncertainty, and she took his hand as an act of reassurance. The Dolphin Dog came out when Pania opened the door to her room and the dog licked Fitz's hand as a gesture of recognition. These two simple things began his journey back to health and mental well-being.

For the first two days Fitz didn't leave Pania's room, feeling afraid and vulnerable. She would go out to her work and come back home in the evening with food, and she would comfort him gently in the night. He began to feel safer and stronger as the days went by, eventually venturing out into the common room to try and immerse himself back into ordinary life again. Most of the people who had been at the party were away on holiday as the occasion of the party had been the end of the university term. This suited Fitz very well as he didn't really want to talk to many people, least of all those who might have experienced his assumed pōrangi behaviour that night. He also thought that peace and quiet would be the best way to make a speedy recovery.

One afternoon when he was resting on Pania's bed Fitz was in a half-asleep, half-awake state and the afternoon sun danced around the edge of his consciousness. Slowly his spirit began to leave his body and drift towards the roof of Pania's room. Fitz realised he was looking down at his tinana from his wairua and if he didn't do something they would be separated and he would die. As he floated, hovering above himself in what seemed an eternity of slow-motion indecision, the weight of his quest became the stimulus which brought him back to earth. Also, as he had straddled the spirit world, he had turned into his mother whose wairua had seemed to invade his own, and if he hadn't come down at that moment he would have lost himself forever to the spirit of someone else.

Resisting his mother's seduction and gradually drifting back to reality, Fitz's dreams of the beauty of the woman and the landscape he had set out to find returned to him in full force. She stood brown and bare breasted before him with the beauty of the land and seascape he had also dreamed as a backdrop, emulating and enhancing the visage ataahua that was herself. The rise and fall of the undulating landscape followed the contours and form of her body, the lightness and shimmer of the sun and elements of the sea and sky followed the wild and free nature of her spirit as it beckoned and called to his own inner spirit, and they danced together in that special place which trysts the night of darkness and evil away.

When Pania arrived home that evening Fitz's belongings were packed and he was nowhere to be seen. Dolphin Dog came over to her, whimpering, as though she was trying to tell her something. Pania, who knew that Fitz would leave as soon as he could, still felt a sense of loss, almost betrayal. She sat down on the bed they had shared for the last week or two and had a little tangi, her thoughts and feelings mixed about this man she had looked after and been intimate with in an intense and very unexpected way. She did not usually let people into her life in such a direct and trusting manner. But somehow Fitz had been different, in some way in tune with her deeper being, and the impact had been immediate.

Fitz arrived back at Yellban to find Pania sitting on her bed. She had obviously been crying and she didn't reply to his over-enthusiastic greeting. There was a long silence between them, which lasted through into the evening. Every now and again Fitz tried to break through it by saying something about why he was going, but it always came out sounding like an excuse or an apology. Eventually Pania said in a low voice which was barely audible and full of hurt, 'So you'd rather follow this dream, this ideal, than stay here with the reality of me.'

'It's not like that,' Fitz replied, at the same time realising that that was exactly what it was like. This new unlevel crossing between the world of fantasy and fact was set before him like a further challenge to his own idea of himself, a moral and emotional stymie. He knew how important Pania had been in his recovery and he had developed a real aroha for her because of that. One thing that he hadn't seen until now was that she also needed him in her life. She had seemed so strong and self-contained; it hadn't entered into his head that she might also feel vulnerable and in need of his love and affection.

Now, as Fitz stood on the deck of the interisland ferry and watched Seatoun and Barrett's Reef passing like some quaint, cold Caribbean vision of postcolonial suburbia, he realised with a shudder the implication of leaving Pania on the reef, as it were. Two images came to him simultaneously. The first was a childhood memory of a small plastic effigy of the famous Māori maiden which his father had made at the factory he worked at. She was bare breasted and sat on a plastic rock, wearing nothing but a piupiu. In his mind this was juxtaposed with a quote from the famous Catholic theologian Thomas à Kempis, 'an humble husbandman that serveth God is better than a proud philosopher'.

In defiance of the theologian Fitz had also chosen to follow his passion rather than live in humility, and in so doing he was risking the fateful power of the undertow from the wrath of the spiritual world. As the *Aratere* moved between the heads of the harbour into the open water the sea swell hit the prow of the ship with a more intense force and raindrops began to fall.

Determined to keep away from alcohol, Fitz steered clear of the boat's bar and headed for the cafeteria. He bought a cup of coffee and a sandwich and sat down at the table, looking out of the window at the seagulls wheeling and diving in the wind. The ship rolled and pitched in the heavy seas and the rain was now quite persistent. Despite his feeling of gratitude and guilt about Pania, Fitz suddenly felt really pleased to be alone. Alone and travelling, two aspects of life he had not experienced much before. A sense of freedom and adventure took over his consciousness and he immersed himself in this unexpected pleasure. He closed his eyes and allowed the heaving motion of the vessel to rock him back and forth as though he were being cradled. In this way he rested in a reverie of non-thought suspended animation for what seemed like several hours. All the heaviness and dross of the previous few months disappeared, and he felt relaxed and at peace.

'I hope you don't mind if I join you?'

Fitz woke with a start. He saw before him an elderly gentleman who gave the appearance of being very tall and formal. Fitz detected a foreign accent of some European origin. Still half-asleep, Fitz could see that the café had filled up considerably and there was nowhere else for the stranger to sit.

'No, of course not,' he answered the man's question. The newcomer sat down opposite Fitz and began eating a meal. It took Fitz some time to reorientate himself back to a semblance of normality, and he was happy that the other man seemed intent on his eating and did not appear to desire any conversation. After a while the man finished his lunch and, instead of getting up to leave as Fitz had hoped, leaned towards him across the table.

'Dreams. You have been having dreams lately, ja?'

Fitz was taken aback and remained speechless when the other man went on.

'I know you, you see. Or at least I knew your father – a great man, your father.'

What happened next absolutely stunned Fitz. Up till now he had not known much about his father, who had died when Fitz was in his early teens. Even before his death the father had been something of an aloof character in the background of the young Fitz's life. He would often come home late from the factory where he worked, or from having a few drinks at the bowling club he belonged to, for in Fitz's younger days the hotels still closed at 6 p.m. So his father was a kind of non-participant in family life, and it was only after he died that the young Patrick Fitzgerald wanted to find out about the man who was so much a part of himself and yet so much in the background.

Now here was this perfect stranger speaking in a foreign accent about the father who, although Fitz had always seen him as an enigma in his own life, seemed in no other way exceptional. But as the old man continued, Fitz did indeed begin to understand the significance of some of the dreams he had had on the overnight train from Auckland as well as some of the Yellban hallucinations.

'I first met your father in Berlin, in 1943,' the man went on, 'I was a young Wehrmacht attaché in the Foreign Office and your father was an SS Colonel in the same area, but in that organisation, unlike other members of his tribe, your father, whose name was Mikhel von Leerig, was a friendly, approachable sort of fellow, and from that time until July 1944 we saw quite a lot of each other both as colleagues and socially. We had both been put in charge of Irish affairs for our organisations, with particular emphasis being placed on making contacts with the IRA, to whom we were supplying arms.

'Gradually, von Leerig revealed to me his grave fears for what was happening in Germany. He told me how he had already saved the lives of many people by using his influence as an SS officer to get passports to Jews and others who were condemned. As we both had young families we had to be very careful not to do anything overt against the Nazi regime which could endanger them. At the same time we could see the disaster that the Führer was leading us into.

'Your father, early in 1944, told me of a secret SS report which had been initiated by Heydrich before his assassination. It spoke of Hitler's 'nicht naturlich' status, which had often been rumoured. Heydrich, who had personal ambition beyond his calling, had found the original damning material which had been cooked up in the Poison Kitchen at Altheimer Eck in 1933 – the perfect address for a newspaper about to expose the Führer's impending insanity, don't you agree!'

Here the stranger had a little chuckle to himself, but soon became serious again and Fitz could not choose but hear.

'With Heydrich's death the SS became even more powerful as Himmler saw one of his principal rivals gone. Your father knew that Himmler had prepared a secret report on Hitler's mental health. This revealed disturbing signs and von Leerig used this to try to influence Himmler to open negotiations with the West to bring an end to the war, as he knew the Reichführer SS understood that the Führer was beginning to deteriorate and Himmler himself had begun to fantasise about his own future power.

'As intrigue and mistrust permeated the Berlin of that year and the war began going against us more and more, von Leerig played an increasingly dangerous hand. He gave his Irish affairs over to another SS officer, von Klagen, son of the poet Ludwig Klages. Ironically, von Klagen resurfaced in Auckland in the mid-1980s, shot by a neo-Nazi group in Aotea Square. Von Leerig was leading a double life which saw him on the one hand becoming a valued and trusted member of Himmler's inner circle. On the other hand he was using this position to steer more people away from the death camps. He was also aware of the plot to kill Hitler, and actively encouraged von Stauffenberg. In his research into the Reich's enemies he had found an untitled poem written by a left-wing Jewish writer called Karl Wolfskehl in 1934. In some unexplained way this prophetic poem touched a chord in this intelligent cabal of German officers who realised that the Nazi dream had indeed made real the abstract idea of the original and had turned man into a superman, a Nietzschean nightmare, and the great nineteenth century European vision of its own civilisation lay in ruins – this was the tragedy of Hitler's legacy: surrealism made flesh!'

The older man here faltered and sat silent for a while. Fitz noticed that the *Aratere* had entered the Marlborough Sounds and the surrounding hills were covered in low fog and mist. The rain was still falling but the wind had dropped and the ship's passage was now sheltered by the land. He felt a sense of disappointment that his first trip across Cook Strait had been interrupted by this Mephistophelian visitor who had completely upset his moho, his third-card mote terra incognito of his pater incertus, as it were. However, the story of his own father was so compelling and the dreams had a reality to them that could only be explained thus. It seemed those who dream are doomed to live their reality. Fitz forgot the South Island landscape as the old man continued.

'Then came the long expected unexpected. The July bomb meant to kill Hitler. Everyone had to think on his feet. First reports had the Führer dead and many Wehrmacht soldiers were ready to stage a coup to oust the Nazi leadership. Then came the news that the Führer had survived and Himmler, the hypocrite, became once again 'mein treue Heine' and the SS became more fervently the avenging angels of their leader. Von Leerig was in a real quandary because he could easily be incriminated in the plot. In the months that followed he devised a way to leave Germany which would ensure that his wife and children were safe and that none of his work in helping people escape the concentration camps would be uncovered.

'His investigations into Wolfskehl had revealed that the poet now lived in a faraway country called New Zealand. Your father had a friend in the Navy, Günter Reisenstuhl, who was second in command of a U-boat.

'Your father, von Leerig, found out that his friend's submarine, U862, was due to make a mischievous voyage to the Southern Ocean to sink shipping off the coast of Australia and New Zealand. Von Leerig went to Himmler with the evidence implicating Wolfskehl as a key inspiration behind the plot to kill Hitler. He told the Reichführer SS that he wanted to go to the other side of the world to kill the poet as revenge for inspiring the July plot. Himmler agreed and told him he would ensure the safety and well-being of his family if von Leerig was killed, a U-boat mission being a particularly hazardous one, especially by this stage of the war.

'It was a couple of months before U862 was due to set sail, so your father contacted Albert Speer whom he heard was trying to get manpower for the armaments ministry. Von Leerig made himself responsible for the SS labour supply of those who were healthy enough from the camps to get transfer to arms-production factories. In this way he again saved many more lives which would have otherwise perished in the fires of hell of Auschwitz and many other of the death factories.

'Von Leerig hoped during this last two months that no one would discover his role in giving information to those who set the July bomb. Fortunately he had set up enough of a smokescreen not to be detected, and he set sail in U862 at some time during the last months of 1944. It was early 1945 by the time they reached the coast of Australia, where they sank a few merchant ships before heading south to New Zealand. The original plan was that your father would be put out in a rubber boat in Auckland Harbour, the city where Wolfskehl was thought to be living. Even though U862 one night made its way right into the harbour, almost to the city itself, the captain deemed it too risky to surface as there was a naval base at Devonport and they would soon be tracked down. Eschewing the temptation to sink a nice, juicy freighter, U862 left Auckland and travelled down the coast to Napier. Here the submarine surfaced long enough to let von Leerig out into a rubber dinghy on his mission to "kill the poet–Jew traitor".

'Whilst the town of Napier was under blackout, from the U-boat the sailors could see an occasional car headlight going through the night, and it was from these that your father got his bearings. His kameraden farewelled him with God-speed and Heil Hitler and he rowed silently toward the shore as the undersea vessel slipped away into the dark.

'As von Leerig neared the shore he threw a weighted package overboard. It contained everything that identified him as Mikhel von Leerig, SS officer and German citizen. In place of these documents he pulled out his new passport and other identity papers which bore the name Michael Patrick Fitzgerald. He had got them from a dead IRA man. Fortunately his host had been from Belfast which meant that the passport was British, not Irish, which would make things a lot easier in this 'little Britain of the South'.

'Not much is known of your father's movements after this period until the day he died in the mid-sixties. Of course he never intended killing Wolfskehl although he did send him a postcard in 1946 with the cryptic inscription 'How can poetry be written after Auschwitz', which he signed from Meister 'Boy' George, Cosmic Circle of the Secret Germany, found amongst Wolfskehl's papers after his death in 1948. A handwriting expert verified it as being your father's hand against SS documents in the Simon Wiesenthal Centre for War Crimes. They are still trying to track him down to put him on trial despite overwhelming evidence against their case – your father was in the SS, therefore a criminal in their reasoning.

'We do know that he was in touch with some Italian Fascist who left his son vast amounts of gold in a 'Guilt Gilt Box', which his son used to atone for the sins of his father by supplying poor people in Auckland with footwear and medical services. It wasn't exactly Mussolini's millions, but it was a healthy sum and it helped a lot of people.

'In case you are curious about your half-brother and sister and step-mother back in Germany, well, Himmler was as good as his word and had them well set up and cared for in Dresden, a city considered to be among the safest in the Reich as refuge for women and children. However, like so many others your family perished in the firestorm caused by the allied bombing of that beautiful Baroque city in February 1945. And of course Chicken Man himself, Heinrich II, died of eating a poison bird seed when his own delusions became too real and he could no longer live with either. If that isn't symbolist poetic justice, I don't know what is! Those who live by the words, die by the words!'

Fitz felt somewhat dizzy and confused and needed a cup of coffee. He excused himself after asking the man if he wanted one also, to which he replied 'Nein, danke,' and all Fitz could think of was 'Gingernuts' and had to suppress a violent desire to laugh uproariously and uncontrollably. Swallowing his laughter he went over to the self-service, semi-circular buffet and purchased a coffee and a roll. Feeling and thinking a thousand jumbled, tumbling thoughts and sensations, he returned to his table.

He almost dropped the tray with the food and drink on to the floor. The realisation that his father's friend had gone shook him. Fitz looked around, frantically trying to locate the person who had told him all the strange, bizarre facts about his father and about his dreams. He sat down slowly, hoping the man had just gone for a piss or something. Realising that he hadn't eaten for several hours, he ate ravenously but without tasting. As he sipped the coffee and time slipped by he knew that the older man was not going to return.

Exhausted, he stared silently into his own thoughts. There were so many questions that needed answering. The man he had known as his father all these years had existed as a quiet presence in the background for so long. Fitz had only been seven or eight when the news had come that his father had collapsed near the Penrose Railway Station. One memory he had kept all these years was how sensible his dad had been to pull over to the side of the road when the blood had burst in his head and allowed dreams and death to flow in.

He remembered his father as a man of few words, and when he did speak it was with an accent which Fitz had presumed was Irish. But now everything had changed, and nothing had changed – another unlevel crossing! Fitz had to look anew at his whole psychological and emotional landscape. Everything he'd ever known or thought about himself was irrevocably transformed, while the material aspects of time and place stayed the same. Amidst all these details and abstracts of this new perspective on his life, one image began to take shape and haunt his inner perception. The image of his German brother and sister being incinerated sprang up into his mind, the ashen bodies huddled close to each other and their mother as they perished together in their safe haven on the River Elbe – a delicately pretty picture etched forever in the blood and fire of a tragic Dresden vase in Fitz's inner kiln of memory.

'Sorry mate, time to go.' The steward was wiping down the last of the tables. 'If you don't hurry we'll be heading back to Wellington soon.'

Fitz realised that they had reached Picton, had been there already for over a quarter of an hour. So lost in his thoughts had he been, he hadn't noticed the *Aratere* docking. All his fellow passengers had already left the ship. Again he felt a certain annoyance that he had not been able to enjoy and savour his arrival in the picturesque little town which was the gateway to Te Wai Pounamu, the South Island. Instead, he had to now hurry, gather his things together and find the railway station so he could catch his train to Christchurch.

2

When Fitz walked out of the ferry terminal and on to the streets of Picton he found himself in the kind of picture-postcard seaside place that you read about in travel articles. On his right-hand side were the railway shunting yards where the freight trains are made up of the wagons coming off the ferries from Te Ika a Māui. On his left hand was the bay and the park which led up to the main part of town. Following the rail tracks he found his way to the railway station and checked in. There was about half an hour before the Coastal Pacific Express left, so he decided to wander the streets to fill in time.

Walking up the rise towards the town's main street, Fitz saw at the top the large, old-fashioned veranda of the hotel. His first instinct was to go in for a beer, however he denied this instinct for fear of what he remembered of Yellban. The memory made him shudder, as though a shadow had crossed his grave. Instead of going further into the town he went across the road and through the Memorial Archway to the Glorious Dead, down on to the grassed area which leads to the bay. He went over to a drinking fountain where he cupped his hands together and drank some water to go with the pills they had prescribed at the hospital to stabilise his condition. He sat down on a park bench and watched the people going by and the boats and the water taxis coming in and out of the various jetties and wharves. Suddenly he felt very tired, not just from the medication.

The sun shone without alternative on the water and Fitz's eyes were led by the sparkling ripples to a large elongated black shape lying in the water about half a mile away to his right. He couldn't believe what he was seeing. Here, in the middle of Picton Bay, was U862 about to surface over fifty years after the war had ended. Was his father on board? Fitz stood up in a state of shock, wanting to warn all these families with their young children to get away from this Nazi sea-wolf. Yet he did not want to betray his own father by alerting the authorities. As he gained his feet a cloud crossed the sky and the bright water became momentarily dull, allowing Fitz to see properly the gutted hull of an old wooden ship which lay half-submerged in the distance where he thought he had seen the submarine.

Fitz almost reeled backwards at the absurdity of his hallucination. Looking over to where the 'U-boat' had been, an area with a backdrop of lush green wooded hills, he thought back to how he had noticed when he was checking in at the railway station that the weather had lifted and now after nearly half an hour the whole Picton sky was blue.

'Railway station! Half an hour!' he shouted almost aloud to himself. His train was just about to depart as he burst on to the platform waving and gesticulating like a wild man. The guard, who was ready to blow the whistle, signalled to the driver to wait and Fitz leapt aboard. As he entered the carriage his fellow passengers, who were already settled into their snug positions for the journey with books and music headphones, looked somewhat askance at the late arrival intruding on their comfort. Fitz looked at the seat number on his ticket and was pleased to find that he was in a double-facing four-seated area by himself. He had no inclination for any kind of phatic communion or small talk with anyone and as the train slowly pulled out of Picton Station he gradually calmed down and prepared for the long journey ahead.

As the train crossed the road crossing just south of the town, it was going slowly enough for Fitz to observe a late-model Mercedes waiting for the train to pass. He caught a glimpse of the single passenger in the chauffeur-driven car and it was, he was certain, the man who had spoken to him on board the ship. Before he could react, the train had gone over the road and was heading away into the valley where only the railway goes, leaving the highway to its own route.

Fitz set himself into the rhythm peculiar to the melancholic motion of the railway. His thoughts began to emulate the rocking and rolling of the train as it gathered momentum, gentle and steady. The train and the medication conspired to seduce him towards sleep. Soft, transparent images appeared in his mind, but they were indistinct and left almost the moment they arrived. Even the pictures of the woman and the place which were the purpose of his quest could not hold, and they dissolved into indistinct shapes and colours. The centre let go and he dreamed he was falling down the long shaft of Te Wai Pounamu into a bottomless pit of oceanic wairua.

Clickety clack Wairau River clickety clack, clickety clack Opawa River clickety clack clickety clack. As Fitz slowly woke the train too slowed down and within a minute had stopped at Blenheim Station. He looked out of the window and saw many people having their luggage checked and preparing to get on the south-bound express. He tried to imagine where they were all going, but again his mind began to suffer from some non-specific virus which seemed to cut the idea-Apaches off at the synapse-pass. The clock inside the station office, which Fitz could just see by craning his neck to the right, read 2.10 p.m. and the next minute the whistle blew and the train made its way through the south part of the town slowly, click clack Taylor River click clack, through Riverlands and then burst out on the open rail road. Fitz fell asleep.

The train slowed click clack Awatere River click clack as it arrived in Seddon half an hour later. Fitz woke with a start and saw a small town. It began to seep into his perception how different Te Wai Pounamu was to Te Ika a Māui. He saw for the first time the landscape and the lack of people. In some psychological way the two names of the islands hinted at the difference, one being the catch from the sea of a man-god, the other being the place of a coloured spiritual stone, unlike the Pākehā signs which hinted only at two separate geographical locations.

Two men got on the train at Seddon and were seated in the two single seats opposite Fitz across the aisle of the carriage. While Fitz was glad they were not placed in his four-seated area, he was still annoyed at the proximity of the two. They were both dressed in suits and ties and as the train went slowly click clack over the Starborough Creek click clack, they called the steward over and ordered drinks. Fitz looked out of the window and prepared for the longest non-stop part of the journey. Like the wind which rushed by alongside the railway tracks Fitz's thoughts found it hard to settle, as though he were haurangi without being drunk, as though the wind rushed through his mind not allowing his ideas any peace.

Clickety clack Hog Swamp Creek clickety clack ' ... aliis conventibus qui Fancy Balls dicuntur, King's dick.' Fitz, half asleep, heard the strangely familiar language of his neighbours on the other side of the carriage.

'Non convertus vulgo dictus Fancy Balls, quoties minus honesti simt,' replied the other, and Fitz wondered what vulgo dictus had to do with the honesty of the South Island main trunk railway and as the train went clickety clack Blind River clickety clack he drifted back into a fitful sleep ... cum omnibus ...

Fitz woke in a panic clickety clack Cattle Creek clickety clack, the words 'Festum SS Petri et Pauli, cordis ...' had permeated his sleeping consciousness. By the time he had become fully awake the second man was rejoining with ... 'expendis erectionem, ea qua decet reservatia et obsequio, SS mo, et Dunedinensi habentur.'

'Edita in Sessione tertia SS.' The two men and their coitus began to disturb Fitz. Not only could he not decipher the language they spoke, the constant reference to the SS was, to say the least, unnerving, especially in the light of the conversation on the *Aratere*. Coupled with what seemed an obvious reference to Dunedin, Fitz's paranoia was complete, for it was that Southern Edinburgh he was bound for in pursuit of his dreams, and it was his dreams which had got him into this nightmare of self-knowledge and self-deceit.

Lake Grassmere passed by unlike any place he had ever seen before. Despite his inner turmoil he couldn't choose but look at this odd mixture of lunar landscape and Stalinesque salt mines, the Siberia of the southern moon. Clickety clack Flaxbourne River clickety clack the homererotica of his neighbour's lustig-pream and earnest rhoemboidering nazi – arm me with jobs, arm me with confidence! A kind of Zeitgeist Zimmler of the mind of the Neo-Kashubian Kabbalah Z.Z.Z. knight of the long knaves Prophet, where the magpie dawdle dawdle waddle fowles its own nest egg clickety clack Needles Creek clickety clack Mirzas Creek clickety clack Waima River Republic clickety clack Woodside Creek clickety clack Kererengu River clickety clack – get off the Günter, this is no shunter but a full-blown low-speed express zug zug zugging its way between the bridges of Valhalla and the inevitable Deadman, streaming southwards away from Bethlehem with a PLEACH, male and female, in its wake. Fine again is the weather and here is a prayer for everyone when they come and rejoice!

Fitz got up and went to the toilet for a mimi. He closed the cubicle door and locked it. He was away from the pōrangi thoughts and feelings engendered by his two fellow travellers and their homage to catatonia. Fitz looked out of the toilet window and saw for the first time that the train was now right down on the coast line. He watched for a while the beautiful Pacific Ocean as its waves rolled in and folded on to the shore.

Clickety clack Washdyke Stream clickety clack, the railway and the road huddled together on a small shelf of land between the sea and the Seaward Kaikoura Range which now loomed spectacularly up on the other side of the carriage. As Fitz resumed his seat and the train rounded the point and crossed the clickety clack Clarence River clickety clack.

'Sexenta flumena Europae,' said one of the Latinos. 'Sex vel ad minus quatuor ejasmodi.' The second man laughed and made the motion of pulling a sword from a scabbard in a melodramatic fashion.

'Gladicoma duxit e vagina ut penes secaret,' he said, and then said in English, 'all along the banks of the six hundred rivers of Europe.' And they both chuckled with laughter as they drained their glasses.

Fitz observed them in a detached, more objective way now. Looking closer he realised that they were two old priests, probably on holiday together. He watched them with affectionate amusement. This was probably the first time they had been able to speak Latin together for many years. He remembered, with some humour, his father's excuse for not going to church with Mum and him had been the fact that they no longer said the mass in Latin.

'Who wants to belong to a religion you can understand,' he would laugh to Mum's chiding. But this never explained why he didn't come to church before they stopped the Latin!

Then one thing which Fitz remembered from the old days of being taught by nuns made him aware of the absurdity of his paranoia earlier on the train. In liturgical terms the letters SS in Latin meant that saints were being talked about. Fitz didn't know whether to laugh or cry. His vision had been so blackened by the conversation on the ship that he had immediately seen these two old boys as two black angels sent to further torment him. Clickety clack Rakautara Stream clickety clack.

'Hujus anni indiximus, praesertim quad vocant Cricket et hujusmodi,' said the younger priest.

'Tunc anagramori enim largitories, exhibaemut de istius qui Māori Volcanictus,' replied the older one, although to Fitz they both appeared quite ancient. They seemed to be talking about a game of cricket and something to do with things Māori. Fitz felt ashamed and dirty for his own thoughts. He wanted to jump off the train at the next station, like Sebastian Dangerfield when he discovered people were watching him in a lascivious manner on the train to Dublin when he himself was the groper! Clickety clack Hapuka River clickety clack.

'Dolorem capere ex aliqua re.' Fitz decided to look out of the window at the natural beauty of the sea and sky. Driftwood as big as telegraph poles was washed up on the sandy shore, a barefoot girl waded in the water and a large, fluffy white cloud suggested a ghost horse and rider slowly drifting across the blue prairie of the firmament. In and out of this scene wove the Latin words and the sound of the train crossing another bridge, 'Cupiditate alicuius rei accensum, inflammatum esse.' Clickety clack Harnets Creek, the train was on the outskirts of Kaikoura and slowing to a click clack Middle Creek click clack.

Fitz looked over towards the two men, more to see the town through their window than to see them. One was saying, 'Nuntium remittere alicui.' The other looked thoughtfully at his friend and then made a sudden gesture, throwing his hands up in the air and proclaiming, 'Sed Mannum de tabula!' As the train stopped at Kaikoura Station both the priests stood up, one clapping the other on the shoulder and saying, 'Come on Jonah, let's go and get a taste of whale-watching.' They both gestured a good-humoured farewell to Fitz and left the carriage to find their luggage.

3

Stepping down from the train Fitz decided he needed to stretch his legs for the few remaining minutes they would be at Kaikoura. Looking northward along the platform he was overwhelmed by a sight he had never seen before: snow! The great mountain range that dominated the area was covered in a luminous white which gave the whole immediate inland landscape an ethereal air. He looked with a childlike wonder at this phenomenon and felt overawed by the presence of such natural beauty. The absolute quiet and stillness of the scene took him quite by surprise and he almost felt himself falling at the overwhelming sight.

Coupled with the contrast of the blue sky and the blue-green hue of the sea on the other side of the railway station, Fitz was in a state of unanimated suspension as though the coldness of the air had frozen him and the surrounding scene into an eternal freeze-frame of internal pictorial delight.

'Come on mate,' said the guard, tapping him on the shoulder. 'Good thing I remembered your face or we would have left you here.'

Fitz got back on board. The carriage seemed to be fuller and he noted with dismay that two people sat in his previously unoccupied four-seated area. Making his way down to his own place, he excused himself as he crossed over in front of one of the newcomers to his window seat. As the train moved slowly away from Kaikoura Station heading south, it turned in an arc across the bridge whence Fitz could see down in the heart of the old township. To him it looked like a mini Atlantis, ancient and underwater, and all the coloured cars were different species of tropical fish, darting hither and thither through the empty, submerged buildings.

Feeling tense and nervous Fitz tried not to make eye contact with his new fellow passengers. He had hoped click clack Kowhai River click clack to be left alone and he felt the proximity of the two people to be intrusive. As the express picked up speed he noticed with some relief that they showed no desire to converse with him. Indeed they seemed totally self-absorbed. Fitz thought that perhaps they were a honeymooning couple, which would suit him down to the ground.

Fitz settled into a kind of daydream that incorporated the sunshine outside and the colours of the sky and water. Together these elements conspired to keep out the dark, disturbing aspects of his life which hovered around the edge of his consciousness. Whenever a suggestion of guilt or an evil thought threatened to permeate his soul, a sparkle of sunshine would dance around his mind and dissipate the threat of despair and blackness. The motion of the train clickety clack Ewelme Stream clickety clack lulled and soothed him, and even the southern small mirror image lakes Rotoiti and Rotorua, which threatened to re-surface his great-grandfather's ordeal in the buried village during the Tarawera eruption, couldn't break the clickety clack Kahutara River clickety clack spell of magical contentment.

The train entered a tunnel and Fitz fell asleep. He awoke again briefly at a sign which read Goose Bay. Fitz was conscious long enough to realise that the sign was one of the bordered railway signs which used to designate a railway station in the old days. The block semi-Gothic upper-case lettering seemed to capture a lost era in New Zealand, as opposed to the modern lower-case coloured Tranz Rail signs which are used nowadays. Fitz felt the vague, sleepy sense of something significant about the contrasting signs and, as he struggled against sleepiness to understand the metaphoric insight that appeared to be suggesting itself, sleep won out and he fell into that sweet void which builds life anew. Clickety clack Ote Makura Stream clickety clack, the train caroused on down the coastal strip, leaving the road which turned inland at Aoro.

Clickety clack Aoro River clickety clack the train became a canoe. As the levels of the lake rose and fell at once the canoe was stuck on the muddy floor, and all of a sudden the waters rose high above their normal levels so that the flax was sunk beneath the surface. The one-man train-canoe was then extended carrying at times two, then four, then up to thirteen passengers who each carried the head of a dog. Clickety clack Okarahia Stream clickety clack then reversing back the image returned to the bush railway track where the earth rumbled and crumbled and the sky was set alight reflecting the buried pink and white clickety clack cleverley turning inland the canoe train crosses the Conway River clickety clack, Hundalee roadway and down the other side of the valley clickety clack Open Creek clickety clack not far from the Greek, but it's clickety clack Waingaro Stream clickety clack waiting at the lights, know what I mean!

Still, the same scary monsters of Tarawera loomed up as the train raced into the late-afternoon landscape. The shadows were lengthening all down the line and the colours became starker. Out the window in a waking moment Fitz saw a collection of beehives in a paddock and the instant he closed his eyes he was back with his tipuna who was a young child, being pushed by pram away from the buried village of Wairoa. Even as a small boy his tipuna had understood the reason for the eruption of Papa had been because the tapu of Tamahoe had been broken. Where the atua had fallen the young men had taken honey from wild bees to their old chief Rangihehuwa, who lived at the foot of the Pink Terrace. And now, as the train canoe crossed clickety clack Leader River clickety clack, Fitz understood why bees never stung him: because his tipuna had refused the tapu-breaking honey.

One Tree Hill on the right of the train, poet's tree hill, Parnassus, on the other as the Delphi Express passes through the upturned U2 spy plain of North Canterbury, and with or without you the rhymes of the ancient marooned of antiquity are forever frozen in the same carriage seat, nearly but never touching as the echoes of Auckland volcanoes and chainsaws reverberate in soundless 'leave it to psmith and skeat' still life clawtitudes – take the Eh, boy! Train to the middle way tao and then is my advice! Then now the savage reminder of the Black Hole of Calculator new write by olde left brought Fitz to an eye-opening shudder with barely a 'do I wake or sleep!' The train clanked over a bridge clickety clack Waiau River clickety clack and Fitz remembered without ever having known, that it was indeed 'the bloody business of the deed, MacBeth' who had murdered sleep. Bugger! The first word is the deepest, as a baby I know.

Swampthing clickety clack over Swamp Stream clickety clack and the train is a train again, then the train in Spain pulls into the Mina Station at exactly 5.15 timetable time when the last train to Port Chalmers and the third last to Papakura used to leave, by jove I got it! A large sheep with short, thick wool waits to be Sean and indeed can be seen one naughtigal mile off – it's the blokes who are nervous round here!

By now the darkness was almost complete and Fitz could only see a thin, almost imperceptible golden line in the distance on the other side of the carriage where the sun had gone over the horizon.

As the train gathered momentum, having gone over the click clack Crystal Brook click clack the babbling of his fellow traversers had ceased and Fitz realised that they must have alighted up in smoke-free Cheviot. The train was now moving as if on the homeward run and the faster it went the slower and less frequent were Fitz's thoughts. Clickety clack Hurinui

River clickety clack unbeknownst to the dazed, dreaming Fitz the train passed the inland fish with the damaged breathing apparatus named after the quiet Beatle's hairdo, Arthur. Fitz's thoughtlessness amazed him, he was almost back to his old self! Click clack Omihi Creek click clack, the carriage lights were bright and cheerful as the train pulled in to Waipara Station.

Leaving at one after 6.06 come on baby don't be cold as ice with that upside-down number, Fitz had never felt cold like it as an icy blast blew in the carriage window which he shut click clack Waipara River click clack the train was now lolling, almost amberleying along with the certainty of homeward bounding clypt ticket for the destination, one knight stands as another night falls clickety clack Kowhai River clickety clack and although the landscape outside was as black as witch and could not be scene with the naked I, Fitz sensed that it was a very different place of colours and shapes than he had ever experienced before. The flat, river-crossed land with its unable-to-be-seen last late autumn colours and hill-country backdrop of the centre of Te Wai Pounamu was so different to the fish belly and waterlogged Te Ika, and the early snow on the foothills could be baringly glimpsed as a luminous darkness outside the whirring windows of the train clickety clack Stoney Creek clickety clack and Fitz was falling asleep again as the train went click clack Ashley River click clack and entered Rangiora. Only twenty-five minutes to Christchurch. Only one half an hour to the balm of non-travel as the diesel locomotive enters the full cranky revolutions of its inner sanctum followed by the liberal half-revolutions of the click clack Cam River click clack, weeeell ya know we all wanna change the worllleed.

One person got on the train at Rangiora even though it's normally a stop to set down passengers. He was a tall, angular-looking man with a Samuel Beckett skull mask and an Anglican church dog-collar. Much to Fitz's consternation this distinguished, elderly looking genitalman came and sat right opposite him in his four-seated area.

'Good evening,' said the mock-priest.

'Kia ora,' Fitz replied in an aloof tone, hoping the man would realise that he didn't feel like talking.

'Travelling far?' asked the other.

'I don't know,' answered Fitz almost inaudibly.

There was an awkward silence for a moment, but the newcomer seemed determined to converse. Clickety clack Cust River clickety clack, ' ... at the end of the journey,' he was saying, the first part of his sentence had been drowned out by the train crossing a bridge. As the train whisked through Kaiapoi the man said, 'Are you travelling tomorrow?'

'I'm leaving for Dunedin in the morning,' Fitz replied. He felt somehow defeated by his attempt to remain silent and decided to talk to the fellow seeing that there was only a quarter of an hour or so left before getting into Christchurch.

'Funny place, Dunedin,' mused the priest. 'Very strange. There are some odd spiritual aspects to the Edinburgh of the South – what makes you want to go there?'

Fitz explained about the dream he had had as the train thundered and rocked CLICKETY CLACK CLICKETY CLACK hurriedly across the lengthy Waimakariri River bridge CLICKETY CLACK CLICKETY CLACK and approached the outlying suburbs of the city.

The pastor pondered the Fitzdream. At length he said to his startled companion, 'Did you know that Dunedin is the one place in the world where the disturbed spirits of the murderers who perpetrated the most terrible crimes from the last great European war, World War Two, go to work out their karma.'

Fitz was speechless. The dream crossed the reality of his thoughts: while this wake-a-day world looked fine again outside the train window, inside the absurdity of an ancient Māori Hillkilljoyler, a wry-call to armies-belokwnees suburboon ban on that unkind of thing if there ever was, 'Ko Niutienis haharuru (the laughing owl, in all its wisdom) un-laleish the Ala lala boom te, eh, of the mind!'

But the priest proceeded, thus taking Fitz out of himself in a non-epileptic way, as they are wont to say. 'So it seems that many of the present-day population of this southern city are still imbued with the spiritual malaise left by these ghosts and ghouls. There is an existential undertow that needs some kind of reverse reality to counter the inherent evil of this situation.'

Fitz felt totally unnerved. All this bizarre talk about the city he was heading to when considered alongside his dreaming in full voice sangfreud, Oi, Oi!, sent his fancy reeling! (and you know what happens when fancy reeling!)

'What is needed in my opinion,' the priest continued, 'is the formation of a Gestalt Gestapo to go down to Dunedin and help the citizens of that beautiful city to rid them of a problem they don't even know they have!'

Fitz felt threatened and confused as the train blew its crazy whistle, heading towards another phantom-pregnant Irishtown Railway Station on the Coastal Pacific line.

On the platform at Belfast stood the Irish junkie, G. N. Morphy, who had spotted the train of thought coming a mile off clickety clack Styx River clickety clack, and Fitz saw from the window the lighted house boat waiting to take the souls of the dead to the underworld. In this world it's not a question of whether it begins or ends with bangs or whimpers, but who pays for the crossing ... the user. Obviously!

The Protestant priest leaned forward towards Fitz and said in an eerie tone, 'The artist Dürer predicted the Nazi era in Germany several centuries ago. He said of the German character, "Whosoever wants to build something insists on employing a new pattern the like of which has never been seen before." What the Nazi experience did was invert from creative to destructive these forces of striving for originality in everything. So all the images from the Third Reich amount to a kind of dark mirror of the Andachtsbilder art. These iconoclastic pictures of the suffering from the concentration camps are the opposite to what the devotional art of Dürer and his contemporaries strove for.'

The train was now deep in suburban Christchurch and the backyards of the houses were lit up from the kitchens and bedrooms. Fitz sat stunned and confused by this clergyman's revelations with their intensity and directness regarding his own recently discovered situation. It was certain that the priest was unaware of the conversation that Fitz had had on the *Aratere* but it was such a direct hit on the general area that Fitz couldn't but suspect a kind of metaphysical conspiracy. Like a pillbox for sentries on a faraway station on the Trans-Siberian Railway, the station at Addington, now Christchurch Central, stood waiting in the middle of an industrial wasteland to welcome the passengers from the world, headpieces filled with the straw of travel, to New Zealand's second-most-populous city.

The train pulled slowly into the station and Fitz got his bag down from the rack, wondering why there was no through service further south. When he turned back to look down the aisle he realised that his companion was no longer to be seen.

South
9
unlevel
crossings
2
6
tū te
nakohu
te tereina
3
HOKITIKA
PART 5
OAMARU
1
DUNEDIN
8
4
ki te Tonga
17

1

Patrick Fitzgerald arrived at the Addington Christchurch Railway Station early. He had had a sleepless night in the cheap hotel he had stayed at and he just wanted to get on the move. His lack of rest was due to the guest in the room next to him, a raving, crying drunkard who called himself a novelist and who was right off his nut on angst and alcohol. On his way to complain to the hotel's sergeant at arms, the night porter, Fitz had seen his noisy neighbour's door ajar. Looking in he saw a pathetic sight. There was a Māori-looking man in his early forties crouched over a desk at an old typewriter. A half-empty bottle of whiskey sat teetering on the desk's edge, and the whole room was lined from end to end with empty milk and juice cartons. A ghetto blaster wailed out the plaintive freedom anthems of Bob Marley and on the wall was a single poster of Che Guevara.

'Kia ora,' Fitz said, and the writer gave a paranoid start. 'I wonder would you mind turning the noise down a bit, both the music and yourself!'

'Ko wai koe, e te whakatoi pōrangi!' the man replied, standing up and turning on Fitz aggressively. The look in his eyes was both glazed and one of defiant challenge. When he stood up Fitz noticed that he was a lot bigger and more threatening than when he was hunched over his writing table. A tense, almost frightening period ensued until Fitz remembered his own behaviour at Yellban. He then decided to be conciliatory towards this strange individual, knowing it would mean giving up a much-needed night's sleep. Fitz told the man his name and then held out his hand as a gesture of friendship. Muttering to himself, 'Ko Te Arawa mangai nui, nei,' he finally took

Fitz's hand and shook it perfunctorily. He then gestured to Fitz to sit on a tiny stool next to his chair at the desk. 'Haere mai, e noho, e hoa, whakarongo mai!'

The man then launched into a tirade which lasted over two hours. He first told Fitz his name was Haki Maroke Kuha. As though he were some grey bearded loon, he held Fitz in his thrall. The language used was a mixture of Māori and English, both spoken imperfectly and in a circumlocutious manner, almost pretentious in its effect. Every now and then he would pour himself and Fitz a measure of whiskey into two crystal tumblers. The single bar heater burned with a low heat and the smell from the empty milk cartons, which had obviously remained unwashed, permeated the already foul and pestilent air.

The gist of what the man had to say was that he saw himself as the new Christ coming to save Aotearoa from spiritual, economic and social decay. The pile of disordered, yellowing, typewritten papers on his desk he referred to as his 'Manifesto for the New Write', and it began with the humble words, 'In the beginning were these words!' Fitz saw through a somewhat hazy blur engendered by tiredness, whiskey and medication the title on top of the first page of the manuscript 'Karawheta Ahau: He aha i riro ai hei Kairaukau Pakaru – Nā, Haki Maroke Kuha.'

As the train for Dunedin pulled into the platform Fitz remembered the final words of his friend the night before. 'Get out of here ya fucking big mouth cunt, I tell you I will build the New Jerusalem!' he had said as he drained the last drops from the whiskey bottle and fell backwards on to his small, dilapidated single cot. Fitz had then gone zombie-like to his own room, feeling the full effects of his drink, drugs and sleeplessness. He lay in a catatonic yet fully aware state until the first dawn rays invaded his darkness and took away his overstaying dreams. Now here he was about to embark on the next leg of his journey and he felt numb and indifferent to his dreams and his reality.

The platform was packed with early morning travellers and Fitz felt a certain distance between himself and his own body as he twisted the knob of the carriage door open. An internal unlevel crossing took place as he boarded the train. As he moved in a split second from outside to inside it was as though he had walked through a plate-glass window in slow motion and each of the fragments from the shattered glass had embedded in it a piece of his body and soul. Like crossing the invisible line from north to south, Fitz disappeared from the platform on to the train as though from life to death.

Fitz re-emerged alive and well in the aisle of the carriage of the Southerner. Where he had been in that split second of non-existence, that black-hole eternity of doubt, he neither knew nor cared. He was now fully reconstructed and looked around for his seat on the train. When he finally matched his ticket with the reality he saw that there was already someone sitting opposite his seat. Unlike his previous reaction the morning before when the two priests had sat too close for comfort, this morning Fitz felt glad of the prospect of the company of a fellow traveller.

As the train gathered momentum, travelling through the southern suburbs of Christchurch like a Hornby trainset through some child's unfamiliar bedroom, Fitz picked up the literature provided by the railroad company. He followed with his eyes the new and alien landscape he would be passing through. Unknown names like Rolleston and Studholm Junction and Goodwood and ... Goodwood. He remembered the long-ago song of a dream: this was the place he would first see her. But he had already enquired of the guard where the Southerners would make their unlevel crossings to exchange crew and cabin staff and he had been informed that they crossed at Merton. 'They haven't crossed at Goodwood for twenty-odd years mate,' the railwayman had added before moving on to help someone else with another irrelevant inquiry. Fitz had felt for a moment crestfallen. Were all these dreams to be unreal? Were they all to be lacking in substance, sent to mock and tease his very sanity and existence?

'Travelling far?' The words seeped into Fitz's reverie with a welcome infusion of reality.

'Dunedin,' he replied in the hope of a normal, non-controversial conversation as a foil to all the previous encounters thus far on this odyssey. By this time the train was rollicking through Burnham and the other fellow was saying ...

' ... going to see my folks. I'm not going very far, just to Ashburton, go down a couple of days a week. The old man's getting on, he's got a bad ticker, and Mum's just experiencing the first signs of Alzheimer's, keeps forgetting who she is and why she turned the oven on, things like that – could be dangerous, eh. But, I like going down on the train, eh, makes a change even though it's only a little over an hour's journey, you know ...'

Fitz looked at the perpetrator of the Kiwi soliloquy with a certain ironic admiration for such unaware solipsism. But seeing that he was in no particular mood for conversation, or traumatic revelation, or paranoid disembodiment, he let his good companion continue in his secular, unpriestly fashion ...

' ... Dun's sandal was placed over a certain indelicate spot as we stopped him in full whakapohane flight and we were all singing beautiful, beautiful brown eyes, we'll never love old blue eyes again! And Dun sang 'I Did it My Way', as we good-naturedly threw him in the paddy wagon. But it was during the 81 Springbok Tour that my police career reached both its pinnacle and its nadir. I was in the red squad and we were the first to use the long batons and shields and the German helmets ...'

Fitz suddenly experienced an overwhelming sensation, a change of perception which evoked a merging world of faint but unfathomable proportions. For a fragment of a second the train turned into a moving marae. As it thundered across a river bridge Fitz saw all the passengers sitting on mattresses on the carriage floor waiting for the pōwhiri and the whaikōrero with the ghost of old Māori railway station names arranged in geographical ranks, the first of which was now being experienced karikiti kiraki te kēhua o te Teihana Rerewe o Rakaia karikiti kiraki … .

Fitz shook himself in disbelief as the carriage interior changed back to its normal seating arrangement. This latest unlevel crossing, with its cultural and personal implications, had him really bedazzled. As the train tumbled through Chertsey dud and repeat, dud and repeat, Toby or not Toby on a tractor seat, woooowoooo motion, Fitz decided to tune in again to his police-academy graduate friend who was still reliving the 1981 Tour de Farce for Muldoon's re-election. ' … at Hamilton. That was the defining moment, when the protesters stormed on to the park and as the flares and spears shone we were vilified by the rugby fans as much as we were by the other mob …'

'It must have been quite frightening,' said Fitz, remembering the TV and newspaper images.

'It was. Although for me the issues were a lot more clear-cut than what we had to deal with at Bastion Point – that was a real awful thing to be part of. The way we had to remove all those people: women, children and, worst of all, the old ones – and from their own land! Terrible! Makes you feel like a real heartless bastard, almost inhuman. That was the first time I had any misgivings about my career.'

The man sat in thought and Fitz too found he had memories he had forgotten. He said to the man opposite, 'I remember one of the younger fellas in the factory where I worked coming in after a big demonstration during the 81 Springbok thing full of excitement. He said he had been with the ones who had tipped over and set fire to an undercover police car on the weekend. It was on the front page of the *Herald* that Monday morning. We all razzed him in the smoko room, but even though most of us had no interest in politics there was an underlying admiration for him, even though he'd really only done it as a gang prospect rather than a political act as such. There was a lot of disenchantment amongst ...' Fitz stopped in full flight when he realised the train had pulled into the Ashburton Station and his friend was standing up and getting down his bag from the overhead luggage rack.

'Good to meet ya mate, hope you have a good journey!' the fellow said, shaking Fitz's hand and heading for the exit. Fitz stood up and stretched his limbs. He walked down the carriage and surveyed the platform from the door of the train.

2

An announcement came over the train's intercom system that there would be a delay of approximately twenty minutes. A goods train had broken down further south and a new engine had been sent to bring it in. Fitz walked along the platform of the Ashburton Station, thinking how low and long the roof of the building was. Inside the station were a few of the private local businesses which had become common in many of the remaining stations throughout Aotearoa which was the aftermath of Prebble's 'Save the Rail' campaign of the mid-eighties. Fitz looked across the main tracks to the desolate scene: once-busy, bustling railyards where the empty lines lay unused and rusting now.

The call over the intercom had reminded passengers who wanted to stretch their legs not to leave the vicinity of the station. Fitz wandered from one end of the platform to the other and then went around to the front of the building to take a look at the township itself. With one eye on the station clock and checking to see if there was any sign of the stricken freight train, he decided that it wouldn't hurt to walk into the main street for a few minutes. The first thing he noticed was the wide openness of the main street – so different to most of the towns of Te Ika a Māui. Crossing the grassed area he made his way over the road and on to the footpath of the main shopping area. People seemed to look at him with a certain amount of suspicion and he noticed that they all dressed quite differently to himself. There seemed to be no Māori- or Polynesian-looking people in this place. Fitz went into a coffee bar which was just over the road from the railway crossing south of the station. From here he could see when the goods train arrived and he would be able to dash across the road in time to get back on the Southerner before it left. The place was almost full with people meeting friends for an early morning tea. Fitz went to the counter and ordered a black coffee and a date scone. The person serving appeared to be somewhat reluctant to be either courteous or efficient towards him, and as he said 'Thank you,' and picked up his tray he was answered with a begrudging grunt and saw a kind of knowing sneer on the face of the woman who had given him his order.

Feeling insulted and somewhat bemused by his treatment Fitz struggled through the crowded café. He wanted a seat near the window so he could keep an eye on the train and he came to one which had only one person sitting there. All the others were full and he got such an unfriendly feeling from most of the occupants that he felt he could not approach them anyway.

'Mind if I join you?' Fitz asked the elderly lady who sat at the table.

'No, of course not. In fact I've been expecting you. It's a good thing your train was delayed or else I might have had to come for a ride to Timaru and back. My name is Marie Murdock by the way,' the woman said, holding out her hand in friendship. 'Don't be surprised, I won't eat you!' said Marie. 'Herr Frisch and his chauffeur called by last night and told me to make sure your journey was proceeding correctly. Herr Frisch told me he'd seen you on the boat from Wellington and I was most intrigued. We've been wanting to meet you for many years.'

Fitz sipped his coffee in a daze of surprise and incomprehension. As the old lady talked on he barely registered what was being said to him. She was telling him how his father had helped her escape Berlin in 1943.

'Mind you, he wasn't always the good man he later became. He was a Nazi fanatic for many years in the early days. Up until he had some sort of vision he was an ambitious SS man, which is why later on he could do what he did – he was one of Himmler's favourites, you know. But Hilda knows the full story. You go and see her when you get to Dunedin.' She handed him an envelope and told him to open it when he got on the train. She went on talking about her life in New Zealand since she arrived in the early forties. She had married into a local landed family who had done well because of some early trickery at the expense of the Māori people in the region. In recent times this had begun to work against them and ... Fitz looked out towards the railway crossing and saw the barrier arms coming down and the light from the engine of the goods train coming into the loop, with the crippled engine and the rest of the wagons following. The train whistle sounded and Fitz stood up from his seat.

'I must go or I'll miss the train. Don't get up,' he said and held out his hand to the delicate old woman's clasp.

'Goodbye dear,' the old one said, 'I owe my life to your father and it has been a really great thing seeing you. By the way, don't feel too upset about the reception from the people here. I was here for twenty years before they took me into the fold. You better run now – give my love to Hilda.'

Fitz walked out of the door of the café. He turned and waved a last goodbye before crossing East Street to the station. Boarding the train he returned to his seat just as the Southerner's whistle blew. As the train pulled clickety clack out and gathered speed through Tinwald Fitz looked around to see if anyone had replaced the cop in the seat opposite. He felt good because no one had and he opened the envelope slowly. He gave an almost audible gasp of surprise. Inside the envelope he found two thousand dollars in fifty dollar notes. When he had recovered from the initial shock of finding the money he also noticed a piece of paper which read 'Hilda Burstein, Flat 1, 113 London Street, Dunedin.' Also in the envelope Fitz found an Iron Cross and two SS lightning stripes and a smaller hand written note saying, 'I loved your father in younger days – he gave me these when I left Germany – M.M.'

As the train rattled through Hinds Fitz felt the inner turmoil of his thoughts almost equal the juxtaposed reality of the temporal world of the events and people he had met since leaving Auckland, as though the inner and outer worlds were beginning to marry.

3

Looking out of the window of the carriage Fitz caught sight for the first time of the faraway beauty and grandeur of the Southern Alps. The snowy peaks and sheer height of these mountains were unlike anything he had experienced before and for a while he was lost in the otherworldliness of the physical world. With the motion of the train adding to his reverie he began almost to levitate in a slow orgasmic consciousness rarely achieved in this day and age of perpetual emotion and stimulation. Fitz was in a trance-like, semi-spiritual realm of nirvanic completeness and he relished the experience. There were lowering, dark clouds to the south as the train went karikiti kiraki Rangitata and swung south-east towards the coast, past the turn-off to Geraldine, coal black as a raven. The coastal cloud began to enshroud the train as it passed karikiti kiraki Orari and on down through karikiti kiraki Temuka. Fitz felt like he was carrying an ancient sacred fire to defeat some spiritual enemy which was struggling for possession of his soul through the undermining of his mind by dreams and visions which would drive his passions of te umu kaha o te aroha, as though he was mākutu and thus himself magical also.

Karikiti kiraki Arowhenua, the place of te poka o te whaea of the wahine moemoea aroha whose urupā could almost be seen from the train, and it was also the place where the whenua o te tama was buried across the river. Fitz felt a strong pull from the past and from the future, the women and the children of his life, and as he looked around he saw that the carriage had again turned into a marae as the train passed through the place of birth and death, te mamae me te aroha i tēnei wā, nō reira.

'E ngā mana o te rerewe, e ngā reo o te tereina, e ngā hau e whā o ngā pāhīhī, tēnā koutou, tēnā koutou, tēnā koutou katoa.' A man with a tokotoko was welcoming everybody from the many places of the world to this railway journey. He pointed out the place where lesbians bathe near the shade of a cabbage tree. 'In the shadow of sweet Caroline Bay,' he said as the Southerner curved around beneath the embankment leading into karikiti kiraki Timaru Station, whence Fitz could see through the train's window the tall, round petrol-storage tanks in the industrial wharf from the top of which the town looked like a surreal Mediterranean montage with the snowcapped mountains of the Alps far in the distance, in the late morning sun.

It was just after a quarter to eleven in the morning when the train left Timaru, almost half an hour late. Gathering momentum quickly, as though trying to make a defensive gesture to critics of rail travel by defiantly making up the lost time, the train was bolting along by the time it went through karikiti kiraki Pareora. The desolate sands and the crashing breakers heightened the karanga which welcomed the new passengers to the train. The wero was a bit constrained because of the lack of space traditionally needed to lay the challenge in front of the manuhiri, but once the evil spirits had been sent packing by the pōwhiri everyone was feeling relaxed and happy on this marae o te rerewe – karikiti kiraki Makikihi, and the sound of the contented voices of the travellers was like an expectant murmuring of the branch of a river as everyone waited for the mihi and the whaikōrero to continue.

KARIKITI KIRAKI Waitaki KARIKITI KIRAKI. As the train thundered across the longest rail bridge in Te Wai Pounamu denoting the borderlands of Otago, a waiata could be heard rising above the din of the machinery from one of the 'songbirds', the women, who was singing a lament for the once-pure waters now polluted by industrial and agricultural waste. The speeches continued with a kaumātua talking about the fact that much of the railway land was given to the country by Māori only on the condition that trains, even the great express trains, would have to stop even at the smallest country stations if a Māori from the local iwi wanted to get on. He spoke of how far from the original spirit of things the Pākehā government had gone.

The speaker reminded the assembled that this marae train was being sent to address that by only recognising the ghost stations with Māori names between Ashburton and Palmerston.

As the train raced through karikiti kiraki Pukeuri he held aloft a piece of black stone fashioned in the shape of a crucifix and asked the assembled to join him in a prayer to the Lord that some day the railway stations would be returned to the official Tranz Rail Timetables as in the Tiriti.

With the whole train resounding to the music of a waiata tapu, the Southerner entered the outskirts of the township of Oamaru. Fitz had been so overwhelmed by being a part of this amazing journey that he had forgotten all about his own particular sorrows and confusions. Being on this fantastic voyage, whether it turned to erosion or not, had lifted his wairua so much that he found himself singing along to these hymns to the silence fully in tune, despite the fact that he'd been told by the nuns at an early age that he couldn't sing. He remembered reading somewhere that the Chinese word for music translated as 'enthusiasm for life' and it was this 'ngakau whakapuke mō te ora', it was this feeling that was the basis for his following the dream he had of the woman, because it was exactly that emotion which she engendered in him; and for a moment she stood there beside him, singing. He felt a lust for life which he had seldom had in his twenty years of factory routine, which had been more like hypnotising chickens! Even the food of a diety of apple only eve and God knows what, made him feel close to her as the train pulled karikiti kiraki into Oamaru Station, and made his quest seem even more sacred, as though of honeydew he had fed.

For a while the train resumed its normal seating arrangements and Fitz sat in the empty seat on the left side of the carriage looking out at the sea across the largely abandoned Oamaru railyards. As the train pulled out the guard announced that on the last stretch the train had made up five minutes and was now only twenty minutes behind schedule. He added, 'The fact that we are late will be good news for one of our passengers, because we now won't be crossing the northbound train at Merton, but at Goodwood where our crew will swap over.'

At first the words washed over Fitz and he didn't comprehend what the train manager had said. He had been looking out the window as the train clanked over the curved rail bridge to the south of the town. Engrossed in the marvel of the olde historic whitestone precinct which had in recent years been lovingly restored, he was watching a man riding a penny-farthing bicycle dressed in a three-piece suit, with a fob watch and a top hat, as if to say I am not a number I am a free lunatic, and the news that the Southerners would cross over at Goodwood only slowly penetrated his consciousness. As the train made its way up the hill through the city's botanical garden region and on into the southern suburbs, Fitz suddenly felt a tormented hope, and pleasure, and a wild expectation. In a little over an hour he would know if his dream had any substance and his thoughts, fed by the sweet waters of remembrance of dreams past sent his mind and feelings reeling, tumbling into a tailspin of fear and delight, as though from the lodge of Deborah! Karikiti kiraki Waireka, the tereina now began its long and winding railroad to Dunedin after its straight-line run through Canterbury.

The marae train was back on track karikiti kiraki clickety clack like a tall, lean tōtara whose station had just been crossed, a man was giving another whaikōrero in which he expressed his sadness that the haerenga would soon end for the tereina o te marae. Then, pointing his tokotoko at Fitz, he said that as one journey ends so another begins. He intimated that Fitz had been chosen to come south to rid the area of a terrible curse, and guided by the spirit of aroha he would cleanse the darkness and bring evil to him who thinks evil. Karikiti kiraki Maheno, the unfastening of the rock-island line of dreams was beginning to send Fitz spinning inside and out! And as the stream of words and images karikiti kiraki Waimotu went by his Koni Atu Island of the mind he found that the very rock on which his ideas were founded was floundering and almost swept away.

'He mōhio takewe! Hei koni atu te hinengaro, nō reira!' The speaker was up close to Fitz now. 'Haere atu ki te wairua kino! He toiora ki a koe, e tama! Kia ora ki a koe, kei te rapu i te aroha, nō reira!' As the train rumbled down the valley south of Moeraki, where adze boulders love sleeping in the sun as cats do, and no road moves but goes west of the border in bolder times, the speaker points karikiti kiraki Kartigi Katiki, to the poupou which adorn the top of the carriage walls and as he speaks a waiata springs up from the people, encouraged by his words ...

like an omen
an albino ruru which fans
its pure white wings wide-
open as far as they will

... Fitz felt elevated, and the heady mixture of the song and the sight of the sea and the sand and water and road which lay well below this stretch of railway incited in his feelings and thoughts the overpouring of natural sensations, beyond the ordinary, yet born out of it more than words are worth. As the waiata continued he had a very distinct sense of déjà vu coupled with a portent of the future.

one thousand miles
is not a long distance
for dreams to travel

chorus   he moemoea haerenga nei

dreams have been known
to circumnavigate the earth

and even blast off into outer space

chorus he moemoea haerenga nei

rā huritau
ki a Aroha tāu
takoto iho ki taku moenga

chorus he moemoea haerenga nei

me he ika au ki a koe, auē, auē, awatu
ki a Riro i He nei
e muri ahiahi
ka hara mai te aroha

chorus he moemoea haerenga nei

he moemoea haerenga nei
hi auē hi!

As the Southerner rounded in a long, slow semi-circular motion the foot of Puketapu, Fitz looked up at the summit which dominates the local landscape and saw the famous cairn atop the hill. All the people of the marae train were beginning their hariru and hongi with the people who would continue the journey further south. Fitz realised that the song which had just been sung, and which had turned the whole train into a movement of music and magic and aroha, had been the poroporoaki of the travelling tangata whenua o te rerewe. Fitz was laughing and crying, he had never before felt so much at home in the company of others. Even the slow, grinding comradeship of his fellow factory workers had not engendered such closeness although he had known them for so long. That had been more the shared sorrow of forced capitalist labour, whereas this had the excitement and the elevation of the spiritual realm so often neglected in today's dialectically materialist society. As the train pulled into Palmerston Station the man who had spoken the final whaikōrero and initiated the waiata came over to Fitz. Holding out his hand in friendship he gave Fitz a hongi and said to him, 'E hoa, you have been entrusted with a great mission. Your dreams have brought you here for a reason, and the woman who came to you will help you fulfil this destiny. A great sadness has come to this part of Te Wai Pounamu and, despite the economic and social advances of our people, the spiritual malaise and darkness remains.'

He handed Fitz the black greenstone crucifix, which had been held aloft by the first speaker just north of Oamaru, and said that this would protect him in his future struggles.

'But you must find this wahine moemoea and work together. The pounamu will help you as it is of an ancient wairua fashioned into a Christian symbol, and both are for the overpowering of evil. Haere atu ki tō mahi, haere, haere.' The koroheke got down on to the low platform. He shook Fitz's hand one last time and said, 'One clue is that she was born in this town.' Then he crossed the road in the direction of the Pig Root and when Fitz looked away along the railway line which curved with the shape of the platform and back again, the kaumātua and all the other people from the marae train had disappeared. Fitz got back into the carriage, which had returned to its normal seating arrangements. All the carvings and mattresses had gone. The marae ātea had been replaced by the buffet section of the carriage. Fitz gained his seat exhausted and incredulous. Everything looked so normal and undisturbed. He tried to distract his thoughts by looking out of the window. A tereina utanga sat waiting in the loop beside the Southerner for the green signal north. Made up mainly of flat-deck container wagons with a few of the old box style wagons towards the back of the train, it provided Fitz with a bit of visual interest until his own train began to move.

The marae train, whose name was Tū Te Makohu from Kāti Mamoe, echoed in Fitz's consciousness so that the Southerner made the sound of te tū te tū, te tū te tū, riding slowly over the individual sleepers as it pulled out of Palmerston. Fitz was so tired now that in a short time he fell asleep.

4

Fitz woke with a start! The train had stopped and the low sound of the stationary diesel engine seemed to be twice as loud as normal. In a panic of realisation he saw that the northbound Southerner had already pulled alongside his own train. Looking out of the window he saw the sign designating the GOODWOOD railway loop where a station once stood. The train must have been there several minutes and when the northbound one blew its whistle he realised that it was about to leave. He ran to the door at the end of the carriage and opened it to try and get a better look at the people in the other train. Putting his head out he saw up the track that the northern lights had turned green, and as the northbound Southerner began to slowly pull forward he caught a glimpse of her from the doorway of his southbound carriage.

Waving and yelling like a mad thing Fitz tried to catch her eye and it was just as the moving window began to become a blur that the woman in the other train saw Fitz trying to attract her attention and waved in time for him to realise that she had seen him too! As his own train began its first heavy, jerky movements forward and both trains gathered momentum in opposite directions Fitz felt an ever-rising sense of exhilaration matched in intensity only by his feeling of confusion and stupidity. Almost every detail which had happened in the dream had now really happened, that much was true. Fitz had lived and relived that dream so many times that he knew that what had happened was a true replica of the dream-event.

But how could this be? Surely that woman was someone responding involuntarily to the antics of a stranger on another train, as a child waves to an engine driver when a train goes over a level crossing. His train had by now pulled out of the loop and was rocking along the main line. He felt the movement gently mocking his inner turmoil, the side-to-side motion resembling the cocktail of images and emotions he was experiencing. Now the train was climbing into a steep struggle uphill towards the Tumai Overbridge.

Fitz seemed to become disembodied yet simultaneously grounded at this unlevel crossing. The train itself appeared detached, almost floating above the rails as it now sped downhill, passing through the township of Waikouaiti, past the swampy ponds, towards the Merton Bridge over which it made a cascade of noise, its whole being shaking, the wooden piles and stays beneath stretched to their fullest by the weight and sway of the vehicle.

Then, as Tū Te Makohu made his way following the ancient Māori pathway which curves in a long arc up towards the sky at Puketeraki and through the rest of coastal Otago, Fitz had another sensation of dream recognition. The heavy chugging echo of the diesel engine reverberated around the early afternoon hills as the Southerner made its way through the cutting just south of the railway crossing towards the steep, winding cliffs. The deep, steady shaking sounds sent him into dream memory. Looking out the window as the train rounded the frog-pond at O'Connell's farm, he knew that underneath the blanket of afternoon mist which had set in, lay Parimoana, the place he had dreamed of, his tūrangawaewae o te moehewa. As the train passed through the small village, which off to the left looked as though Heathcliff might appear at any moment, Fitz felt the sea and the sky and the land separating into their own distinct forms beneath the cloak of grey darkness which now made them appear as one. This eerie early afternoon twilight town whose maunga, Mount Charlotte, lay shrouded in the mysterious mist of his dreams, welcomed Fitz as one of its own.

The barrier arms lifted as the train passed the crossing south of Parimoana and went in a downward semi-spiral movement through Omimi and on through the seaside resort of Warrington. Fitz looked out blankly at Blueskin Bay which was below the low cloud and mist cover. There was even a long sliver of light shining out towards Doctor's Point as the train rocked and rolled loudly across the Evansdale Bridge and headed past the salmon farm through to Waitati. Fitz felt a heady mix of this beautiful landscape intermingle with the fusion of his double fantasy dream realism. Within the space of half an hour he had seen both his dream of her and his dream of the place transformed into palpable experience. And while these verifications had amounted to little more than rail surrealism, like a scene from an O'Shea movie which validated the underlying nature of this weird Aotearoa country, it had actually happened!

The train was making its way through the backyards of cribs and bush as it wound upwards through Michies Crossing and into the little pine plantation before its breathtaking uphill hillside ascent, where the line is so high above and so close to the sheer drop to the sea before entering the Cliffs Tunnel and safety. The Southerner now followed a long, curving line past The Gums and on around in a broad semi-circular sweep through Purakanui. From the idea to the incident, from the dreaming to the technofunkolour magic Nazism of Gerigarcia Borges plucked directly from the exile's years in South American jungles. From his father to his mother, from twenty years of factorial labour to two months' dissolution of the marriage of heathen and hell, and now the reality of a train rushing headlong into the bishop's mitre hat tunnel plunged into Mihiwaka darkness.

Busting out into sunshine and wet, dripping ferns and fronds of the bush above Deborah Bay, the train seemed almost eager to get on with its southern journey after all the twists and turns of the Coastal Otago line. South of Dunedin the landscape would flatten and the lines would straighten into Southland. The optimism of the train and the sunny winter weather which manifested itself on the south side of the Mihiwaka Tunnel infused Fitz with a less introspective outlook. He decided to just look out of the window and enjoy the new landscape which he had never before experienced.

Coming out of the Carey's Bay Tunnel Fitz reflected on the beauty of that bay with its colourful and quaint fishing fleet. A new sight caught his eye as the beauty of the stonework on the Iona Church, perched high above the Port Chalmers township, made a striking contrast to the modern utility of the container wharf. One monument to God and one to Mammon, Fitz thought. Port Chalmers itself looked from the train like a scene from one of those movies set in Wales or the West of Ireland, and as the train clanked over the concrete road bridge and down into Sawyer's Bay, Fitz had the idea that he might actually be in some sort of strange movie and he laughed softly at the thought.

Hurtling out of the tunnel at the south end of Sawyer's Bay Station the train went out on a causeway of its own with the road curving away to the right so that the train was alone out in the middle of the water of the Otago Harbour. Fitz noticed the ancient dredge that was employed to lessen the silt in the narrow shipping lane which led from Port Chalmers to the other port at Dunedin City. The water was choppy and seemed to change colour from emerald green to black and blue as the clouds whipped the wind along the skyline. But the train was making up lost time clickety clack, the train was making up lost time clickety clack, and the strange female forms which comprise the Otago Peninsula across the other side of the harbour appeared fleeting and elusive.

Passing through St Leonards the train rejoined the roadway and the land again, hugging closely to the side of the sombre hills which lead into Ravensbourne. The yellow dust of the fertiliser works piled high in large bins gave a surreal industrio-art feel against the hill, itself half quarried away. Fitz caught sight of the large oil tank installations as the rowers from the local rowing club pulled back the water with their oars. The train went over the Water of Leith river bridge which at this point is more like a concrete open sewer than the beautiful babbling brook it is further towards its source. However, Fitz liked the giant concrete slipway. It evoked images of an earlier, less abstract age in that it had a certain hard-nosed honesty about its demeanour.

The Southerner was now surrounded by old houses and rundown industrial buildings as it slowed down for its approach to Dunedin Station. Pulling into the platform at 2.11 p.m., over ten minutes late, but having made up more than ten minutes' lost time on the journey from Ashburton, the announcement over the station's loudspeaker said that the train would be leaving for Invercargill at 2.15 p.m. Fitz gathered his possessions and stepped down into the cold crisp air of a Dunedin afternoon. To him the station seemed a magical place with its beautiful bluestone outer walls and its tiled concourse with the stained glass windows of the Blessed Virgin train. He was lost in its majesty and intricacy of design which had kept much of the original feel, even though it had been recently turned into a middle-class glass menagerie and a sports museum. There were many people rushing hither and thither and Fitz became quite disorientated after all his travel and strange experiences. He accidentally bumped into a man who seemed to be waiting for someone. Fitz apologised and was about to move out through the main doors into Anzac Square, when he looked again at this man who appeared to be looking back at him with a gesture of recognition.

9
the
2
sow
of
PART 6
3
hades
5
1
8
unlevel
crossings
4
17

1

Patrick Mika Fitzgerald and Paul Te Ariki Calvert walked through the dark streets of a late-afternoon winter, turning briskly into George Street. Looking north towards Mount Cargill, which had now almost disappeared beneath the snow-laden clouds, the spire of Knox Church appeared as a beacon pointing to their destination. Fitz had now been in Otago for over a month and was living out at Parimoana, the place he had seen from the train window and had recognised as the location from his dreams. Things had moved quickly since his arrival in the south and as time passed his mission was becoming more and more urgent. The one thing he was finding both elusive and frustrating was that he had not yet met the woman he had dreamed, the woman on the north-bound Southerner, the woman whom the kaumātua had signalled would be necessary to fulfil his destiny.

Turning into London Street at the intersection where it meets Pitt Street and the main street, Calvert and Fitz ascended the steep, winding road. The footpath surface was beginning to ice over. Snow began falling lightly again, and the austere beauty of the city underneath its white blanket filled Fitz with a sense of wonder. Pulling from his pocket the piece of paper which had been given to him by Mrs Murdock in Ashburton, he looked at the address of Hilda Burstein, checked it and said to his companion, 'Not far now, e hoa.'

'Look out!' Calvert yelled as a slipping, sliding car headed down the road and over on to the pathway for pedestrians, coming to rest as it hit a fence post only metres away from where the two friends were walking. 'Boy, that was close!' Calvert said. Fitz nodded in agreement. Both men went over to see if they could assist the driver. It appeared that the impact had knocked him out, for he was slumped over the steering wheel.

However, what Fitz and Calvert found when they got to the car and opened the door was even more chilling than the air outside in the Dunedin streets. The man in the car Paul recognised as a kaumātua of the local rūnanga. He was well known for his outspoken opposition to the skinhead neo-nazi groups which had sprung up in this part of the country in recent years. When the wharepuni of one of the city's marae had been burned down a few months before and racist slogans and swastikas painted on an adjacent wall, Hemi Te Kaha O'Sullivan had been very vocal in calling these people to account and to justice. Now here he was with a knife in his back, dead at the wheel of his car. Further up the road Fitz saw two shadows disappear around the corner in the direction from which Te Hemi's car had come, but because of the conditions underfoot it was useless to try and chase them.

Calvert chanted slowly a short karakia and Fitz crossed himself with the greenstone crucifix, offering up a short prayer for the spirit of the dead man. Calvert pulled out his cellphone and made an anonymous call to the police station, telling the details of their find in as few words as possible. Quickly both men attempted to eliminate any fingerprints or other things which would lead the police to their whereabouts. It was snowing quite heavily now so footprints they might have left would be covered over by the time the police got there. Both men looked back one more time as they entered Hilda Burstein's gate a few hundred yards away from the crashed vehicle. As Hilda opened the door to them they could hear the wail of the police sirens making their way slipping and sliding on the ice towards the scene of the murder.

2

Fitz had met Calvert a few days after arriving in Dunedin. They were standing in line in a coffee-bar queue in the Octagon and Fitz felt a stranger staring at him. When he turned around to see what the purpose of this gaze was, Calvert said, 'I remember you. You're the one who bumped into me at the railway station.'

'Sorry,' Fitz said. 'I –'

'No, don't apologise,' Calvert said. 'It was partly my fault. I was watching you. I thought I knew you somehow. Anyway, would you like to join me?'

That afternoon they ended up sitting in the downstairs coffee bar for several hours. They talked and listened to each other and consumed endless cups of coffee. Fitz told Paul about his life in the factory in Auckland and his mother's death. He told him of his extraordinary journey and all the strange adventures of the mind and in reality which had accompanied his recent travel. He could see Calvert becoming more and more interested, as though he was somehow personally involved in this story of Patrick Fitzgerald, who up to now had been a perfect stranger.

Calvert seemed particularly absorbed in that aspect of Fitz's story involving the man on the *Aratere*. He listened intently, nodding almost knowingly at various points of reference. Finally he asked Fitz, 'Did this Herr Frisch mention a man named von Klagen?' When Fitz, who had to think about it for a while, did remember that the man had talked about a von Klagen who had been shot in Auckland's Aotea Square in the 1980s, and who had been somehow related to von Klages, a Berlin poet friend of Karl Wolfskehl, Calvert seemed overwhelmed. He went white in the face and fell silent for several minutes.

'Von Klagen was my father,' Calvert said almost inaudibly. 'I was there beside him when he was shot. It was the first time I'd ever met him.' Both men sat quietly, realising the enormity of their common bond. The tragic fascism of the sins of their fathers split their inner and outer worlds. The guilt and despair of their fragmented souls fought for possession of them. A parade of deathly images and bestiality polluted their vision and, as if at once, they both felt the pull of darkness upon their immortality.

'Where are you staying?' Calvert eventually broke the mood with a practicality.

'At the Leviathan Hotel along the road,' Fitz said, 'but I want to get out to Parimoana. I dreamt about a place like it once, and when I saw Parimoana from the train the other day I was sure that it was the place in my dream.'

'Well come and stay in my flat in London Street tonight.' Calvert said. 'My wife is away up north at the moment seeing her whānau, and our daughter is staying with a friend. Tomorrow we'll drive out to the coast and see what's what.' They both got up and walked back along Dunedin's main street, Fitz looking around at everything that was so new to him. They talked well into the night and their kōrero was only interrupted when Calvert's wife rang to see how he was.

Calvert had some work to do at the university the following morning so it was mid-afternoon before he and Fitz headed out through Pine Hill and on to the northern motorway. Dark clouds had been gathering all morning and by the time they hit the road Dunedin and the surrounding hill suburbs were almost covered in black, thick formations of foam-like substance. As the car rose above the city and on to the motorway proper Fitz turned around and looked back on the dramatic Gothic scene and asked his friend to pull over to the nearest shoulder of the roadside.

With a perfect view over the city the two saw the most extraordinary event. The sky was now so dark that it resembled night, except for several large rays of pale light descending golden, elongated and diffused throughout the lower regions of the sky towards the southern suburbs. Reaching skywards the many church spires of the Edinburgh of the South went up as though to greet this lowering apocalyptic cloud bank, which sank slower and slower like a large zeppelin docking. However the further down it sank in the sky the more closely it revealed its true incarnation. With ever-increasing clarity the two friends were witnessing something truly horrific. 'The Sow of Hades,' whispered Calvert hoarsely. He turned to Fitz with a terrified look on his countenance. 'The Sow of Hades ...' he repeated, and Fitz looked away from his friend and back towards the apparition.

By now the cloud formation was so low and the sky so dark that the city of Dunedin had almost disappeared. As Fitz looked closer he could see the manifestation of a gigantic female pig whose heavily laden teats touched the rooftops of the Dunedin buildings. She looked like she was suckling the city, feeding it a heady brew which would poison the very air. The sight was so real that Calvert had to take Fitz's arm to prevent himself from faltering.

Within a few moments the wind came up and the cloud patterns changed. Fitz and Calvert got back in the car and continued the journey without saying a word. Their surreal feeling of the day intensified when the motorway entered into a forested area reminiscent of postcards from Germany. Both men felt the heavy pleasure of memories of their Nazi fathers, adding to the already strange atmospheric and landscape conditions. Looking north from the highest point of the road at Pidgeon Flat, the clouds had lowered, and it looked as though snow would fall as soon as the wind dropped. Leaving the

Kilmog Road at Evansdale, Fitz had the feeling that he was time-travelling backwards by car, not train this time. As the winding, twisting coast road made its way up and down the terrain in a series of unlevel crossings he remembered his recent train-trip entry into this landscape a few days before.

By the time they got to Parimoana it had begun to snow and the darkness was almost complete. Turning into Russell Road Calvert gave out a stifled curse as he realised his friends weren't at home. But he knew where the key was kept so they let themselves in. They spent half an hour or so chopping wood for a fire and by the time they sat down for a cup of tea the snow was falling heavily.

'We won't be going anywhere tonight,' said Calvert. The warmth from the fire was now beginning to be felt and they opened the bottle of whiskey they had bought at Evansdale. As the fire burned they heard the mournful call of an evening goods train going through the village below, blowing its whistle in a train's lonesome blues fashion, and the night enclosed them.

At length Fitz inquired, 'What was that Sow of Hades business?'

Calvert took a deep drink of whiskey and said, 'It's something which is tied in with your gift of dreams. In many ways the Sow of Hades is part of our joint destiny. When I first came south, after my father had been shot, I was in a similar position to you. Hine and I had just been married and we had a child. We had originally gone to Wellington, but, like you, I had been plagued by dreams for many years. Knowing my father had been an SS officer meant that some of my dreams began to make sense. However in some respects it left more questions than answers. I began to research the Nazi mythology and it became quite scary. After a few years I was able to apply for a job at Otago University as a junior lecturer because of my knowledge of the esoteric occult. Anyway, to cut a long story short I found out about things that were happening down here which were really quite strange. And the Sow of Hades is one of those northern hemisphere apparitions so pregnant with meaning and menace that it really makes me feel afraid, something which doesn't happen often.'

At this point Calvert stopped for a while and just stared into the now brightly burning fire. Fitz leaned over and poured them both another drink and the liquid mirrored the feeling of heat and danger both of them were feeling from the fire and the talk. Fitz stood up and went outside for a mimi. The snow was now falling heavily and the whole nightscape was covered in white, only met in intensity by the blackness of the sky. Fitz was held as if in a spell. Not caring how cold it was he stood out on the edge of the pathway, looking in the direction of the sea which he could hear breaking over the rocks at the bottom of the cliffs down past the village. The snowflakes were large and fell heavily on to his big black overcoat.

'You OK?' Fitz heard Calvert's voice calling as it broke through the enchantment in which the darkness and the snow held him. Reluctantly he made his way back inside. 'I had an idea while you were out there,' said Calvert. 'The people who live here have a small hut out the back of the property. I'll ask them if they will let you stay there in exchange for a little work around the place. At least that will be one of your dreams come true. You haven't told me about the other aspects of your dreams yet – are they that bad?'

Fitz had so far avoided talking about the woman, partly because he didn't want Calvert to think how stupid it sounded. How could you explain the thing at Goodwood, for example? But there was something else which held him back, something instinctive, mysterious and slightly unnerving which Fitz didn't understand, and yet it was real. He shrugged it off by pouring another drink and saying, 'So is this pig, it sounds so absurd when you call it the pig from hell, doesn't it? Is this uwha poaka o rarohenga some sort of harbinger, or what?'

At this all seriousness left the conversation and Calvert burst into a fit of uncontrollable laughter. It wasn't what Fitz had said, but the way it had been enunciated which had sent Calvert into spasms. That mock kind of high intellect which Fitz was always on the verge of parodying and emulating at one and the same time meant that often the most mundane utterance could take on a pseudo-profundity which one could only admire and make fun of simultaneously. And of course the whiskey was just kicking in at that time.

Fitz and Calvert ended up snowed-in for two more days. The ice on the motorway into Dunedin had made any travel treacherous and even the old Mount Cargill Road had been closed, which was most unusual. During that time Paul took the trouble to inform Fitz about the background to the racial attacks on local Māori people and their property in recent times. Three of the marae in the Otago area had been attacked, one of them being totally burned to the ground. Old people had been abused and children had been threatened on their way home from school. Right-wing fanatics had insinuated themselves in every walk of life in the south, especially business, politics and, in a most unlikely area, the arts. Slowly they had gained the trust and respect of the community. Now, Calvert was sure they were ready for something big.

'In England they call that kind of gradual takeover of local institutions by neo-nazi groups the process of osmosley!' Fitz had said, during one of their discussions.

'Any more jokes like that and you vil be shot!' retorted Calvert.

One of the main things they tried to get to grips with was the comment the Anglican vicar had made to Fitz on the train to Christchurch. 'And he really believes that this is the place in the world where the Nazi souls escaped to – very curious,' said Calvert. Thus far the outward manifestation of this was the thuggery and arson already alluded to, but now that Calvert and Fitz had seen the Sow of Hades a deeper, more disturbing element had been introduced.

'What if it was just an unusual cloud formation?' asked Fitz.

'Let's hope it was,' replied Calvert.

Finally, the conditions got better. The people who owned the place had returned earlier as they were coming from the north where road conditions were a lot better. They agreed to Fitz renting the hut, so he came to live in the place he had dreamed of. It was a strange feeling, but at this particular time there was little room for contemplation. If Calvert's theories about the ancient Teutonic myth of the Sow of Hades were correct, thought Fitz, a great catastrophe was looming, and when Calvert inferred that the sidereal clock was ticking towards a day of doom suddenly the significance of the Goth and Ghoul party at Yellban began to make sense. And both Calvert and Fitz had the seeds of doom within them from their Nazi fathers. Their challenge from the gift of dreams was to find out which side was real and which side of the spectrum was false and seductive.

3

Hilda Burstein opened the door and seeing two rather dishevelled, rough-looking men she became alarmed. Because of what had happened a few moments before when they found the stabbed body of Te Kaha O'Sullivan in his car, Fitz and Calvert were still in a state of shock. They stood there in front of the elderly woman, speechless. After what seemed an age, but was probably no more than a few seconds, Fitz spoke.

'I have a message for you from Marie Murdock.' The old lady's eyes lit up immediately and she said, 'Come in, come in, willkommen – it's very cold out there.' Fitz and Calvert were ushered into a tastefully decorated living room. While the flat was quite small, the overall effect was spacious. A bookcase displayed several volumes of classic literature, plus some beautifully leather-bound tomes all in German and obviously very old. Hilda Burstein herself was a woman of great decorum and grace. She must have been over seventy years old, but because of her immaculate appearance and grooming she seemed more like a woman twenty years her junior. A piano adorned one corner of the room and there were three or four nicely framed original art works on the wall.

'And how is Marie? We were in Berlin together, we even went to the same night school to learn typing,' the old lady said. 'So many things have happened since. So much turmoil and sorrow. Ah, but you young men don't want to hear about that old stuff. Do you want coffee?'

When they answered yes, Hilda Burstein went off to make the drinks. She returned, and while the coffee brewed Fitz and Calvert began to relate their story. After they reached the Sow of Hades incident, Hilda went and poured the hot, welcome brew and came back saying, 'Why is it suddenly Nazis reappear in my life? I escaped them once, and now here they are again. Actually, the big irony for me is that the real Nazis never touched me at all, even though they did kill everyone in my family – but they never touched me. I had to come to New Zealand to be mistreated.' She stopped here and looked for the reaction from her guests.

'Yes, I can never think of my New Zealand husband without thinking of the words written by Primo Levi in the concentration camps – "If from inside the lager, a message could have seeped out to free men it would have been this:

Take care not to suffer in your own home what is inflicted on us here." Imagine the irony I saw in the fact that my husband's favourite beer, which he consumed as he beat me senseless, just happened to be Stein Lager!' Saying the two words separately and deliberately, Hilda shuddered from the memory as she gave a mirthless laugh.

Fitz glanced furtively at Calvert who looked away, avoiding his friend's involuntary gaze. Fitz suddenly realised how close he and Calvert had become over the last month or so, how much they shared, and also how he'd never really had a close friend before, at least not since becoming an adult. He felt a real sense of aroha towards this man, and he hoped that nothing would ever come between them. Even those friends he had known all the years working in the factory remained very much on the surface – drinking mates, good people, but there had never been any depth or understanding of a more profound need. And looking after his mum had really precluded anything but the most superficial relations with women.

'Anyway,' Hilda broke from her own reverie and through Fitz's, and said, 'you two young men haven't come here to listen to the ramblings of an old lady.'

There was a silence, and from outside in the dark night the flashing blue and red lights of a police car could be seen in a dark area of Hilda's flat. The three of them looked at this corner of the living room, and the two men wondered if they had left any trace of their presence. Eventually, Fitz said, 'We have come to see you because Mrs Murdock said you could help us.'

Both men then told Hilda about their fathers, who they were and why they needed to know the background to their lives. They also told her of the fears they had from the events of recent times and how they felt that something strange and terrible was about to happen. Hilda sat listening, her face looked tired and old but still alert, and it had a certain beauty in its aged wisdom. Tears began to show in her eyes as all the horrors of a lifetime passed through her spirit. But she also felt a kind of freedom and catharsis. In reliving her life in Berlin she began to remember the good things and the good people at both ends of the political spectrum before things had turned hateful. Even people who became devout Nazis she remembered with affection from her maiden years. What had happened, what had gone wrong? She laughed when she remembered how in 1938 she was working in the office of a government ministry, Albert Speer's father had come walking out of his son's office exclaiming in bemused anger, 'You've all gone completely mad!' But the laughter was tinged with bitterness and sadness.

At length, Hilda excused herself and left the room. She returned with a pile of letters and papers bound by a rubber band. 'Both Mrs Murdock and I were very fond of your father,' she said turning to Fitz. 'In fact you might say we were rivals for his affections at one time. If only I had known he had come to New Zealand ...' her voice trailed off. 'Anyway, he gave me this letter before he helped me escape from Germany. He drove me to the border personally. We pretended we were lovers on a weekend jaunt – can you imagine?'

Hilda went to the kitchen and brought in fresh coffee. Pouring it, she continued. 'Von Leerig and I talked a lot on that trip. He trusted me and it seemed to help him to unload his burden. He told me how he'd had a vision which had revealed the reality to him of what they were really doing in the SS. When I asked why he stayed, he explained that because of his position of trust he felt he could help a lot more people by remaining. "Like I'm doing for you today," he had said to me. He was a poet, you know,' she said and handed Fitz a paper from the pile. 'Read this,' she urged.

Self Deception

Snow was falling on the small railway station
The ground was as cold as the air
The only heat rose from the engine's boiler
Whose steam billowed out of its funnel
Spilling over on to the platform
Obscuring the already chaotic scene

Our guards were rounding up old women
Children, and lame and crippled men
Herding them into freight wagons
As I crossed the mesh of railway tracks
Towards the Belsen-bound death express
Out of the crowd came a small boy, smiling

The child was dark and Jewish-looking
And one of our men was yelling at him
To hurry up and get into the boxcar
When suddenly the boy turned away
And became light and ethereal looking
He floated off into the approaching evening air

As the vision joined the engine's rising smoke
I realised that I was watching myself
All those years ago at this station, waiting
To get the train home from my school
Catching a final glimpse towards the clouds
The evaporating image smiled back down

von Leerig

Fitz read silently, astounded. This poem was exactly, to the word almost, the dream he'd had before he left Auckland. He read it several times before handing it to Calvert. Hilda watched them both. After a time she said, 'Tell me, this Herr Frisch, what did he look like?' Fitz described the man on the interisland ferry as best he could remember. The woman went, 'Mmm,' at various intervals during the description. Suddenly, she said in a strange, unearthly voice, 'Mein Gott!' She had gone a pale, ghostly white and had slumped forward in her chair with her head in her hands. Calvert and Fitz looked at each other in a perturbed, uncomprehending way. Eventually, Calvert said in a gentle voice, 'What is it, Mrs Burstein?'

'Will you stop calling me that, please! Burstein is my maiden name – the name of my beautiful family, who were put to death by those bastard tyrants, just like your von Oven here. What a name for a Nazi, von Oven. Grotesque!'

Fitz and Calvert were upset and bemused by this sudden outburst and looked awkwardly around the room. Hilda sat rocking herself slowly, a long, quiet moan coming from her. All these years she had tried to forget. Even her husband's brutality had taken her mind off the terrible memories and phantoms in a perverse way. But now here it was, over fifty years and twelve thousand miles away, and it had caught her.

Eventually, Hilda looked at the two guests and said, 'It is worse than I imagined. I have tried to ignore it but now it is up to you two to redeem yourselves and your fathers' memories, to free their souls from purgatory as it were. I knew both von Leerig and von Klagen. As I have said it was von Leerig who I worked with in the Propaganda Ministry and it was he who got me away soon after the July plot. Von Klagen was far more of a selfish, vain man. I'm sorry,' she said, turning to Calvert, 'but he had one redeeming feature and that was the great love he had for your mother. Oh, the outrage which that affair caused in Berlin! But now this Herr Frisch, who you, Fitz, met on the boat is, if I'm not mistaken, really von Oven and, believe me, wherever he is there is trouble. I was with him and Goebbels the night they discovered your father and Albert Speer's names on the list of potential leaders to take over when the bomb killed the Führer. At that time Wilfred von Oven was Goebbels' chronicler and it was only Speer's and von Leerig's closeness to Hitler and Himmler respectively which saved their skins.'

Fitz and Calvert began to feel quite uneasy. It was the first real encounter with the fact that their fathers had actually been friends and confidants with these people in real life.

'I have in the last twenty years or so had a very strong and increasing feeling of dread about this part of the world where I found exile. What you have told me tonight, along with recent events, confirms my fears. The so-called random mass killings at Waldronville, Aramoana, and the Bain family murders, coupled with the burning down of marae and the threats and assaults on local Māori people in Otago all point to the madness that was Nazism. Now you are telling me about the Anglican priest's notion and the Sow of Hades visitation, and to top it off von Oven's reappearance – all this points to something big and highly volatile about to happen. It is up to you two to uncover whatever it is and stop it!'

As the two left the old lady's flat and went out into the cold, each man had his own dark thoughts which seemed to match the night. Walking in the opposite direction from where they had discovered the body in the car, Calvert broke the silence by saying, 'You'd better stay at our place tonight. The roads north will be impassable by now. You'll have to sleep on the couch but it will be a good chance for you to meet Hine and our daughter.'

Fitz agreed. He had bought a car with some of the money Mrs Murdock had given him and he had no inclination to drive it into a ditch or over a bank on the coast road in the icy conditions. Also he was looking forward to meeting his friend's whānau. 'The good thing is that we are just up the road at the top of London Street,' said Calvert and they made their way carefully along the iced-over footpath.

4

Fitz knew he had fallen in love with her the moment they met. Hinengaro Te Riro i He was standing over the coal range in their dark flat making a stew, stirring with one hand and holding a book she was reading with the other. Fitz was struck dumb by her beauty, and by the knowledge that it was HER. She looked up from her study and Fitz thought he could detect the sense of recognition in her eyes that he had seen in the dream, and thought she faltered slightly.

Calvert said, 'Darling this is –'

Her husband's introduction was interrupted by their daughter calling 'Muuummm ...' from the other room.

'Kia ora,' she said to Fitz. 'Mind stirring this for a while?' she continued, handing him the spoon and heading off to the daughter's bedroom. Fitz stood there dumbstruck, holding the wooden spoon she had given him. Overwhelmed by his own emotions, he stared blankly into the Rotorua mud-pool stew which bubbled and plopped, plopped and bubbled in the pot. Why did it have to be Calvert's wife? He felt that awful sickening agony and ecstasy simply being in her presence was to give him in the future. He had never felt such palpable intensity of emotion before, but without any way of expressing it the result was a bland, neutral, apathetic exterior.

'Are you all right?' Calvert asked Fitz. 'You look like you just saw a ghost.'

Fitz didn't hear a word his friend had said, and Calvert had to repeat it.

'Oh,' said Fitz, 'oh yes, I'm fine. Just a bit cold and tired and overwhelmed by what's happened.'

'Yes, I must admit I'm a bit blown away by it all myself,' replied Calvert. Fitz looked at his friend and again thought, why the fuck did it have to be his wife, of all the bloody women in the world!

Fitz didn't sleep very much that night. He lay awake on the sofa in his friend's living room, the heat from the coal range keeping the Dunedin cold at bay. Every time he closed his eyes Hinengaro came into his vision. She had only come out once since he got there to apologise for not being more sociable, but their daughter was having some difficulty at school and by the time Hinengaro had sorted her out she was very tired. 'Nice to meet you Fitz, goodnight,' she had said. She seemed to look at him a second longer than would have been normal for a stranger, and then she was gone. Calvert stayed up a while longer, but sensed that Fitz didn't want to talk anymore and went to bed.

The only time that Fitz did sleep that night, he dreamed of her. The dream was so vivid and real and alive that he felt it was more real than things were when he was awake. Together they walked, Te Riro i He and Patrick Miki, through the twilight city. Everything seemed exact and yet dislocated. The old Stock Exchange building was still standing and the pre-neon illuminated clock flashed an iridescent flicker of colour on to the tramlines. It had been raining and the streets looked washed and clean as only summer rain can do. The time flashed again – koata pahi i te ono karaka – followed by the date – te tekau mā ono o ngā rā o Hune; ko te tau kotahi mano iwa rau mā whā. It was their first walk together, and they clung to each other like barnacles. As the 6.15 tram to Caversham went clanking past they saw a notice that the mayor had asked that the

Order in Council for the Andersons Bay tramway might be hurried on.

They walked further away from their time out to be together place, still locked arm in arm. She was explaining to him how some young women suffered a kind of dying by inches. 'That is the only way to describe hundreds of bloodless girls who are slipping slowly but surely from simple anaemia into a decline,' she was saying. They walked past the bank towards the Octagon. Looking in the window of J & J Arthurs they saw some all-wool Colonial Tweed Suitings for only £2/15s/0d. 'That's cheap,' Hinengaro said, and as they moved further along George Street they discussed the idea of going for a coach ride to Highcliff and Sandymount. 'Let's go next Tuesday – it's only 1s/6d each way,' Te Riro i He said to Miki and everything went red like a lightning flash with colour. Hinengaro Te Riro i He and Patrick Miki were both in love and they walked as if on air. Indeed, the local newspaper said as much as they swung back towards the Octagon, 'truly much is in the air', to sit silent at the foot of the Poet's statue.

'Doomsblay maybe amidst the smoke of battle, but there is no battle in the smoke of Juno, and Wai Rongoa now holds ten special gold medals,' said Fitz as they walked quickly past Dallas and Watts. It was getting dark now and the last tram up the valley would soon be leaving. What with the death of a footballer and Bibles in schools Fitz could feel the city re-enter his mind and he wished she had been with him. He carried her through the hard-nosed day of a labouring man and her beauty was so strong that he wept inwardly ...

Fitz woke up with the image of her in a long, flowing, early century dress and hat walking down the Boulevard de Dunedineaux, holding his arm as they went window shopping. The absurdity of such a vision made him want to burst out in laughter. The shadows and light of the living room gave a certain surreal aspect when married with his dreams. He fell asleep again and his waka entered into the strange seas of another moemoea o aroha. This time she came to him brown, bare breasted, laughing and radiant. They felt each other's presence as earthbound, yet beyond the confines of obstacles – as manacles released from chains, the uncertain yet true manu o aroha hou was about to express its new freedom when Fitz woke up to the sound of the phone ringing ...

'I'll get it!' Calvert yelled and came running from the bedroom.

After the snow and rain of the previous night the weather had created a new world of sunshine and colour, as though the world had been reborn. Fitz wanted to get out of the Calverts' home as soon as possible, certainly before Hinengaro got up. 'Are you sure you're alright to drive?' asked Calvert, 'you don't look like you slept at all last night. I'm sorry, but the sofa was the only place ...'

Fitz quickly assured him that it had been fine. This new feeling of almost contempt he now felt for his friend horrified Fitz, but he couldn't help it. 'I'll call you later,' he said to Calvert, and added awkwardly, 'tell your wife it was nice to meet her.' He found that she was a love whose name he dared not speak.

5

As Fitz drove back to Parimoana all he could see was her. She was in the sky, she was the other side of the sky! And even the elements spoke her name, the wind whispered Te Riro i He and he could hear te hau some way off, coming from the sea, bringing the sky and the ocean ever closer – i He. Fitz could see, looking back to the south, her form in the ancient land; her head, her breasts and her pregnant belly full of the promise of new life. The wind grew cold as the last light of the following evening was lost, and he went inside for the physical warmth from the fire he had lit in the house. The owners were away for a few days so he had the place to himself. The flames flickered but he did not feel warm. He felt cold and alone, cut off from his source, his mauri, which she somehow shared.

The phone rang and it was Calvert. 'Are you alright? I haven't heard from you since you took off – I've been worried about you because you didn't say goodbye or leave a note. Anyway, I've discovered something really important. In a week's time there is going to be a meeting at the hall in Port Chalmers of an outfit called the Wahnfried Society, which is ostensibly a club set up for the appreciation of Wagner's music. But it's just a front for the Dunedin neo-Nazis. I got a letter from them inviting me as a guest of honour – can you believe it? It's because of my father. You also received a similar letter, or at least I assume it is. It must be this Frisch/von Oven fellow's doing. I've given it to Hine to bring out to you later tonight – she's visiting a friend out your way and it seemed like a sensible idea. I'll try and get out to see you tomorrow to talk about our strategies if we go to that meeting ... Fitz, are you there? Are you listening?'

Fitz was stunned. She's coming here! Hinengaro Te Riro i He is coming here – tonight! Fitz must have been thinking out loud because Calvert answered, 'Yes, I told you she's going to bring you your invitation. Anyway, I must be getting on with a few things, our daughter Amiria is going out tonight and I've got to drop her off. See you tomorrow, probably in the early afternoon.'

Fitz managed to mumble some sort of normal-sounding reply and goodbye. She was coming here; they would be alone together! He sat by the fire in the main house smoking his pipe and musing upon the fact that she would soon be there. He felt the slow-burning fuse of his passion for her, which had burned like a coal-seam fire since he had first had those dreams about her back in Auckland. This passion began to ignite in his heart and fanned out through his whole body permeating every organ, every pore and then into his wairua. The flames from the fireplace lapped and licked dangerously at the edge of his consciousness as he sat alone in the lowly lit room.

In a gesture of disbelief, subdued excitement and anxiety he shook his head. He walked outside to watch the last of the twilight as the sky darkened, bringing it and the ocean ever closer so that their indefinite lines met at the horizon. He calmed himself by saying a karakia which addressed the land meeting the new moon, and aligning this with his calling to her ...

twilight brings its gradual descent
of the night to Parimoana – the sea,
the clouds, touch – merge, and the trees
turn ever-darkening shades of green

the last residue of crimson lies stretched,
elongated across the horizon
and these things seen in you
are also mirrored within my soul

thoughts of you are repeated over
and over again, ever changing
with the days, ever increasing
with the same subtle blend as landscape

colours and shapes sometimes clearly
defined, sometimes barely discerned
and sometimes, when memory's unturned
just the darkness which is complete

the light beyond is te marama
who, when she shines, touches softly
the silent sleeping soul of the earthly
unseen world, alive with light

beyond those tall trees, that rising
darkness and sensuous non-colour
of strange, stark colours
lies the profound aroha of our waka

te pō
te pō
te pō aroha
the moonlight world
of our understanding

As Fitz stood outside in the darkness he could see the light beginning to filter through the trees at the bottom of the hill. But it was not the light from the rising of the moon as he had initially thought. The yellow beam intensified and the sound of a car's engine could be heard coming closer and closer. It must be her!

6

Pulling into the driveway of the place where Patrick Miki Fitzgerald was staying, Hinengaro Te Riro i He felt a kind of thrill. A thrill of the unknown and of excitement. When Calvert had asked her to deliver a letter to Fitz when she went to Parimoana to visit her friend Apikara, she had felt apprehensive. Ever since she had seen him waving from the southbound Southerner at Goodwood she had known he was the one. Later that day on the marae train north to see her whānau, her kaumātua had told her he had seen a man who would accompany her – what the wise one didn't tell her was that he would be a friend of her husband. And even though she and Calvert had stopped the lovemaking part of their marriage some time ago, she was still a loyal wife, a devout Catholic and not into 'sinfidelity', as she jokingly called adultery to her friends.

Getting out of the car on to the dimly lit footpath, she could hear the sounds of the silence of the countryside – sounds that you couldn't hear in the din of city life. The crickets and the frogs calling, sheep and cattle sharing their goodnight lowing, a horse snorting, and the sound of a far-off goods train making its way northwards around The Cliffs past Purakanui. The smells in the air carried themselves on the same breeze which brought the sounds. Smells of animals and the smoke from the winter fires of the neighbourhood. All her senses came alive.

Making her way towards the house she gave a yelp as she knocked over something and in the half-light saw the black sockets of the eyes of a sheep's skull looking up at her from where she had kicked it to. She then noticed that the whole pathway was adorned with these grotesqueries, all in a row mounted on various rocks and poles. She gave a little shudder at this parody of Turuturumokai. Then from the slightly open window of the living room came wafting through the night air the smell of freshly brewed coffee which seemed to reassure her.

Composing herself she stood at the front door, putting off the moment for yet another minute. Then she knocked as quietly as possible. 'Come in,' she heard Fitz's voice calling, as though it were a hundred miles away. She opened the door and went in. Fitz was sitting in front of the fire with his back to the door. He had a book in his hand and was smoking a pipe the aroma of which, although she did not normally like or condone smoking, seemed to excite her. 'I won't be a minute. I'll just finish this paragraph.' Hine felt the warmth of the fire. She wanted to go over by it and feel safe and secure, but this charade of Fitz's prevented such immediacy of comfort and intimacy.

Slowly Fitz took off his glasses and got up, putting the book to one side. Hinengaro glanced at the title – *The Guermantes Way* – and wondered what on earth that could mean.

'Would you like some coffee?' Fitz said, after what seemed a long time.

'Yes, please,' Hine answered awkwardly. As he handed her the drink she noticed that his hands seemed to be shaking, the coffee spilling on to the saucer. She thought to herself, poor devil, he's as terrified as I am, and she almost burst out laughing. She pulled her chair nearer the fire and they both sat silent for several minutes.

When they did speak again it was at exactly the same time. 'Paul rang – asked me to – said you would – deliver a letter!' They both looked at each other and then burst out into great gales of unstoppable laughing and crying.

They embraced, and Hinengaro, for so long loyal and loveless, felt the possibilities, the first feelings of being human and beyond. Taking the unlevel crossing of their love from tapu to noa across that unbridgeable gap and deadly schism caused by the original sin, the wilful transgression of the knowledge of good and evil, she knew that it was love which healed these deep wounds in our souls, not duty or dreams. They explored each other as though they were ancient travellers and as he caressed her neck, her breasts, her face, she was transported by delight and passion. Kissing, moist of mouth, the juices of her body and her spirit flowing freely, Hinengaro let go. She felt him rise within her as the gentle flames from the night by the fireside bring warmth and light. She felt the beauty of their aroha lighten her as they shared each other's touch and grace in an embrace which sent through their bodies and into their wairua electric currents coming from the ancient impulse to belong. At the moment of release Hinengaro thought to herself, 'We dare not hold on too long, we dare not let go,' and she gave out a cry of pleasure and separation which comes from the only belonging.

What lingers on had only just begun. The love that dared not speak could only whisper small, soft words: fingers half touching, telling of a longing to understand.

Like the waves of heat wafting out from the fire as they lay naked and replete in each others' arms, Hinengaro let the waves of thought and feeling soak into her healing spirit. In the night by the fireside, bright sparks and gentle flames brought more warmth and light. The mānuka which took so long to grow soon burnt, adding to their inner glow, the mystery deepened and the pain they were left with receded with the darkness.

They lay together in their waka aroha, letting the waves of sorrow, waves of joy wash over them. Eventually, she lifted his heavy, factory-worn hand from her breast and she extricated herself from his embrace. 'I've got to go now,' she said softly. 'Miki, we've got some difficult times ahead. You, me and Paul have been brought together for a purpose. We must forget our personal jealousies and disenchantments and work together. At this point the purpose is not clear, but –' she watched his gaze upon her as he was watching her getting dressed. He had a look of rapture on his face and she felt loved and desired for the first time in many years. 'But,' she continued, 'I'm sure it's got something to do with this.' She handed him the letter which had ostensibly been the reason for her visit. 'And I'm sure that you and Paul have to share your destiny. As for what happens between us, at the moment I feel we are now noa and that our crossings have been levelled – we must now concentrate on unselfish things.'

Hinengaro stood at the door and sang a waiata in a voice which could only have come from the angels. She felt Fitz weep inwards.

> The seeds of the trees
> Which separate us
> Are planted again
> But each time
> We are apart
> We grow together
> Like an unseen river
> Beneath the surface
> Of our lives
> The aroha
> Is between us
> As well as the distance

Before she left, Hinengaro Te Riro i He took a small pounamu from the pocket of her skirt and went over to Fitz with it. She kissed him, their lips held together like beaks, she put the greenstone in his hand, and said, 'He iti noa iho, nā te aroha.' She then turned, threw her hair back as a gesture of strength and kaha, and walked out the door into the cold night air. For a brief moment she sat at the wheel of the car and had a tangi. Then she started the engine, backed out of the driveway and headed towards Dunedin along the coast ghost road.

7

Fitz woke with a start. The shadows which played across the wall from the embers of the dying fire startled and disoriented him. Large animals and birds came into momentary existence. The horn of the skull of a goat crossed the roof and the wing from a stuffed hawk flew over his shoulder. The fire had little warmth left in it and he shivered with the cold, but his body and his spirit were aglow, as though he was shining on the inside. His memories of Hinengaro were strong and of a rare and sensuous nature. As he thought of her opening up to him to dispel the magic of dreams, giving him a reality which was far stronger and more magical, he realised his dreams were like a mirage to a hungry and desperate man dying of thirst. The beauty and nourishment of the palpable food of love – taste and smell and touch – had been as sustaining as real food and drink. He felt satiated and complete.

Fitz just wanted to go on feeling this fabulous world into which he had entered. Yet she was no longer with him, and the separation hurt like a wound. Slowly he got up from the position where she had left him by the fire, took the blanket she had covered him with, and he dressed. He knew he wouldn't sleep much that night so he built the fire up again, then went outside and chopped some more wood. He felt the power, the kaha which she had given him surge through his being as though her presence and their lovemaking had infused a kind of immortality in him. It was like his wairua had been crossed at just the right level with his physical being.

Making himself a cup of hot, strong coffee Fitz began to feel restless. He wanted her here, beside him. He walked outside into the night and saw that it had begun to snow again. It looked quite special, the large flakes cascading down, down out of the dark, dark night like clusters of silently exploding stars. Going back inside he tried to settle down to reading the book he was pretending to read when Hinengaro had first arrived. But somehow it wasn't a Proustian night. He flicked impatiently through the pages, randomly stopping and moving on. Fitz had never been a reader and the books in this house belonged to someone who had far more of an intellectual disposition than he did. He was about to put the book down because he felt he couldn't understand a word of it, his restlessness notwithstanding, when he happened upon the sentence, 'For when we are in love, all the trifling little privileges that we enjoy we would like to be able to divulge to the woman we love, as people who have been disinherited and bores of other kinds do to us in everyday life.' Suddenly, Fitz felt a great affinity with this Proust. Despite the almost indecipherable use of the English language, he felt in this one phrase he had found a friend, someone who understood what it was like to be in love. He had been let into a world of words from which he had previously felt excluded. And, like so many other things, it had been his love for Hinengaro both in dreams and in reality which had opened the door.

Fitz began with great difficulty to read part one of *The Guermantes Way*, having repeatedly to go back over words he couldn't comprehend. When he got to the bit about 'every forest has its spirit, as there is a nymph for every stream', he thought it was just like Māori mythology in relation to the concept of mauri. He was amazed that someone from Europe could understand such things! The book went on, 'sometimes hidden in the heart of its name, the fairy is transformed to suit the life of our imagination by which she lives', and Fitz thought of how in such a concrete way Hinengaro had come to represent desire to him. As he read on, contemplating how he might win some, if not all her affection from now on, he was suddenly sent into mortal turmoil by what he saw on the following page. Reading, 'yet the fairy must perish if we come in contact with the real person to whom her name corresponds', Fitz felt a real sense of anxiety and panic brought on by these words. His ignorance and innocence which had allowed his mind and spirit to soar so high in dreams now plunged him into a free-fall of fear. Crestfallen, he threw the book aside (that Pandora's box of knowledge, that square-shaped apple of the understanding of good and evil), just missing the fireplace, where he had probably, subconsciously wanted it to go. Fitz felt caught in a trap with his superstitious mind, his limited education and his newly found passionate nature.

Building the fire whose flames now flickered and leapt, he thought of Hinengaro's love as the only thing in the world he ever wanted, yet the circumstances of their lives meant they must be separate. His passion to be joined with her could bring down the heavens. The heavens answered with an icy blast outside that shook the house. 'Like your Master's kingdom, our love cannot be of this world.' This was the question of her ever-present absence in his life.

It was now the middle of the night. The wind had died down and, as the fire burned on, Fitz went out of the house. The rain and snow clouds had cleared away and the moon sat silent in the sky over the sea, above the cliffs of Parimoana. He looked at te marama, the moon, flooding the sky with its light: diffuse, organic, milky.

Returning inside, Fitz thought he might as well just lie down on the sofa and sleep in front of the fire instead of going back to the hut, which would be freezing. On the table he noticed the letter which Hine had delivered, but decided not to open it until the morning. He lay down, his happy and sad thoughts of her washing over him. Before he fell asleep, he remembered how beautiful and powerful and complete he had felt being inside her, and how sadness comes from the only true connection which had chased Te Kēhua o Aroha into reality.

8

Hinengaro woke in the middle of the night. Her sleep had been full of strange, disturbing images and dreams. Her husband lay sleeping quietly next to her and she felt the warmth and familiarity of his presence. But everything would be different now. She remembered the flames and the shadows dancing together in the room. The smell from the mānuka gum that oozed out over the hot, burning logs had mingled with the natural aroma of sex coming from the out-pouring of male and female elemental juices. Slipping her hand gently down through her lush pubic hair she felt the little ridge of flesh rising to meet her touch and memory. The full molly-honey river of her teke began to flow as she imagined Fitz there with her, inside her, holding her strong and gentle. Calvert stirred in the bed and Hine realised she must have been moving her body a lot. Not wanting to wake her husband up, she took her hand away from herself and let her thoughts and feelings subside, until she lay motionless and calm, and the remembrance of her and Miki's combined taste and smell passed in and out of her consciousness.

Lying in the darkened bedroom as the first light of dawn began to rise slowly above the darkness, Hinengaro Te Riro i He realised the enormity and the necessity of what had happened. Drifting between dreams and sleep, she found herself wandering alone along a desolate beach. Fitz stood solitary at a river mouth and she could see he was wearing a military uniform of some description. She went up to talk to him, touching him softly on the arm. She then saw he was holding a child who had been badly wounded by a bullet. The horizon had an unnatural, ethereal glow – like a sunset in reverse. Hine took the silent, bleeding child from Fitz and he jumped aboard a tank which was headed towards the front. She was overcome by the stillness. He saluted her in a half-reverential, half-mocking manner and as Fitz and his comrades turned into a cloud of dust she was shocked to see he was wearing an Iron Cross with a swastika held in the talons of an eagle. The scene then changed to te tekau mā ono o ngā rā o Hune, ko te tau kotahi mano, iwa rau mā wha, and as the tram to Maori Hill clanked along George Street they looked at each other and burst out laughing. 'We missed our tram again, eh Miki!' she said. 'Oh well, we wouldn't want to be the only Māoris living in Maori Hill!'

'Anyway, is the game worth the candle?' Fitz mused enigmatically as they walked further back arm in arm towards the Octagon, where they sat silent at the foot of the Poet's statue. This was the first day they had walked out together and both were wearing their nicest winter DRESS MATERIALS, which they had purchased from THE DUNEDINERS, Dallas and Watts. Hine laughed as she recalled to him how she had just made the late letters guard's van of the port train at 2.30 that afternoon. 'I told him in the epistle in no doubtful language the result after taking Dr. Morse's Indian Root Pills,' she said almost in hysterics.

Having a discreet shot of Wolfe's Schnapps (for kidney ailments, naturally) they walked, arms linked, along the streets of Dunedin. Hine felt happy and light, and as they planned a trip by horse and coach together the following Tuesday, to Sandymount, she almost forgot her husband and child and the family obligations which stood between them like trees against the horizon. They were happy.

Suddenly the dream darkened, as though the Sow of Hades had descended, her dark shadow throwing everything into evil contrast and premonition of the winds of a terrible century ahead, looming. She had reached te wāhi moemoea and felt afraid as the winds blew hard out along the coast telling of the thousand miles and the millions of murders – a face floated before her from the steam cloud of a locomotive's boiler. She followed it and saw its moko engraved on its surface. The moko told an ancient story of Abelard and Heloise and their ill-fated love. He ended up a ball-less theologian and she a nun ... Kei te kata nei anō, kua mane te ngakau, a te mutunga o tāua koa he pōuri ... the cloud face, smiling down at her, was that of Miki leading her closer and closer towards the cliffs which overlook the sea at Parimoana. And then she was falling – falling down all the years from 1904, down the thousand miles from Tamaki-makau-rau to Otepoti, through the murderous fog which was the Sow of Hades, over the wild cliffs of Parimoana, falling, falling and he keeps calling me back again ... 'Wake up, Hine! Wake up!' It was her husband calling her. 'You must have been having a nightmare. It's alright, darling,' he said, and she held him close and he stroked her hair soothingly.

9

Fitz and Calvert met again in the Octagon coffee bar. They had been invited to a special evening of the Wahnfried Society as guests of honour, and Calvert had earlier told Hilda Burstein this. She looked worried and thought they must be up to something very big. 'Be careful, the two of you. This Wilfred von Oven is one of Goebbels' creations: obviously charming, but not to be trusted. He will fly in all directions. Take care that you don't become Androcles in reverse when you enter that lion's den.'

'How's Hinengaro?' asked Fitz, as nonchalantly as he possibly could, yet feeling that every word he spoke came out sounding false and exaggerated.

'She's fine – well, she's been a bit out of sorts lately, not sleeping, that kind of thing. She says she has lots of strange dreams and I sometimes find her waking in the night crying. She hasn't been like that since we first met. Anyway, she's gone to a hui tonight at the Kaikorai Marae, which should take her mind off things.'

Fitz immediately thought te kēhua o aroha, she must have inherited his own dream reality during their unlevel crossing, their lovemaking. He had wondered why his own dreaming world had subsided since she had been with him, and this was the reason! They had spoken to each other once on the phone since the evening they had spent together. There had been an awkward conversation in which they had agreed to see each other again at a later date. She had jokingly intimated that people should see a marriage-guidance counsellor before they embarked on a relationship, rather than when it was collapsing around them. 'I must go now,' she had said. As he heard the click of the phone in its cradle, he suddenly felt very alone and vulnerable, as though part of him had gone ...

'Raisley Calvert, an old uncle of mine, knew what words were worth, Fitz. Yes, there's a man who knew the difference between a nun and a whore!'

Fitz had no idea what his friend was talking about. In his reverie about his phone call to Hine he had lost the thread of what Calvert had been saying. He thought, with a certain amount of contempt (for which he immediately felt remorse) how fucking easy and urbane and unctuous husbands were. Both men agreed to go to this Wahnfried Society meeting to see if they could get some insight into the intentions of the group and to find out if they had been responsible for the recent attacks on Otago Marae. They felt if they could use their positions as the sons of real Nazis to get rid of the curse of this ring of misfits and weirdos and thugs they would have to do so.

As they drove out to Port Chalmers along the winding and twisting roadway in the Calverts' old Triumph the two men were strangely silent. Both of them knew in an intrinsic, unspoken way that the other was thinking of Hinengaro Te Riro i He. Calvert, of course, knew nothing of his wife's liaison with Fitz, but in some instinctive, elemental insight he suspected that her recent change in behaviour had something to do with Fitz's presence. And knowing and not knowing this had brought the two men together, making their already naturally strong bond even closer. The deep, heavy sound of the car's engine seemed to emulate and facilitate the measure and mood of their thoughts, as though preparing them for the impending confrontation with their fathers' pasts.

The car swung right, over the level crossing between the station yards and the tunnel which takes the trains through to the port itself. Going up the hill and turning left into Currie Street, both men felt a sense of awe and dread as they saw the lighted hall and heard the strains of Wagnerian music coming from the far end of the street. Calvert had smoked a joint in the car on the way out which Fitz, fearing the worst, had declined. Although he had not had to take medication for a while now, and since his lovemaking with Hinengaro he had felt a lot better about himself, the memories of Yellban were still fresh in his mind, and this situation was weird enough without adding to it.

Getting out of the car Fitz and Calvert gave each other a final glance of solidarity across the roof of the Triumph before walking towards the crowd entering the main doorway of the hall. At the entrance the music was so loud, the dark resounding notes coupled with the heavy Germanic language had an intoxicating effect from the start. The two guards on the door were patched members of the Mongrel Mob and, as they checked Fitz and Calvert's tickets, the realisation that their colours of black, red and white were the same as Nazi colours sent a chill through Fitz. At the same time it made him want to burst out laughing at the incongruity of white supremacists employing an ethnic gang as bouncers. Not daring to look at Paul, who would obviously be thinking similar absurdities, Fitz moved further into the hall. The sobering thought that the

Mongrel Mob were not that far removed from Rhoem's S.A. Beer Hall brawlers brought the desire to laugh to a halt. The noise from the music outside was muted in the interior of the building, so that when the speeches began the audience could hear everything perfectly well, while giving the outside world the impression that the maestro's operas were the main reason for the meeting.

The hall was almost full, the seating arrangements were like that of a theatre. Draped all around the room were large hanging flags, some of which were ordinary Nazi swastika varieties, interspersed with those of SS divisions such as Wotan, Siegfried and the Schutzstaffeln Adolf Hitler. Most of the people in the hall were dressed in formal evening wear: the men wore suits and bowties, and the women wore long, tasteful gowns as though dressed for the opera. The dark lighting and the presence of Mongrel Mob guards at intervals around the room gave a distinctly oppressive feel, but this was offset by the gaiety and animation of the respectable, well-groomed crowd who sipped champagne and talked to each other with easy familiarity. The man who Fitz recognised as Herr Frisch from the *Aratere* came over and, pouring two glasses of Moët, introduced himself to Calvert as Wilfred von Oven.

'You seem surprised, mein freund,' he said to Fitz. 'One can't be too careful, hence the invention of Herr Frisch. Oh! By the way the story I told you about your father is unfortunately true in the main. We lost a good man in his betrayal, but we don't want to lose his son also, ja?' He tapped with a spoon on his glass. 'Meine Damen und Herren, I would like to announce the arrival of our two guests of honour this evening.' He turned and indicated in the direction of Fitz and Calvert with an out-stretched hand, 'Herr von Leerig und Herr von Klagen, the juniors!' A kind of hush went around the room followed by an at first tentative and then open outpouring of clapping and cheering. Glasses were refilled as the official speakers began to take the stage.

The podium was flanked by two guards dressed as birds of prey, personifying the traditional eagle of German militarism and might. They stood holding symbolic spears in their talons, their wings spread as if ready for flight. The *Götterdämmerung* provided a dramatic backdrop, and a large banner with an eagle holding a broken cross was at the back of the speakers. High above a further banner proclaimed WAHNFRIED in gold embroidered lettering six feet high. People listened enraptured as a young dark-haired woman came on stage and sang an aria as the incarnation of Erdna. This was followed by a recitation, rather than a musical version, of the reply to Wotan's question, 'Who art thou, brooding spirit?' Fitz thought this speech seemed to reveal both the appeal and the destructive nature of the Magic Nazism Movement, the spell and the curse under which people like his father had fallen. It was von Oven himself who stood before the audience to read the epistle, as it were. The silence was electric as he uttered the words ...

All that was I know
All that is I know
All that ever shall be done
This as well I know

Erdna the name I bear
The fates my daughters are
Danger threatens dire
This had drawn me near

Hearken! Hearken! Hearken!
All that is shall end
Heed ye well, ere dawn of doom –
Beware the cursed Ring!

Von Oven stood quietly, resplendent in his bohemian garb. Obviously influenced by Goebbels' philosophy that politics should be entertainment, as opposed to Hitler's 'hit them hard and often' approach to propaganda, this aging, well-preserved relic of the Third Reich began to introduce the people who would address the faithful. Firstly, he indicated the head of the Samoan Nazi Party, Aelolea le Fanau, whose lecture would be entitled 'Through a Class Darkly: The House by the Khurch-yard'. Secondly, Ida Barron-Munchausen would discuss the contribution to German Kultchur in Aotearoa by her mother and mentor, the eminent scholar Führer Frau, Vida Barron.

'Then, we have a very special guest, Dr Olda Juenger, who will discuss his father Ernst's work in the field of alpine lilies, their evolution and survival as a metaphor for the Führer's Thousand Year Reich!' This drew wild applause and von Oven at this point began a speech about his own vision of the future. He started by saying the first Nazi experiment had been over-ambitious and in the wrong part of the world. Quickly, he added, 'This is not a criticism of our beloved Führer, but a postmodern realisation that 'Think Big' projects do not work unless they are established initially in small cellular networks. Over the past several years we have seen in this country, Aotearoa, the acceptance and implementation of right-wing economics. Now, we in the New Millennium are poised to fulfil the Führer's vision much more easily than was the case halfway through the last century of the old millennium. The Führer lit the flame and we carry the torch into the new Thousand Year Reich with the confidence and assurance that this time the fates and providence are truly on our side.'

Fitz and Calvert looked at each other uneasily as they found themselves rising to their feet along with everyone else and giving the Nazi salute to the sound of 'Sieg Heil! Sieg Heil! Sieg Heil!' As old habits die hard, one of the Mongrel Mob sergeants at arms was heard just slightly behind the herd, yelling 'Sieg Fucken Heil!' and was then seen to go red in the face and turn away sheepishly as he realised his involuntary indiscretion had been picked up by his more 'civilised' patrons. Looking out over the mini-headed multitude, von Oven, now in the incarnation of Rübezahl, felt with satisfaction and pride the effects his words had wrought. He thought to himself – 'Today Port Chalmers, tomorrow ...' After all, this was how the Führer himself had begun. Even though he, Rübezahl Wilfred von Oven, was now old he could at least sow the seeds of Hades in the new generation. He saw Fitz and Calvert sitting in the front row and felt a great sense of destiny that he had delivered to the movement the inheritors of their fathers' dreams.

Fitz shifted uneasily in his chair when his hand brushed against something which was sticking out of his pocket. 'Damn!' he thought. He'd forgotten to post the letter he'd written to Pania and Dolphin Dog at Yellban. They had kept in contact, and she was saying how much her dog was missing him, yelping every time she saw the photo he had sent them. The tide of high green grass emotion had subsided in the bierhaus and von Oven continued with his introductions of the speakers. 'Then we will have Mr Hashimoto, otherwise known as Job Bones, the man who instigated Honshu's successful Unemployment Strategy. The more people who are jobless in the market economy, his theory goes, the sooner radical political change can come. Complacency and full employment are anathema to National Socialism because people do not take to the streets if they are well fed.'

Fitz got a real shock when von Oven introduced the following orator. 'Herr Haki Maroke Kuha is raising the currents of the New Write literature. He has done great work for our cause and will be well rewarded. Despite what the intellectuals say, Herr Kuha will be our Minister of Kultchur, an appointment my former boss would certainly have approved of – read, to hell with it!' Fitz remembered the drunken, raving, out-of-it author in the Christchurch hovel and shivered at the thought of his having power over anyone, let alone what books may be read in the home! 'Finally, we will hear from our spokesperson on ethnic and women's affairs, Ponsetta Phyllis Stein, who despite her name, has worked tirelessly for the party in both South America and The Kingdom of YETE.'

The lights dimmed and a soft spotlight descended like a ray entering the side window to the crypt of a cathedral. In the delicate shimmer von Oven stood. His pose was that of a man who carried a heavy weight, but who bore it with a passion and strength which accompanies those destined for greatness. He began his speech quietly, hoarsely, almost inaudibly, as though the very words were weighted with doom. 'Now,' his hushed voice echoed through the microphone and mingled with low strains of the beginning to the 'Ride of the Valkyries' which was playing over the speaker system outside the hall. 'Now comes the most difficult of my tasks. Before I hand you over to the other speakers,' he paused, drinking in the admiration of his followers, 'there is a grave and profound truth I must share with you. As you all know we are in this part of the world for a reason – and that reason is to begin yet again, sans bullet, the work left undone. We chose to come to a small, out of the way country, Tasman's Ultima Thule no less, to work out our karma, and in the prophetic words of Erdna, "All that is shall end, heed ye well ere dawn of doom!"'

Von Oven's voice began to rise as the music outside increased in tempo and volume. This time the sound had been turned up in the hall as well. 'Kia ora, they say in this country. Now echo the call from the kameraden of South Amerikan Magico Naziano – 'Que Hora!' – and the answer is, 'The time is NOW!' I, because of my name and with the blessing of the

Führer before he died, have been sent to baptise the world, to change the evil hearts of men and women in a flood of fire.' His voice pitched and undulated with the rise and fall of the music. 'We are in the early stages of our divine mission, and as with all our works we invoke the inspiration of artists and poets to guide us. The Fischl Policy we are implementing at this time is that of 'The Black Palms Still Buffing Boots'. This entails lone acts of terrorism carried out by fringe members of society, those disaffected and deranged by the pressures of modern capitalist society.' The crowd became louder and louder, like the swelling music of the *Götterdämmerung*.

Von Oven continued, 'The Black Palms SS is a suicide squad dedicated to our cause and willing to lay down their lives for the Neo-Millennium Man, and to facilitate the world wide web of lies for the induction of the Thousand Year Reich. Aramoana, the Bain killings, the burning of marae buildings, all these are part of our strategy, and of course the blame can never be traced to us because the psychiatric or criminal histories of these individuals are such that they are seen to be outsiders, marginalised and sick people. Even as I speak ...' the music, the swastika emblems of the flags, the pageantry and the bizarre staged performance of von Oven himself, all these conspired to intoxicate and exhilarate the passions of the audience, so that when von Oven uttered the words, ' ... even as I speak one of our suicide bomber kameraden – trained in Lebanon as a legacy of 'Operation Eau de Cologne' in the 1950s when Krupp was courting Nasser – is at the Kaikorai Marae on just such a holy mission.' It took even Fitz and Calvert a few moments to turn their minds to what had been said.

'Hine!' Both the men said her name simultaneously with looks of terror and concern on their faces. Their initial impulse was to run out of this crowded hall of ghoulish zealots, but they realised that would be dangerous. Fitz whispered to

Calvert to move slowly but swiftly, and they both walked past the enraptured faces of those believers who were listening to the rhetoric of murder and destruction; those respected pillars of society who are able to smile as they kill, and sleep at night secure in the comfort of other peoples' dreams.

As they reached the end of the hall they heard von Oven thanking and invoking the Sow of Hades, saying that her recent visitation to the dark Dunedin skies had been a validation and a sign that their years of exile had not been in vain. As the mad ranting was eclipsed by the increase in volume of the Valkyries riding to their gruesome destination, Fitz and Calvert left the Valhalla of deathshead ideals. Coming upon the Mongrel Mob sentinels they almost faltered. But they gave them a Nazi salute at attention to which the gang members replied in kind, adding, 'Fuck off honkies,' for good measure as they giggled to themselves. Then Fitz and Calvert got into the car and sped off down the Port road towards Dunedin and the Kaikorai Valley. 'Come on! Fuck you, come on!' Fitz kept saying to the car, and Calvert who was driving, was puzzled by the desperation in his friend's tone of voice. After all, it was his wife whose life was in danger, not Fitz's.

10

Hinengaro Te Riro i He had been in the kitchen of the wharekai when she first heard the commotion and smelled the strong stench of burning paint. She had been doing the dishes with the other women at the hui, and was sitting down, a tea towel draped over her shoulder, thinking about a quote she had seen in a recent *Reader's Digest* – 'love at first sight explained by a previous existence'. Apparently, it was some ancient Latin or Greek phrase and the article had explained that it was a philosophical concept which dealt with why some people just seem to know each other as soon as they meet, as though they had been lovers in another time, like invisible partners. It went on to explain about something called 'imago therapy' which helped couples understand each other's attraction by the image that they had as individuals of what the perfect man or woman would be. Anyway, it was something like that. Hine laughed at herself for even wanting to think about such rubbish. However, she had noticed that she looked at women's magazines for clues about such things since she met Fitz. The recent changes she had felt within herself had meant that she was feeling sentimental and open to new things again.

Now she was running towards the wharenui. People were screaming, children and old people were being herded along the corridor away from where she was heading. Where there is smoke, there is fire, Hine thought to herself, smiling to herself at the banal aptness of such a trite phrase at a time like this. The idea flashed through her mind that this quote also had implications for the wider picture of her and Fitz, and she said to herself, 'I know,' thankful that there was enough noise and chaos around her for no one else to have heard. She heard two loud BANGS and realised they were gunshots. Opening the main door the flames leapt out at her and she became aware that the whole wharenui was alight. She could hear someone groaning, obviously wounded or hurt, calling from inside the living room of the marae. Hine made her way towards the sound, holding the tea towel over her face to prevent smoke inhalation. 'Over here! Over here!' she could hear the voice of a woman calling. The smoke was now thick and the flames intense and Hine tripped on an overturned chair, hitting her head on the floor as she fell. The coughing and calling of the other woman had ceased and Hine, almost delirious, became completely oblivious to the increasing danger of the fire now threatening to engulf her.

Semi-conscious, Hine watched the smoke which billowed around her begin to suggest tangible forms, to evoke the dreams she had been having of recent times. Fitz's face floated gradually towards her and she knew that he was the one she had met in a previous life, as this life was about to leave her. The wind blew hard out along the coast, whipping up the water, sending chunks of sure cliffs crashing to the sea below. One of the main beams from the roof of the wharenui crashed down, pinning Hinengaro in the position she had fallen. Her thoughts were picked up by te hau, who carried them soaring southwards over the dark and stormy hills, taking them gently down the valley to reach her lover as a whisper.

Coughing from the smoke which began to fill her lungs and yawning from the tiredness of sheer exhaustion, Hine felt a sharp burning and throbbing in her head. The flames were now at her face and trying desperately to free herself she suddenly remembered the new life which was beginning to grow inside her. Even if she didn't survive herself, that baby must! With all her remaining strength Hinengaro jerked her legs painfully from under the wooden beam which held her, and with a great effort of will she freed herself. The colours, the heat and the pain all intensified as she staggered towards the direction she had come from, having just enough energy to call out, she coughed violently, yelling, 'HELP!' and as the foggy smoke-billowing image of Fitz embraced her, she collapsed and everything went black.

11

Fitz sat down to read the *Otago Daily Times* the following morning at the Octagon Coffee Bar. Calvert had gone to the hospital to see Hine and was going to meet Fitz there afterwards. He looked again at the photograph of him pulling a battered and bruised Hinengaro from the flames of the wharekai at the Kaikorai Marae. He wondered at how beautiful she looked even in such circumstances. The headline of the paper read: 'Another Police Shooting'. The report went on to say that the arsonist who had tried to burn down Kaikorai Marae the previous night had a history of mental illness. After setting fire to the main meeting house the man, whose name was not yet available, had presented a firearm, aimed it at an officer, and was then shot. He was found to have explosives strapped to his body. Fitz read on. A stalwart of the local Māori community, Mrs Hine Calvert, had gone back into the fire to rescue someone who she had heard calling for help and had herself been overcome by smoke. She, in turn had been rescued by a friend of the family. The caption for the photograph read: 'Mrs Calvert pulled out of the burning building by Mr Patrick Fitzgerald.'

Fitz flicked randomly through the newspaper. The smell of coffee was strong and reassuring. He ordered a plate of bacon and eggs and just as they arrived, their aroma permeating the area around him, his eye caught a small headline on page nine. 'Wagner still popular.' Fitz read the one column item which described how a hall in Port Chalmers had been turned into Valhalla for an evening. A group calling themselves the Wahnfried Society, who are dedicated to the enjoyment of the great German composer's works, plan further excursions into the music of Wagnerian proportions. A spokeswoman for the group, Mrs Ida Barron-Munchausen, daughter of the Otago University lecturer in the German Department in the 1940s and 50s, Vida Barron, said that they were attempting to recreate the great theatricality of Wagner, with costumes and sets like a true stage production. Guest speakers had been a highlight and it was hoped that live operatic and orchestral performances would ensue.

Fitz ate his brunch, turning time and again to look at the photograph of Hinengaro and himself. Later in the day he would go down to the newspaper office in Lower Stuart Street and order a good photo-print copy of it. Whatever happened, it would become a taonga wherever he went in his life. He saw Calvert descending the staircase, and as his friend came over to him Fitz knew that Hinengaro would decide to stay in the marriage. The closeness he felt to this good man was that of a brother. In such a short time they had shared so many close and strange things.

'How's Hinengaro?' asked Fitz, as uninvolved as possible.

'Recovering well, thanks to you. You saved her life and neither of us will forget that. By the way, nice photo of you two in the paper today. Hine can't stop talking about it – now, if I were one of those suspicious type of husbands ...' Calvert let the sentence lapse, laughing and clapping his friend on the back.

'Have you seen this?' Fitz asked, showing Calvert the story on the Wagner meeting.

'Yeah, I even went and reported the fact that we were at the meeting to the police. They didn't even want to know. Too many prominent people involved, I guess. It's easier just to blame some poor bloody psycho who's down on his luck. Anyway, I intend to keep investigating my father, your father, all of them, until I come up with the hard facts behind the charade. It can't happen here they say, but it is happening here and it's up to us to bear witness and stop it before it goes any further. What are you going to do now Fitz? Do you want to stay in Otago and work as a research assistant in my department? That way we could uncover the truth of the extent these bastards have already prepared this New Millennium Reich of theirs.'

'Depends,' said Fitz. What he didn't say was, that it depends on whether Calvert's wife wanted to be with him or not.

land of the long white cloud

It was a few weeks before Hinengaro Te Riro i He was able to meet Fitz alone. She was feeling a lot better and when they went to their time out to be together restaurant she looked healthy and radiant. Gently, she took his hand and immediately the great surge of vitality and ora which she engendered in him shot through his whole being like a life-restoring injection. She said, 'E Miki tāu, kei te hapū au.'

Fitz was stunned. He wanted to cry, he wanted to laugh out loud. A great joy and sadness washed over him. This was their final unlevel crossing. She said, 'Miki, I cannot be with you. I have thought about it – I've thought about nothing else since I found out I was pregnant to you. I love you profoundly, you have given me back my life – no, I don't mean when you saved me in the fire. You didn't save me then, our child did. No, I mean you restored my wairua by loving me. You brought me dreams and poetry and I will always be thankful for your koha.'

Fitz went to pull his hand away, but Hinengaro held it firmly.

'No, don't withdraw from me, I need you more than ever now that I've decided that we must be apart. I need to know your aroha is there for me and our child. I need to know that you won't desert me just because I must live with another man.'

Fitz looked across the table at this woman. Her beauty was so strong that he wept inwardly. She said, 'I want you to come and sit with me in the cathedral in Smith Street so that God can see us together and give us His blessing and forgiveness, even though we have sinned gravely in the eyes of the Catholic doctrine.'

They walked arm-in-arm together up Stuart Street, turning left and allowing themselves to be enveloped by the large bat-like open wings of Saint Joseph's. Sitting together they felt so close, as though God had blessed their union. It was like they had gone to heaven together or it was like being on God's marae – that is, it was a place where their aroha belonged. Like their Master's Kingdom, nothing could keep them together in this world – but, in the other realm which was eternal, everlasting and they could be there for ever and ever.

'Paul is a good husband and a good father, Miki – no, don't take it the wrong way, darling. I will tell him you are the father later on, maybe when the child is old enough to go to school. For the moment he and I are getting on well enough for him to think that he is the father.' Fitz felt impotent with rage and incomprehension. She held his hand tightly and continued, 'That is a gift you have given us, also. Through loving me you have opened up my ora, and now my life is flowing again. Our daughter has really noticed the difference, also. Everyone attributes it to the near-death experience I had in the marae fire, but you and I only know the truth and that's our taonga.'

They held each other in a long, loving embrace and then she was gone. Fitz stood on the cathedral steps for a long time. He was numb and lifeless, like a Haitian zombie. He had found her only to lose her. The dream travelled on and on and on, as though into eternity. His tears of grief and sorrow for the dark soul of the woman he loved flowed, drowning the tree of love as though he was watering a barren vision which would never bear fruit, no matter how lovingly he tended it. Walking back to the town alone into this southern dream-like, nightmarish city, his spirit seemed somehow lighter even though it was the end. Walking these bleak thoroughfares he was consumed by the absolute ugliness of everyone's face, of the dreary desolation he felt now that she was no longer a possibility.

'Goodbye Fitz,' said Calvert, as he saw him off at Dunedin Railway Station. 'It's a pity I can't persuade you to remain and work with me on my research. After all, you and I know more about the subject than anyone in the country. Hine said to say goodbye. She said she was sorry not to be able to see you off. She's got a touch of morning sickness – you did know she was pregnant, didn't you? We're both delighted. It's given our marriage a whole new start.'

The two men shook hands, embraced and gave each other a farewell hongi. 'Look after her, Paul' said Fitz. Calvert felt that the intensity behind these few words and the enigmatic look on his friend's face was a bit odd, but then he assumed that he just wanted the best for the woman whose life he had saved in the fire.

Fitz sat back in the seat of the Southerner's carriage, just letting his thoughts and feelings wash over him. The train headed north along the harbour and even though it was only the middle of the day, he fell into a dark, dreamful sleep ...

Yet again my dreams are filled with you
Hinengaro Te Riro i He
Awakening from your visit of last night
Where we walked a disenchanted valley
Into the grounds of a small church
Whose green spire reached humbly skyward
All other loves have only reached roof height

... Here Fitz woke as the train blew its whistle going through the small coastal village of Seacliff. Not recognising the name and still feeling very sleepy, he slumbered again and the dream-poem continued its journey also along its own lines ...

Your love conspires to keep me downward bent
While I wrestle with ...
... my unquitted passion for you
Which inspires in me such feelings
And thoughts, and indeed, deeds

That to contemplate them for too long
Would send me reeling, mad incarnate
Of some ancient unknown ...

... The train jolted Fitz awake as it began to move forward. Looking out the window he saw the sign which read MERTON. He could see the southbound train in the loop, waiting for his train to head up the main line now that the crews and cabin staff had changed trains. Fitz shook himself and settled down to sleep as his train clanked across Merton Bridge.

We are together only when the waking world fades
And reason has lost its light of day
But, while I sleep in your arms
I do not wake in them

Auē! Auē! Auē!

... Again, Fitz was woken as the Southerner blew its whistle as it approached the level crossing at Goodwood. The northern light was green up ahead as the train sped towards Christchurch ...